GU00838485

DEVON L
Please return this book on or bef
Renew on tel: 0845 155 1001 or

First Published in Great Britain 2014 by Mirador Publishing

First edition: 2014

ISBN: 978-1-910104-24-8

Mirador Publishing
Mirador
Wearne Lane
Langport
Somerset
TA10 9HB

CAVALIERS & CORRUPTION

BOOK 1:
LOYALTIES CROSSED

By

Barbara Hilton

1   *The house on South Street*

Ellie shifted her weight and swung off the horse, calming it with soft words as she held the reins and pulled her hood forward to cover her dark curls. Lifting her skirts out of the mud, she kept her gaze away from a nearby group of soldiers. From their clothes she could tell they were not Cavaliers of the King's side but Parliamentarians; Roundheads, some called them. They were striding towards her and out of the town. She now felt uncomfortable, alone in Great Torrington. To be sure, she visited weekly for the market, but invariably with her parents or others from a nearby farm. Yet only recently she would have enjoyed the solitude of the ride and then the greetings exchanged with folks she recognised. Today, she must appear to belong, as if her home were here. Slim, dressed plainly and leading her horse, Ellie looked like the farmer's daughter she was, with comely cheeks ruddied by wind, sun and rain. Her dark eyes cast sharp glances about. She avoided the bustle of the marketplace, walking down a side lane to Windy Cross, then into South Street. She counted the doorways and looked for the ninth, on the side opposite that where the land dropped steeply to the river. At the adjacent house a candle flickered in a downstairs window and the door opened as she approached. Remaining still, and close by her horse, Ellie watched as several men in the plain wool garments of Parliamentarians stepped from that door and knocked with their fists at the next, further along. It seemed they were visiting every house.

Anxiously, but as calmly as her nerves allowed, Ellie checked the saddle and remounted. She rode along the damp cobbles at an easy pace, making a detour to the top of Castle Hill before returning to South Street which she found to be quiet. At the ninth house she again alighted and, with one hand clasping her horse's reins, she gripped the round iron door-knocker with the other, tapping the strike-plate as gently as possible to avoid unnecessary noise. A moment later the door opened narrowly and through the crack Ellie could see the nervous eyes of a plump, frightened-looking young maid. Slowly the door opened more widely and a candle was thrust forward, illuminating Ellie's face.

'I seek the seamstress,' Ellie said. The maid seemed not to comprehend and Ellie realised that fright and caution both combined might cause her thus to act. 'The seamstress,' Ellie repeated gently and the maid sprang into activity with quick gestures.

'If it be sewing thou needs,' she said, 'tie thy horse.' But instead of allowing Ellie to look after him she pulled the girl to enter, laid the candle on a low table, and then the maid herself led the horse to be tethered at the back.

Ellie waited in the simply furnished room. She could hear the sounds of children and footsteps approaching. A thin, wiry woman appeared, with measuring tape around her shoulders and candle in her hand, as if she had been disturbed from her sewing task. In spite of her leanness she cast large shadows across the opposite wall. 'Good evening, young mistress,' she said, 'dost thou have business here?'

Ellie remembered the words she had been told to recite and spoke them deliberately. 'It be the cloth I be seeking,' she said.

The woman nodded thoughtfully. 'And be it only cloth?' she enquired.

'I be sure my errand be not in vain,' Ellie chanted the words she had remembered.

'But I know thee not,' the woman said, 'how can I be sure of thee?'

Ellie knew this was the time to show the medallion, given by Father Anthony and used as a token. She reached into the pocket hanging from her waist and proffered the small oval of metal, feeling between her fingers the saintly figure it bore. 'We be with thee,' she whispered fervently. Would these words bring safe passage for a priest, perhaps even for Father Anthony himself?

2

2   Journey to a Devon village

Little did Polly realise at the start of her journey that local conflict remained strong in Derscott, her destination, a village with tales to tell.

Travelling to Devon to recuperate from illness, land and space captured Polly's eyes as the train speeded by and she realised just how much she had missed freedom during months spent in London confined by streets, walls and roofs. Her eyes lighted at the ribbon of countryside but draughts of cold February air breezed down the carriage from windows left open above exit doors. Polly drew a soft woollen scarf around the neck of her sweater, saxe-blue in colour that brought out the hazel in her eyes. Her jacket lay in the overhead rack, though increasingly she felt little need for it, with heated air issuing from vents and warming her legs clad in trim dark corduroys. Her features, while still finely cut, were starting to be eroded by the beginnings of lines; laughter lines she liked to think, that would be diminished and her lungs healed, through the stay away from London and the classroom.

Polly was recovering from a severe infection of her lungs and for a time its cause had been elusive. As a result of various tests possibilities had been eliminated and finally a regime of antibiotics had brought the infection under control. The consultant had extended his analytical mind beyond her clinical symptoms and realised from casual comments that she had coped virtually alone over recent months. In avuncular fashion he had commented that relaxation, a change of scene and gentle exercise might complete her cure. At first Polly had thought of using her bicycle as well as walking the paths through London parks for her convalescence, but the welcome in Marion's invitation and 'phone call had determined her choice. This morning, with a lilt in her step, she had closed the door of her Camden flat and set off on her journey with a small case of warm clothes.

This was an early train, nearly full and over an hour out of Paddington. Polly observed young lawyers dressed smartly in black, reading papers for hearings at Bristol and Exeter. Other travellers tapped keys on their laptops and some talked about agreements and schedules. Not all were on business, though. A few, wearing thick jumpers and with rucksacks stowed on luggage racks, were travelling far. She caught snippets of their plans that lay beyond Penzance, as they journeyed for escape on the Isles of Scilly and then to island-hop, birdwatch and botanise. From her seat with its back to the engine, her view from the window was of hedges defining ancient tracks, as fields carved up the landscape. Frost hung in shadows and sharpened edges. In the distance lay a church tower marking a village, its cluster of old stone and rendered buildings, some thatched, swollen outwards by houses recently built with their pristine roofs and tidy gardens.

Feeling comfortable, she realised she must have dozed for she awakened to find, still clasped within her long fingers, the latest message from Marion that she had printed out only the previous evening. She warmed to the hospitality it promised, '*Rest, reading, country walks and home cooking to help you get fit again.*' Her curiosity was growing about the village in which Marion and Luke, her husband, lived and of they themselves. Her friends had moved to Devon several years ago and it was over six years since she'd seen them. Polly had appreciated Marion's helpful guidance and support in the first years of her teaching; and they had kept in touch ever since. Now, Marion inspected schools and Luke, older than she, had retired. Polly recalled friendly discussions with the two of them over informal meals in their rambling old house in Hornsey. She liked them both and hoped that Luke was as pleased as Marion seemed to be about her visit. She speculated about them, about staying in their Devon home and the opportunities she would have for enjoying the countryside. '***Come to Derscott! Nothing happens here***... *you've all the time you need to get better.*' The words lingered.

Light sunshine reflected off golden buildings at Bath. This

early train, routed through Bristol, gave a sweeping view of Bath's Georgian terraces, crescents and the Abbey. No frost was apparent here. The pale mellow stone provided the most beautiful, refined backdrop for urban business, she thought. The contrast with her own school building was marked. Its four storeys of darkened Victorian brick were served by narrow stairways, rising at opposite corners and leading to alternate floors. Students, the wise and nefarious, quickly learned which stairs gave access most efficiently to their destinations. Newcomers, part-time staff and the thoughtless were confused, and easily targeted for mischief. Around staircases, in hidden corners, lingerers and malingerers secreted themselves; a rustle of papers, a match and a smoke. Polly's lips broke into a smile as she recollected the get-well card, signed by the students in her form, which she had slipped into her case. Known in the school as the most noisy group in Year 10, they were both outgoing and affectionate to those they liked. Polly had won their respect, but she imagined they were testing her replacement.

By Taunton a good number of passengers had left and beyond this the journey took half an hour to Exeter. The train passed fields of sheep and some cattle, grazing on barely-thawed winter grass. As the train gathered speed Polly noticed the stone walls and playing fields of a local public school. She looked up to see her neighbour smiling in her direction. 'It be Devon you be coming to?' the woman asked, 'it be my home and be lovely. B'aint always easy, though…' Polly nodded assent, but while glad that the train was transporting her to warm companionship her thoughts had drifted to Haresh. She missed him, more than she cared to admit. She imagined he was smiling for her, his dark-toned Anglo-Indian skin standing out clearly against the albescent tones of late winter in central Europe, with its lingering snow, dark conifers and absence of colour. Her forehead wrinkled as she conjectured his travels, searching out commodities for his business. Sourcing, that's what he called it, in rural towns and villages.

At Exeter she boarded a local train. 'Umb'rleigh?' the conductor repeated after her, 'I'll tell the driver.' Polly looked around her at others on the Tarka line. Most were elderly or mothers with young children and seemed to know the local stops. Polly again checked the lines of print in Marion's message. They would meet only a short drive from Marion's home at a village halt, still some miles along the single rail-track that made winding progress along a river valley, punctuated by small stations. Between fitful showers sudden bursts of sunshine lighted copses of bare trees and meandering streams that separated grazing land. Polly glimpsed cottages, some thatched, and farms with their barns and outbuildings. Eagerly, she looked out for her request stop and moved her case nearer the exit. Finally, the platform appeared; a lonely strip of concrete alongside an old station-master's house.

So this was Marion's local countryside, with hedges, fields and rounded hills, it appeared like a real-life version of an illustration for a child's story book. A stone's throw away lay the village hall and further still a riverside pub and a few houses. She left her case in the shelter, which freed her to walk across the small parking area to look more closely at her surroundings and wait for Marion. *Has she changed much?* Polly wondered, *and for that matter, what will she think of me?* In her haste, she had drawn back her light brown hair into a band at the nape of her neck. Not yet returned to her usual brisk routine, it had been easier this way, but Haresh liked it loose. Made her more carefree, he said, so she untied it on this country platform that was entirely quiet, except for bird-song; it was peaceful. The shoots of early bulbs were pushing through soil in an untidy row of wooden tubs and winter jasmine sprawled along the walls of local stone.

Happy with anticipation, she remembered how far she was from her customary routine when suddenly... she heard the sound of tyres on gravel and her thoughts stopped. She looked around as a small red car pulled up alongside the platform. Marion, dark-haired and trim in a thick jacket that was also red, stepped out.

'It's great to see you!'

'And nice to be here!'

'Let me help; don't go tiring yourself! You look pale. I don't promise sun, but we'll put some colour in your cheeks!' Marion, with cheerful briskness, installed Polly in the car, her case in the boot, and gave Luke's greetings. She started the engine. 'This is the first time you've visited. We're honoured.' Marion drove warily, avoiding pot-holes and ruts in the patched tarmac of the station forecourt before joining the road, which swept over a wide bridge crossing a river, its brown water fast-flowing and its level high after winter rains. Once more in her company, Marion was just as she remembered; her engaging vivacity making her seem younger than her years. Her hair, framing her face, was still brown with only a few strands of grey and she had retained the funny little habit of making assertions yet smiling so warmly they all seemed acceptable. As if aware of Polly's thoughts, Marion, pausing to make a left turn, smiled broadly. 'You must be tired but we'll be home in a few minutes and lunch is cooking.'

Marion pointed out local features as the car, rising from the valley, climbed hills to Derscott. Polly heard where bluebells grew, buzzards perched and the best fishing was to be had. Intermittently, a mist of light rain blew across the windscreen and then the sky cleared to blue. Nearing the village, the church tower rose over the skyline and the lane narrowed between high hedges and a few cottages, huddled together. 'Here we are!' Marion said, turning the car into the short driveway of a square, white-painted house facing the churchyard, in which stood the church.

'What a delightful position!'

'We're happy here,' Marion said, her voice tinged with pride. 'Some people laugh at our being so near all those graves, but we've really taken to the house: it feels like home. We have historic bits of our own but they're hidden beneath alterations of the years.' Smiling, Marion looked up at the slate roof, shiny with drizzle. 'It's lost its thatch, but the windows at the front are old – and that's yours, just to the left.' Polly gazed at the old sash windows placed symmetrically, like a child's drawing, with three windows on the first floor, that in the centre above the porch and front door. Enclosed by hedges the house was screened from neighbours. Polly followed Marion indoors. 'We'll eat in the kitchen when you're ready. That's where we live, you'll see,' Marion said.

Polly, hungry after her journey, took only a few belongings out of her case and quickly gravitated to the kitchen. A big room, it seemed to Polly to occupy most of the downstairs of the house. Windows gave views to the front, along the side and, through a glass-panelled door, into a shabby, comfortable conservatory at the back, with faded chairs and nearby washing machine. While Marion referred to the room in which they stood as a kitchen, it was clearly much more. It might just as well be called a living or a family room. A large, cream-coloured Aga spread against the outer side-wall and radiated fulsome heat across the entire space. Several wood-framed armchairs, rendered indulgent with bountiful cushions, ranged before it. In the centre of the room stood a sturdy wooden table with heavy turned legs that was capacious enough for six to dine, without disturbing the newspapers and bowl of daffodils. Surrounding this space the walls were entirely covered in books and pictures, and cupboards miscellaneous in style but harmonised by cream paint to match the Aga. Marion brought in a bowl of salad from the conservatory and lifted a substantial casserole dish from the Aga. As she raised the lid, mouthwatering aromas of winter root-vegetables alongside lamb of melting softness percolated the room. Polly could imagine dining off the smell alone. It was a virtual meal, she thought.

'There's as much as you want – and more,' Marion said, ladling substantial helpings onto their plates. 'Luke's looking forward to seeing you later. He's with friends today, at a nearby village. Have I told you of his interest in all things to do with nature? It's grown no end since we've been here, because there's so much. They're looking, would you believe it, at lichens in a local churchyard.' Polly was content to listen as Marion's account digressed to their growing family. 'That's our latest; I think I've told you about Oliver?' She pointed to a photograph of a sleeping baby, her new grandson. 'He's a lovely, contented child; his parents are really proud of him and are bringing him soon.' She continued with anecdotes until Polly, warm and replete, put down her fork and sat back in her chair. Acknowledging an opportunity for Polly to talk, Marion said, 'Tell me about yourself, and how's Haresh?'

'He's been wonderful during my illness, but he's away in Europe. I miss him. He's looking for new products, hand-crafted toys, for his business.' She paused to hand over a package. 'This is from both of us, for Oliver.' Polly watched as Marion, unwrapping the paper and tissue carefully, revealed a musical box, lovingly carved and decorated with farm animals. 'Look, you twist it so,' Polly explained, and they listened to its cheerful folk-tune jingle as small models of black and white cows revolved within a border of sheep and hens on the polished, round base studded with foliage and flowers. Marion's face beamed with delight. 'It's charming! Where's it from?'

Polly described how Haresh had found it in Belarus and was hoping to source similar musical boxes on his current trip. 'They mostly make dolls in folk-costumes and some of them play tunes too. We thought it might fit into Oliver's room, for him to enjoy as he grows...'

Sunlight alternated with showers still and they moved from the table to sit in front of the Aga but as the light started to wane, Marion said, 'You must see something of where we are! D'you have a waterproof downstairs? Borrow mine and my boots, and take a stroll.'

Derscott was quiet. Opposite Marion's house was the church. But first, Polly turned to her left, to the cluster of cottages that comprised the village. The dwellings were mostly Devon cob painted white or pastel colours, interspersed with a few of local grey stone. She looked in the window of a shop, the only shop. This sold small ranges of a wide variety of goods, including staple groceries, potatoes, gloves, weedkiller and newspapers, and also provided cream teas and Sunday lunches. While she was gazing at the window, a man stepped out. 'Like one of these?' he asked, presenting Polly with a pink leaflet, headed *DEVELOPMENT PROTEST* in bold capitals across the top.

She smiled gratefully but paid little attention to it, stuffing it in her pocket as she crossed the road and walked towards the church lych-gate.

The path, its cobbles of grey stone polished by countless footsteps, rose towards the church porch and was bordered on each side by gravestones. These stood in neat rows, uniformly aligned east-west, though their shapes and postures varied, and in front of some were bunches of snowdrops or the remains of Christmas wreaths. Polly had known Marion in Kentish Town, London, and wondered how her friend fitted into this very rural community. *It must go back hundreds of years*, she thought, noticing the dates on some of the headstones. Nearest the church they were of local slate, slim but tall and most stood upright, like silent witnesses of her presence. More distant memorials were drifting out of view and she realised that mist was rising around the churchyard. She tried to decipher the inscriptions and persisting, traced with her fingers the lettering on some. The light was failing and as it dimmed, only with difficulty could she recognise that a few headstones were embellished with scrolls and fragments of urns or angels. She paused and looked at her watch. It seemed too early for dusk but here, in the shelter of the tower and the gathering mist, twilight had almost come. She glimpsed a headstone, a few steps towards the south porch, more worn than others and seriously tilted. It was of slate, its laminations rubbed smooth at the corners. While the lettering was faint in part, she could make out the dedication: '*To ELLEN, We be with thee*'. The wind gathered strength and felt cold in Polly's lungs. Shivering, she ceased her exploration. She preferred the warmth of the Aga and Marion's promise of a hot drink, or sherry with Luke.

3   *Father Patrick*

The priest walked close by the trees that fringed the churchyard. The light was sinking and shadows were long. He was glad to have made it before nightfall. The woman's directions had been fair enough. Exmoor he glimpsed to the northeast and Dartmoor from whence he'd come now lay to the south, as he welcomed arrival at this resting place – within reach of Great Torrington, but away from immediate danger. Bent, the elderly figure took the shape of the trees curved from the prevailing wind. His long black habit of coarse woollen cloth flapped around his slight body and caught low undergrowth, so he drew it closer. His tired eyes followed the line of trees around the churchyard and he scanned the gravestones. There was no sign of movement and he seemed quite alone. The only sound was of the wind. As he moved he disturbed dry twigs, but the leaves had long since blown away. He stood on soft turf and knew his feet would leave imprints, but these were barely perceptible now it was twilight and the ground would recover by dawn. The farm lay below the church and there was no time to be lost in finding it. The folk there would be wary of visitors after nightfall and it was almost that time now. He held his few possessions in a tight bundle and clutched them to him. Cautiously, he moved between trees and made for the churchyard walls that provided moderate cover. He rounded an orchard then came upon an avenue that bordered a track leading to the farm.

No lights were visible. He knew that country people were careful of burning tallow and avoided drawing attention to themselves without good reason. He considered each step he made, not through fear – his time might come at any hour and he wished to face the Lord with an open heart – but out of thoughtfulness for man and beast. If he betrayed himself, he risked betraying others both here and further afield and he valued their lives more than his own. He heard an owl overhead and a dog close by, its barking checked by a man's

11

quiet voice. This he was glad of. He did not wish to wake the family if they were already a-bed. He felt cold drops, a fine drizzle, but he was almost at the farm. He had to return the token, the surety he had been given. The girl, Ellie was her name, had given this to the seamstress and he would return it now. He made for the door and although he did not touch it, the dogs sensed him, barked and were quieted again.

'Who be there?' challenged him.

''Tis I,' he replied. His age and weariness showed in his voice. From the door, which was pulled open, two dogs jumped out and circled him, while a rush-light was thrust towards his face. The farmer saw beneath the priest's worn habit an aged man who looked feeble and without the strength the night required. But his eyes were bright, his gaze penetrating and through his wrinkles and frailty, kindness and determination shone.

'Thou be alone?'

'Why yes, I have come to be with thee,' and he pressed the token into Seth's hand.

Satisfied, Seth the farmer called off his dogs who then romped together but hung about at the door, only to be chided again. The priest was led along a passage. Light flickering from a hearth brightened the main hall-room at the left. 'Thou be cold,' the farmer said. 'Catherine, what can we offer? This be a man of God.' The farmer, of medium height and burly, stood aside as the priest entered the hall which, in earlier years, had served as the whole house. Large, it rose to over double a man's height. The roof and its beams were blackened with smoke. The room itself was plainly furnished with heavy wooden pieces that scraped unevenly across the floor that was stone-flagged yet cobbled in part, and dignified with pottery tiles from Barum around the hearth. Burning logs threw light from flames halfway across the room and warmed people and stray animals too. The hens and cats had space enough as well as respect for one other, so allowed each other's presence. Over the fire sat a pot and around the hearth hung heavy hams, drying and gathering smoke, as well as bundles of herbs. Set into the side of the fireplace was a deep oven and from this came the smell of bread as it baked. In a corner, above a small fire that gave but gentle heat, was a small recess that held cream, clotting to a rich consistency. The dogs, used hard in all weathers, slunk back and lay hidden in warm shadows, waiting to be summoned.

In the flickering light, the priest made out the figure of the farmer's wife as she lifted herself from a settle before the fire. Her age must closely match the farmer's, he believed, and while she was not her husband's height, her girth was indeterminate. So wrapped in clothing was she that she looked over-comely and buxom in her padding. Respectfully, she greeted him and apologised for the simple fare she kept, though he was welcome to share all that was available. She busied herself, giving the priest her own place, so that he could be warmed. Then she cut thick slices off a ham and placed them alongside a bowl of hot broth and a tankard of cider, and she and her husband watched the priest as he replenished himself.

'Daylight will do for talking,' the farmer said. 'Rest thyself here, right now. No harm will come, the dogs'll see to that.' Catherine furnished him with a woven blanket on her seat before the fire, made further preparations for the morning, then she and the farmer left him for the night.

4   The Black Horse

Polly had all of north Devon to discover; how much could she find out about its present and past, she wondered?

After a convivial evening with Marion and Luke she had slept long and comfortably. Awake from a dreamless sleep, she recognised her Derscott surroundings and remembered her short walk in the quiet village and churchyard. This morning was still and very quiet, traffic almost negligible, but Marion had mentioned the school bus and said this could bring noise, with parents' cars and children's voices around the rendezvous at the village shop. She turned her wrist to check the time on her watch. It was not yet half-past eight – the hour the bus collected Derscott pupils travelling the five miles or so to the local secondary school. Normally by now she had cycled to her own school and was busy preparing for the day.

She tried imagining Haresh's current activities and calculated the time change to his destination. He had urged her to accompany him on his sales trip to eastern Europe; he had wanted to care for her himself, and make sure she continued to improve. But he knew she was right about the harshness of the lingering winter and admitted she might be better staying closer to home. Haresh might be eating lunch now, she supposed. She puzzled what he would think of Derscott. She'd tell him about Marion's, that it was opposite the churchyard which turned misty, eerie even, in winter's fading afternoon. And she would ask if he'd found further musical boxes or more pop-up toys. Haresh's own flat was a treasure-trove to whet any child's imagination. On her first visit it had certainly captured hers, as she had gazed at his collection of carefully constructed and embellished pieces, some antique and others examples of products he might import. Money-boxes, clockwork figures, chiming clocks, miniature books, trains and houses, they were all there. Pushing aside memories, she realised she could send a text.

She reached for her mobile and keyed in a message about waking in Devon, missing him, and where was he off to, today? *If only*, she thought, and she longed for the closeness of his body, warming her. She replaced her 'phone on the bedside table and looked around the room. More awake now, she heard the tell-tale responses of an old house to its owners at the start of the day: the creak of a floorboard, squeak of a door handle and gurgling of water running through a network of pipes. She knew that Marion and her husband were about.

First she heard the bus, with the unmistakable sound of its heavy brakes. Then came the young voices, followed by those of parents, calling reminders to their children and greetings to each other. By now, Polly was dressed and as she drew apart the curtains she caught sight of the rear of the bus, starting on its way to Great Torrington. A tap on the door heralded the arrival of a tray with a cup of tea, an orange cut in sections and Marion smiling. 'You're already up! And after all those promises to take it easy.'

'Oh, but I am taking it easy!'

'How did you sleep? Were you warm enough?'

Happily, Polly described how comfortable she'd been and, checking her watch, added, 'And just think, it's almost time to be registering my form and...'

Gently, Marion interrupted. 'Well, now you're ready, come and have breakfast. Luke's partial to bacon, and I've put an extra strip in for you, as well.'

Luke pulled his chair to one side and made way for Polly. Always a generous, warm-hearted man, in retirement his girth had increased to match his nature, but his mind was as sharp as ever. He chortled over reviews in the daily paper and asked Polly's opinion. 'Yes, I suppose we miss going to some of the big-name shows in London,' he said, 'but we manage pretty well. There's a lot going on locally and we can always stay overnight with family if there's something really special. Anna and David are only in Walthamstow.' He relished his bacon, hot and crispy sandwiched in soft bread, and patted Marion on her arm. 'The benefit of a guest,' he added.

Beside her husband, Marion was diminutive. While Luke

had always towered over her, now he engulfed her. *'There were three ravens sat on a tree* (and they be us),' he added the explanation for Polly's benefit, continuing, *'They were as black as black might be, And one of them said to his mate…'*

'What shall we for breakfast take?' Marion interspersed a line of the jingle.

'Bacon,' Luke chorused with her. Then he grinned, wiping the remains of his sandwich from his fingers. 'D'you know the ditty, Polly? The words are slightly different, but…'

'Luke, Polly will think we're crazy.'

'We are!' Luke admitted happily.

'Don't take any notice of him, Polly. Anything you've been looking forward to? That's much more important,' she said turning to her guest.

'Don't imagine my wife is short of ideas. She has a veritable itinerary mapped out,' Luke commented.

'I'd like to know more about Derscott and around where you live,' Polly said.

'I'd suggest a walk,' Marion said, 'but the forecast is mixed. Let's start in Great Torrington, it's the nearest small town and has 'history'. We can plan more when we see how the weather develops.'

'Count me out if it's a shopping trip, but you're welcome to join me this afternoon,' Luke smiled impishly, 'the ground's sacred, I won't lead you astray.'

'He's inviting you to spend the afternoon with lichens in the local churchyard,' Marion explained.

'How does the saying go? *The history of England is in her parish churches*,' Luke ruminated and returned behind his newspaper.

Polly copied Luke and made a sandwich with her bacon. Thinking back to her brief walk in the churchyard, her curiosity increased. Then Marion distracted her and they busied themselves preparing for the short drive to the local town.

The Torrington car park occupied a magnificent site, high above the river. Drizzle, blown on a south-west wind, hampered their visibility as Marion's car slowed to a halt.

'Let's wait a moment, it may clear,' Marion suggested. They watched other cars and their occupants but the misty rain, far from lifting, strengthened. A car pulled into the space adjacent and without hesitation the occupants emerged. At first Polly thought their appearance was a distortion, caused by the rain and condensation within the car. The men seemed to be wearing leather jerkins over their shirts, with heavy cloaks swinging from their shoulders and trousers that were pushed into tall leather boots. The women had on long woollen skirts, coarsely-woven bodices and some had hoods to cover their heads while others wore simple cotton bonnets. Marion saw Polly's surprise at their quaint costumes. 'They're gathering,' Marion smiled, remembering other similar events.

'Whatever for?' As Polly spoke, the men donned wide-brimmed hats with high crowns and the group moved into the shelter of buildings at one end of the car park.

'Re-enacting local history,' Marion started to explain. 'Torrington was a hub of intrigue in Civil War days, with a battle that ended in the blowing up of the church, no less!'

'How extraordinary! How did that happen?'

'Oh, it was gunpowder; they didn't do things by halves,' Marion said. 'By tradition the town was on the King's side – it was Royalist and had been held by them. But towards the end of the Civil War, when things weren't going their way, they stored gunpowder in the church. It was probably the safest, driest place they knew. However, the Parliamentarians (or call them Roundheads, if you like) got the better of them and imprisoned a huge number of Royalist Cavaliers – several hundred, they say – in the church. The tale is, the gunpowder was accidentally lighted and the whole lot blew up. Of course, the church crumbled, many men were killed and the Royalists utterly defeated. It was a turning point of the war in the West Country.'

'And the only battles most people hear about are Naseby and Newark,' Polly commented.

'Maybe in the rest of the country, but they haven't forgotten about 1646 here.' Marion peered again through the windscreen. 'This drizzle could be with us for hours, I'll tell you more over coffee. Does that sound like a good idea?'

Marion led Polly down through the small covered market. At a café, tables spilled out, above which conversation floated, laced with Devon burr, but all the chairs were occupied. 'Let's try *The Black Horse*, instead,' Marion said, 'that's full of history too.' They crossed a corner of the square and stepped over the threshold of the inn, into its cobbled interior. Already it was busy. Marion ordered coffee for them at the wood-panelled bar while Polly found a small table in an adjacent room with a log fire. Joining her, Marion recognised familiar faces. 'Laura, hello! My friend Polly is staying with us. Polly, meet Laura.' Laura's well-groomed appearance contrasted with Marion and Polly as they shook droplets of rain from their waterproofs and straightened their thick sweaters.

'Nice to meet you.' Laura's politeness did not completely mask a touch of embarrassment. 'D'you know Joe, a friend of Mike's and myself?'

'G'day to you both. We had a little business to discuss, and this is convenient enough.' Courteously, Joe moved chairs around to accommodate them all together.

Polly thought he and Laura made an interesting couple. Laura's light hair was shown to its best advantage in fashionable style and complemented by the clean lines of expensive knitwear in soft colours. Polly tried counting the rings on Laura's finely manicured fingers and was uncertain whether they totalled eight, or more. Joe looked like a man in his sixties, or perhaps a bit older than that. His grey hair was brushed back tidily above a weathered face, one which could show concern, Polly thought. But now he was smiling, relaxed and confident, in contrast to Laura's slight nervousness. He sported a comfortable tweed jacket over a checked shirt with a knitted tie. He joined readily in their conversation about a wide range of topics: local events, various coastal initiatives, energy prices and, most fervently, prices at the local cattle markets. His knowledge was extensive and he gave apt examples from his own farming experience.

'Joe's being modest about last year's successes,' Laura interjected.

He smiled. 'All in a season's work,' he said.

Polly, enjoying contact with a world she knew little about, enquired about the breeds he kept.

'Well, for beef there's Devon Red, but I've tried some European stock, Limousin and Simental, as well.' He spoke comfortably of the land and weather conditions before the conversation veered to gardening, local events and sights for Polly to visit.

With happy exchanges she did not notice the passage of time until Joe signalled his need to return. 'I do my best to be home for lunch, I'm sure you understand,' he said, giving his apologies. Their coffee cups drained, Laura and Joe went their separate ways.

'I haven't shown you as much of Great Torrington as I'd hoped,' Marion said as they returned to the car. 'It's a friendly place and there's more to see. We'll look around the church next time and there's the site of a castle too.' The rain had eased and they glanced at the sky, hoping the weather was settled for a dry afternoon.

Back at Derscott they hung their damp jackets in the hallway. 'You'll never guess who we met,' Marion greeted her husband.

'Oh, so you've seen Laura's fancy man?' Luke teased in response to Marion's chatter. 'She keeps him quiet enough, you've done well,' and he added wryly, 'he was more interesting than my lunch, so we'll picnic, I expect.'

'We're eating healthily, that's the truth. And you don't know about Joe and Laura, it's all supposition. She's devoted to her husband; it's just that he's working away,' Marion protested as she spread slices of cold meat, together with salad, across plates.

'Eh, we're deluding ourselves. Joe's loaded and wants to make more.'

'I think it's just a case of his wanting to use his talents.'

'Never a truer word.'

'Luke, you know perfectly well he cares as much for his wife as any man could,' and Marion explained for Polly's benefit that Joe's wife was an invalid and needed round-the-clock support.

'If he's the paragon you believe, why's he spending this

morning with milady in *The Black Horse*?' Luke responded conspiratorially.

'Luke, Polly will have quite the wrong impression of what goes on around here.' And with that Marion softened her teasing and added further explanation. 'Yes, Laura's husband, Mike, is away much of the time. He's a surveyor, overseeing construction projects abroad. But Luke's just echoing village gossip about Joe cultivating Laura, as well as Mike, to further a building development deal. Mike and Laura haven't been here long and they've sold the farmland which came with their house. Joe's bought some of their fields and the tale is the pair of them, Joe and Mike, are in cahoots to build a lot of houses.'

'Circumspect's a lovely word. I'm just being circumspect,' Luke said mischievously.

'Then did you start these speculations?' Marion fenced, lightly.

'Don't hurt a chap who means well.'

'I don't mean to.' Marion kissed her husband's cheek affectionately, before transferring slices of apple pie to the oven.

Later, their meal completed, Luke spied low sunlight on the south-west corner of the church tower. 'I did offer to show Polly the churchyard this afternoon,' he said.

'And I'll see some lichens?'

'Aye, you'll see a few. You'll need stout shoes.'

'She can borrow my wellingtons,' Marion offered.

Suitably clad, Polly set off with Luke to enter the churchyard that looked well tended and neat. Even though the grass was short after a late autumn trim, it was very damp and footsteps made clear impressions. She thought Luke spoke of the lichens in Derscott churchyard as if they were old friends and she enjoyed his enthusiasm in pointing out good examples that spotted the the grey walls of the church, built of local stone and now weathered and repaired. Polly had heard of lichens before: were they pronounced *lychens* or *litchens*, she asked?

'I'm easy about that,' he said, but Polly copied his pronunciation and said *lychens*. Luke's descriptions and the funny names he gave them caricatured their individual appearances. Polly observed their tiny features, enlarged using a magnifying lens, and her interest was captured. The time passed quickly as she familiarised herself with the colours, shapes and textures that lichens added to various surfaces in the churchyard: the stones of memorials, brick used for patching the church walls, the pathway and even several trees. But gradually Polly's attention slipped; Luke realised she was becoming tired and saturated with information. Guiding her to leave, Luke asked if she had observed any of the quaint inscriptions on headstones near the church. 'Some are curious – and on the oldest stones dates are not always given, y' know.' Egged on by Polly's interest he continued, 'We've been looking into the headstones – by we, I mean the village – because we're keen to keep, not lose, them.'

'Lose a gravestone?'

Luke smiled. 'They'd become sloped, quite badly. It was up to us, to straighten or lose them. The Diocese was worried about safety and didn't want any showing neglect or damage. So we raised the funds and the job's almost done.' And he pointed to the remnants of restoration work that tidily had been put to one side, a sack of gravel and another of sand. 'This'll be the last to be made upright, delayed I 'spect by the weather.' He dislodged a small wreath of hellebores and holly that had toppled across a line of snowdrops, still in their prime, along the base of a headstone.

They were standing next to the very old gravestone that Polly had noticed the previous afternoon. She drew attention to its inscription: '*To ELLEN, We be with thee*'.

'I often wonder about that epitaph, myself,' Luke observed. 'Marion tells everyone that nothing ever happens here. It's not true, you know. We only know the surface of people's lives.' He frowned, trying to make out the writing on a card, still attached to the wreath and his voice softened. 'That's a coincidence, it's to Ellen! But I shouldn't be surprised; she's a bit of a legend in these parts.'

They took a last look at the worn, vertical slate slab, the memorial to Ellen against which Luke gently restored her wreath.

5   *Tom*

Ellie folded her arms within the sleeves of her bodice and felt the wind lift the corners of her cap. She paced by the east wall of the small church and her eyes searched for Tom. He was walking the fields, she expected, and if she delayed longer her own absence would be noted. It was time to return to the kitchen and help her mother, Catherine.

Then she caught sight of him, taking a short-cut through the hedge. She admired him and craved to belong: to have the right to feel proud of his looks, his broad face, ready smile and the swing of his shoulders, developed through taking on much of the labour on the farm as he assisted her father. Yet, even more, she admired his willingness to work with nature and harness its energy, as one season gave way to the next. 'Thou'll wear a path and be caught!' she teased as he approached.

Tom drew her to him and closed his arms about her. 'I've found thee,' he said.

'But it were only last evening,' she replied.

'I worry,' he said. 'All thy trips into Torrington...'

'But I be back, to be with thee.'

He shook his head. 'There be trouble about. It b'ain't be right.'

'I be careful enough.' Ellie kept to herself how she had returned the previous day away from the main route, riding along tracks in the lee of hedges and in places leading her horse to avoiding reaching conspicuous height and drawing unnecessary attention to herself.

'It b'ain' t be right,' Tom said again. He looked out across the landscape. The day, just starting, had a sharp brightness. Too cold yet for the land to warm, the colours were vivid with hard shadows. Sheep strayed across the fields which were bare of cattle, kept inside until spring. Recognising Tom, one of the dogs playing around the farmhouse ran up to him. 'Down, Nemo,' Tom said. 'I know,

'tis time for the rounds, me and thee.' He stroked the dog's tangled coat and walked down the slope, his arm round Ellie's waist. Curls of her dark hair were held back under a gathered cap. He wished he could unloose it, and her apron too.

'Tom,' the farmer called, 'see to the cows, then be o'er and fast to it.' The farmer looked at his daughter and caught excitement in her eyes. It was to be expected, he knew, and Tom was a good lad. He'd be well content to call him son, as he had none of his own. But the time wasn't ready yet and he wasn't in the mood for wasting it either. 'Ellie, thy mother's been asking for 'ee.' Catherine was busying herself with provisions, replenishing her stock and taking account of the needs of both the farm and the priest. They'd best keep him indoors until arrangements were settled for his lodging.

6   Lottie of Lee's farm

Polly was introduced to the family of Lee's farm that was as old as the church itself because she had accepted an invitation to meet the youngest generation of Derscott.

'D'you fancy some fresh company this morning?' Marion put down the receiver and looked at her friend with a mixture of humour and apprehension. Polly, wiping honey from her fingers took another sip of coffee. The ringing of the 'phone had interrupted the end of a leisurely breakfast. Morning light caught a stack of correspondence, accumulated over several days, which Marion had been sorting at one corner of the table. She had removed the daffodils that earlier had greeted Polly and rearranged the jug with branches of witchhazel, its delicate flowers just opening, sweet and aromatic. But now her attention was focused. 'Don't feel you have to, but I'd rather not let Lottie down, myself.'

'Beware, Polly,' Luke interrupted. 'I have responded to similar urgent situations myself in the past. Join me, it would be safer.' And he returned to sections of the newspaper that he'd shared with Polly.

'Don't listen to him!' Marion laughed.

'I'm intrigued,' Polly's gaze passed across them both.

'The local nursery group. It's just around the corner and they're stuck for cover. So many mums depend on it and an extra pair of hands – or two – makes all the difference. It only runs for a couple of hours but Lottie can't manage alone.'

'Yes, I'll come along,' Polly replied.

'Aren't there enough willing young women around here?' growled Luke.

'They could use a grandpop. They'd respect you, you know,' Marion rejoined. 'Fancy coming along with us? And how about Polly's age? Half the mums are her age, and some are older.'

Luke was disgruntled. 'I didn't mean that; forgive an old

chap, Polly. Marion knows how I am,' he said. 'I like her around but off she goes, at the slightest chance. She might as well be inspecting!'

Marion wrapped her arms as far as they'd go around his ample frame. 'I'll miss you,' she said.

'No you won't. You'll have slobbering infants to kiss, instead of me.'

The nursery occupied an old school house at the edge of the churchyard. Faced in local stone, it had a high slate roof above wooden eaves with flaking paint. The glass of its wide, gothic-style windows was almost concealed beneath examples of children's art work. The entrance from a side lane led to a wide covered porch. Already a baby-buggy was parked there.

'That will be Lottie's,' Marion explained. 'Her husband's Ray – they farm at Lee's, just down the road.' She and Polly had arrived by 9.30, allowing time to help Lottie sort out activities before the children came at 10.00. The double doors, painted maroon, were chipped with low scuff-marks where young feet had pushed against them. But they opened into a large, light yellow-painted space. The ceiling, following the angles of the roof, gleamed white. A long carpet strip near the entrance led onto the blue linoleum floor on which a young infant sat, while small toddler-sized chairs were placed in groups around him.

'Oh, I'm so grateful – two of you! What a bonus! Chrissie couldn't manage it and Lorna's away, you know.' Lottie greeted them both warmly. 'And this is Charles, Polly. I couldn't resist his name, you see I'm Charlotte really and have always been known as Lottie. But we say Charles in full,' she said as she introduced her young son. 'I mean him to be my last,' she added wistfully. The child gurgled in response to the smiling faces towering above, his blue eyes and open arms held towards them. It was Polly who picked up a child's plastic tractor from nearby and handed it into his chubby fingers.

'Polly's a teacher,' Marion introduced her friend.

'Well, I'm used to rather older children,' Polly admitted.

'Big oaks from little acorns grow,' Lottie said

enthusiastically. 'Look – that's one of our projects, d'you see the leaves on the poster over there?'

'And today?'

'Oh, I'll show you in a moment. Just help with this, will you?' Soon the room was organised with a small play-house, painting corner and sand trough; an activity for each adult to manage.

'How many are coming today?' asked Marion.

'At least fourteen; Phoebe's in bed with a cold and David's gone with his parents to Exeter. I'm not sure about Christopher, I think his family's back now so numbers could be higher. Polly, I suggest you look after the painting. I let the children choose what they want to do when they come in, and we'll change round after a time.'

No sooner had she spoken than the door opened and two youngsters ran into the room. Lottie hugged them and helped them take off their jackets. Brought by their father he said hello to Marion, who was obviously well known in the nursery. 'And this is Polly, a friend of Marion's. She's a teacher,' Lottie explained.

Polly felt promotion had rapidly come her way in this nursery world and soon was engrossed with her small charges, dispensing paint and copious paper, as well as paper towels. 'I'm new here,' she said, 'make me a picture of your house.' The results came fast and were bold and colourful. 'Does your house have a door?' she asked, expecting it to be at the front. Beth's clear blue eyes looked wonderingly and she pointed to one side. Distracted, her attention lapsed. Pushing away her chair but retaining her brush she ran erratically, first to others in her group then across the sand-play area. Polly, amazed at the infant's speed ran to pick her up and was rewarded with stripes of green across her forehead.

'You look charming,' Marion said, bundling Beth into her arms and inviting her to join her group.

Banging in the play-house and sobbing in the sand signalled the need for quiet time. Lottie walked over to the 'fridge and picked up a large plastic-lidded container. 'What d'you think I have here?' she asked the children. Waiting until they were silent, she allowed them to take their choice of fruit. Story-time followed and later a song. At 10 minutes to 12 noon the adults restored the room to order and the children returned to their chairs, again grouped in circles. With prompting by Lottie they chanted a rhyme for that weekday. Gradually, their numbers were reduced as they were collected by parents. By 12.15 all had gone, except Lottie's own child who, remembering odd words of the rhyme, sang them to himself.

'It's been a good morning, and many thanks to you both,' Lottie said.

'Glad to help, but how frantic!' Polly laughed.

'You're alright for tomorrow?' Marion asked.

'All taken care of. But thanks for asking.'

They waited while Lottie fastened Charles into his buggy, ready for the walk home.

'Ray's in for lunch?' Marion asked about Lottie's farmer husband.

'No, he's at market today. So we've time to ourselves, haven't we Charles?'

Cheerfully, she turned and was on her way.

'Their farm,' Marion explained, 'is almost next door but you don't notice it, for trees.

They say it's as old as the church. But right now, I think we deserve something to eat ourselves. Let's go home.'

Polly, looking at herself in the mirror of her bedroom, brushed sand and bits of paper from her clothes and washed her forehead clean of paint. She felt a long way from her usual routine. She had the get-well card from her pupils displayed on top of the chest but they seemed of another world.

The days passed quickly and drifted into a week, and more. Polly grew used to walks in the dry intervals between light showers of mild rain and she felt her resilience returning. With Marion and Luke she explored footpaths, lanes, tea shops and local inns. Occasionally Polly carried her sketchpad with her and captured views in pencil and soft colours. Evenings were spent quietly, usually with a glass of wine and either a book from one of Luke's crowded shelves or they would draw the blinds to view a favourite programme on TV – Arsenal for Luke or a mystery drama for Marion. Polly had observed that at weekends they both checked book reviews, and from them ordered new titles. Kind-heartedly, they shared some of their best-loved volumes with Polly and more than once they found her dozing, snug and warm in a deep arm chair, her fingers around the pages of a book.

7   *Refuge for a priest*

Patrick gave silent thanks for his safe-keeping and food as he held the bowl in his hands. The porridge: warm oats and hot milk sweetened with honey, filled his belly and he felt strengthened after his sleep. The family, all at their tasks, had left him where he had slept before the fire, its warmth and crackling shared with a dog, several cats and a stray hen, perched for comfort above the hearth. This last night had been the first for several that he had slept in a homely place and he knew not when the next would be. In these troubled times he was thankful for each day and for the kindness of charitable folk. His own part, to pray for peace, he could manage anywhere. His loyalty with the Crown he accepted willingly, though this troubled his conscience because of his natural concern for every man. And he met conflicts when others, on the Parliament side, saw him as their enemy. He was grateful for the safety the farm had provided. Beyond its walls, he was unsure. He hesitated to walk in the light for fear of revealing not just himself but the family as well. If the commonplace rumours were founded, he'd be needing a sanctuary for several days more, while troubles eased. He knew he must seek the church, it being his home, as soon as he could bid farewell to his hosts. 'Ah, Ellie,' he said, recognising her in the dim light as she entered from the scullery with a jug of warm milk that was rich with cream.

'Father Patrick, thou slept well, I trust?' He wondered if he had disturbed the rest that others needed. 'Why, nay, I didn't intend that,' the girl said in reply, 'but we be early risers here and hope that all our commotion did not wake thee?'

Seated here, his appetite slaked and with the fire warming his bones, he felt as much contentment as he'd felt for many weeks. Though his conscience knew the weakness in this, he also recognised he should not stir until plans were made, in order that others were not endangered. 'Bless you, Ellie, I must soon move on.'

She paused for a moment, as if he'd worried her. 'Thou be safe here, Father,' she said, 'I know no better place. And we have a cot that others have used. But I'll take thee by the church later.'

'My Father's house and it be mine,' he replied quietly, but Ellie was silent. Either she had not understood, or not heard, he thought.

'Now, what's this thou be saying?' Seth, with Nemo at his heel, strode into the room. At his approach the other dog, named Toss but the quieter of the two, stirred, as did several cats which Seth banished, allowing the one cat that guarded the cream to remain, as well as a solitary hen.

'My son,' Father Patrick began, 'I bring you danger, and warrant none of it.' His frame was slight, but he crossed his arms over his stomach, full from the supper of the last night, and now a hearty breakfast.

'Nay, I can hardly credit thy worry,' Seth protested. The elderly priest, so benign and gentle in demeanour, was in need of protection not banishment, the farmer believed.

'I understand your view.' The priest knew how he appeared. He felt the tautness of his skin, the stiffness of his aching joints and scratching of his scant hair. He raised himself, pressing down on the table to shift his weight and he walked to the settle on which he had slept overnight. 'I am warm now and dozy with comfort. When the Lord calls, I am ready.' His eyes, as clear as a young man's, caught Seth's puzzled look. 'My friend, look at this.' He carried to the table his bundle. Unfolding rags he revealed a box that was not very large, yet conveyed its import in its fine workmanship and silver clasp. The lid lifted to show compartments and, wrapped in clean linen, a small silver chalice for bread and a phial with wine.

Seth nodded. 'I'll see what can be done. Yet the church is a draughty place and no place for thee to rest.'

'But it is my home.'

Seth had not the mettle to argue fundamentals, the implications of which he could only hazard a guess. He knew

30

others, if they chose, would wage war against the symbols of communion and the church. 'Tom be looking a'ter pigs and then the cows and sheep. This morn I check the bounds.' He described these chores, by way of explanation. 'Give us 'til noon, then I be back and'll help thee willingly.'

Patrick retied his bundle and returned to his seat. He stretched his limbs and settled his head, resting one shoulder against the wooden frame. One cat, followed by another, pushed open the door and found warm shadows in which to doze. The stray hen was joined by another on its roost, where they enjoyed their vantage-point across the hall, into the scullery.

In hardly any time, Patrick felt a light pressure on his arm. Again, it was Ellie. 'Father sent me, if thou be ready. I go with thee, to the church.' Father Patrick shook the sleep from his mind and resting his hand against the wall levered himself to his feet. 'Take this, my arm,' Ellie said.

The priest collected his belongings and looked around the room. Catherine, Ellie's mother, hastened in. 'We be near,' she offered reassurance, but this was more for herself than for the priest, who was happy to be returning to God's house. Ellie led him through the back of the farm. The air, crisp yet mild out of the wind, was invigorating. Strengthened by his rest, he looked gladly ahead, seeing that the church lay directly south-west of the farm.

'My child, this is not how I found the farm, last evening.'

'Nay, thou came a more straightforward and level way, yet somewhat further. Thou would not find this way, if it be dark.' She carried his bundle and pointed out the steps which lay over a bank, by the side of the pigs. 'We be walking alongside this wall,' she said, ''til we meet the tree, then cut over to the church.'

The priest realised that the route the maid was leading him afforded valuable cover in this high spot.

'I be looking about for 'ee,' she said, 'and I know of no-one yonder.' She glanced at the fields which lay below and judged it safe for the priest to traverse the open churchyard.

'Your father?' the priest asked.

'In the church, awaiting thee.'

31

They crossed the cobbled path and cut an arc between gravestones to reach the south-west corner of the church, then walked close to its walls. The warmth of the fire had left him now and the priest felt the chilly breeze. The farmer's dogs caught their sounds and ran from the church to bring them in. 'Thank you, my friend,' the priest said and rested on a carved chest, just inside the door.

The small church was well cared for. The stonework was trim and windows held glass, some with patterned and coloured designs. The font was old and bore a simple arched border as used by the Romans, but much of the woodwork including the rood screen was more recent. Since Lent was still a few weeks away the altar held small posies of snowdrops. At the west end lay the bell tower and to the north a small chapel.

'It all lies afore thee.' Seth spoke truthfully. The entire space was apparent – there seemed no visible nooks or crannies in which to hide. 'But there is more to see! Ellie, take these animals,' (he meant Nemo and Toss, the dogs), 'back home and stay there 'til I find thee.'

'Yes, father,' she replied.

Tom was waiting for Ellie, as she climbed down the steps into the farmyard. 'Hush,' she said, 'mother will hear us.'

'I keep telling thee, I b'aint feel right about thee,' Tom said.

'What dost thou mean?'

'The way thou be taking risks!'

'Why, Tom, he be a man of the cloth.' Ellie tried to brush off his concerns.

'That's reason enough, with soldiers around, and only a short ride from here.'

Ellie raised her arms to touch Tom's shoulders. 'I know thou means for the best, but he be frail and aged. It be not right for him to wander and try his luck, o'ernight. What's to become of him?'

'Ellie!' Catherine, catching her daughter lingering with Tom, felt it was time the pot by the hearth was checked. 'Has the cream been stirred, my girl? The butter's to be churned and the dough, it be rising. I need help with the bread.'

Tom turned to face his diverse tasks. He also knew Seth might call on him to make good a hedge to curb the sheep from wandering. This priest, he acknowledged, was deserving. But after this, there'd be another. Was there any end to it, he wondered – and Ellie it was who took the risk.

8   A secret of Lee's farm

Polly little realised she'd discover a secret of Lee's farm when Marion passed the 'phone across to her. Rob had left for school in glum mood. This was most unlike him Lottie, his mother, said. Apologetic but very concerned, she was anxious for him as he was struggling with a biology project for school. Her tone lifted as Polly agreed: she would allow time for the school bus to return and then make her way to their farm, to give what advice she could.

'I could do to stretch my legs,' Luke said as Polly was about to set off, 'I'll introduce you.'

Marion smiled. 'You're taking this very seriously,' she said.

'The young lad's grade may depend on it! And we don't want our convalescent getting lost.'

'I may get lost,' Polly admitted, 'but d'you know, I'm feeling heaps better, thanks to you both.'

'Good-oh!' Luke held the door for her and they set off along the lane, skirting the churchyard and past a footpath that lay to the left alongside several ancient trees. Suddenly the lane opened out to reveal a cluster of farm buildings around an apron of concrete to the right, on which stood tractors, a four-by-four and two smaller cars. 'Here we are, this is Lee's,' Luke said. 'Look at their front door, now that's an entrance to be admired!' Painted sunny yellow, the colour or the door sang out against the white walls of the house and a patch of garden, itself bordered by neat and low old-fashioned metal railings. At the foot of the door was a tub, planted with primroses in primary colours. Polly halted for a moment, charmed by the appearance of the house that looked so bright and cheerful alongside the other buildings – barns, linhays and stables of local grey stone. 'It's old, ask Lottie. These walls could tell a tale or two,' Luke said. Polly looked across the white-painted cob walls topped by dark, weathered thatch. The upstairs windows, higgledy-piggledy and including two dormers, spoke of different ages, as did those at ground level, with two to the left and three to the right of the yellow door.

'It's certainly got character!' Polly smiled.

Luke lifted the latch on the low metal gate and they walked towards the front door that was pulled open before they reached it. 'I've been looking for 'ee,' a lanky fifteen year-old said seriously.

'Good to see you, Rob, this is Polly,' Luke said. 'Started lambing yet?' For several minutes he chatted with the boy, who relaxed in talking about the few early lambs that had arrived ahead of time, his face breaking into smiles. 'Show Polly, before she leaves,' Luke said, and with a wave he turned and left.

'Mum says come this way,' Rob led Polly into a passageway which seemed to run the depth of the house. As he opened a door on the left, Polly saw a large, dimly lighted space. Two chairs had been set in front of paperwork arranged neatly on a heavy, oaken table. Rob switched on an old-fashioned standard lamp with a floral shade, placed conveniently to throw light on his work. 'It sort of doesn't make sense,' Rob said seriously, by way of introduction.

Carefully reviewing the sheaf of papers, Polly pieced the project together. A laboratory exercise, Polly wondered why he had not done field-work, around his home, perhaps.

'I chose this,' Rob was defensive, 'and the timing didn't help. Little was growing then.'

Polly talked with him about what he'd done and it was obvious he'd enjoyed the practical work and understood its purpose. She helped him to organise his results and think about their meaning. 'I can't do more, because this is yours, isn't it.'

'Oh, I know that. But will you come back?' he asked hopefully.

'Of course, if you need me,' Polly smiled. 'D'you normally work in here?' She looked around at her surroundings. At one side of the room was an expansive fireplace. It took up the best part of a whole wall, with recesses at each side and a heavy old beam above. In front of her, on a sideboard, were family photographs alternating with silver cups and rosettes won at agricultural shows and horse-riding events.

'No! Mum thought this would be best. D'you want to see my desk?'

'I don't need to,' said Polly, helping him to stack his papers neatly.

'Mum said she'd come and see you,' Rob said. 'I'll find her.'

'I thought you'd be better downstairs, there's more space,' Lottie explained. 'Thanks a million for coming round.' She was accompanied by Charles, who was alternately wanting to be lifted into her arms and then wriggling, so he could be put down and scramble across the floor. 'He's in athletic mood today. We'll be a sprinter yet, won't we, Charles?'

'I think Rob's making good progress with his project, he's worked hard collecting results,' said Polly. 'And I've been glad to come round. It's a treat to see your house. It's really old, isn't it?'

'I love it,' Lottie said. 'Sometimes Ray says I married him just so I could live here! It's been in his family for two hundred years.' Following Polly's gaze to the fireplace, she added, 'But it's much older than that. This side of the house was the original hall – you know, entire home for the family. And for centuries they used to cook on that fire. Really early on, in the middle-ages, there was a fire in the centre of the room.'

Polly smiled. 'It's hard to imagine now. So this is a Devon long-house?'

'It's all of that!' Lottie said proudly. 'And like most, it's been altered over the years. But this has been the dining room for as long as Ray can remember.' Retracing her steps, Lottie showed Polly her small office, where she kept paperwork for the farm. 'There's enough of that, you know!' she said, leading Polly further and across a lobby into a large kitchen decorated with children's art-work and cosy with an Aga like Marion's. 'This is where we are, most of the time,' she said. Seated at a plastic-topped table were two young girls, who looked up shyly, their faces shining above bright woollen jumpers. 'Meet Becky and Joy,' Lottie said to Polly and, in the same breath, 'come on, girls, tell Polly what you're doing.'

'Homework,' said the younger, Joy, who giggled. She looked about eight years old. Becky, her sister, was using a calculator and ruler as she worked out the areas of various shapes. With coaxing from her mother and encouragement from Polly, she lisped her explanation about being in her second term at the senior school and each morning catching the school bus with Rob, and she listened seriously as Polly said she'd look for her, from the window at Laura's.

'This side of the house has had various uses. It started as a shelter for animals, and the like,' Lottie said as she continued with her tour. 'Ray's grandparents converted this room from a dairy, not that long since. I'll show you our sitting room.' This led off the kitchen. Square-shaped, Polly's immediate impression was of prettiness, with chintz-covered chairs and pots of African violets coming to life in the deep window-sills. Bookcases full of children's books stood each side of a flat-screen TV that stood inert and contrasted with an upright piano, which had music exercises propped on its stand. 'Both girls are learning now,' smiled Lottie. Through the windows Polly saw parked vehicles; she realised this overlooked the front of the house. With Charles scrambling alongside they returned through the kitchen and into the scullery, with its washing machines, rubber boots, outdoor clothes and children's toys. Lottie apologised for the clutter. 'We're lucky to have the space. But with our four, Ray and me, we need it!'

'You have a really interesting home,' Polly said.

'There's no money in farming, you know.'

'Mum,' Rob paled, embarrassed by his mother's frankness. 'She hasn't told you the best bit,' he blurted out.

'Oh, he won't let go of this!'

'Go on,' said Polly encouragingly.

'We've got a tunnel – under there and to the church.' The two girls had run in to join them; curious about their visitor they looked on, wide-eyed.

'Never!' said Polly, 'is that really true?'

'Well, my husband says so. But the passage is all sealed up now, of course.'

'We read a poem in Year 10, *And where we tread is holy, haunted ground*,' Rob said, 'it reminds me of here.'

'Byron?' Polly suggested and simultaneously Lottie added, in an audible whisper, 'They've got this idea, about ghosts. There's none of them. Definitely no ghosts. Your father and your uncle Cliff say not,' she added, addressing her family.

'But the tunnel?' Polly enquired.

'That seems right enough. And the children love the idea, of course.'

'Mum, I'm not a child,' Rob said.

Lottie, pacifying Rob, urged him to show Polly the lambs that needed care and a new litter of pups. 'They're all from Rob's bitch. Go and show her, Rob.'

He led Polly out to the back and showed her a deep kennel, neatly fenced around. Pride showed in his face. As they approached, the sheepdog Lizzie emerged to greet them, followed by her young brood. 'She's hungry – and look at them all!' The black and white furry pups clustered around her, trying to suckle between rolling over each other. Lizzie licked Rob's hands.

'How many?' asked Polly.

'Six and Dad says we can keep two. Look, that's the last.' One, a bit smaller and with fewer white markings, struggled to find a place. 'We bottle-feed him. Half the time he doesn't get a look in. But he's a real one for trying.'

'Can I touch them?' Polly asked.

Rob shook his head. 'They're not house-dogs. I take care of the mother and she'll take care of them, so there's no need to worry.'

The bright-eyed fluffy bundles darted and jumped so quickly that Polly thought there was little likelihood of catching one by leaning over. 'They're beautiful,' she commented as Rob looked on proudly. 'And what about these lambs of yours? Am I allowed to view them? Then I really must be going,' Polly added.

'Over here,' Rob said and with long strides walked Polly

over to a pen in the corner of the barn. There were three ewes and five lambs, which were bleating and supporting themselves on spindly legs.

'They're so tiny,' Polly said, 'but they look sprightly.'

'Aye, they'll be growing,' Rob said, lifting a bag of feed from which he distributed some pellets into the pen. 'They'll soon be in the field, but Dad's worried 'bout 'em, they've come so early.'

'You know Luke will wonder what's happened to me,' Polly said, 'I should be getting back.'

'Aw, don't worry 'bout Luke. He comes round himself, sometimes.'

'Thank your mother again; I have enjoyed visiting and meeting you all. And let me know how you get on.'

She waved to Lottie, standing by the scullery with Charles, and returned along the lane, around the boundary of the church and back to Marion's.

9   Developments

Polly wondered at developments afoot in Derscott and couldn't rid herself of thoughts of Lee's farm.

'Yes, they're Domesday, you know,' Luke commented as Polly recalled her visit and the underground passage at Lottie's farm, at breakfast the next morning. 'A good number are around here.'

'And this house?'

'Good heavens, no. The front's country-Georgian. When we first came, I looked around and thought I found traces of an earlier dwelling. But I can't be sure.'

'Well, I like to think,' Marion interjected, 'the fabric of the side wall is older.'

Luke shrugged his shoulders. 'It's nice to let your imagination run on a bit, but I reckon they used whatever was at hand.' Turning to Polly he continued, 'We have the deeds, you know. They say it was built for the widow of a rector. His grave's in the yard opposite, 1790-ish. It was close to the stones we looked at the other day.'

'The past seems so immediate here.'

Marion looked at Polly quizzically. 'You don't exactly escape it in London!'

'It's closer here. The children, I mean Rob, told me about a passage.'

'Aye, I've heard that,' said Luke.

'And ghosts too, have you heard about them?'

'Piffle.' Marion squashed the idea. 'You know what children are like.'

'They've still got imaginations, that we've discarded,' Luke grunted. 'I'm open-minded.'

'Piffle and poppycock.' Marion spoke more emphatically. 'Lottie doesn't want her children's heads full of such nonsense.'

'Doesn't mean she's right,' Luke mused. 'I like the resonance the idea brings.'

Polly smiled. 'I like Derscott, ghosts or not.'

'They're about to be displaced,' said Luke, darkly.

'Whatever d' you mean?'

Luke spoke volubly about plans for five or six hundred houses, no mere handful, on a site near Lee's farm. 'So this is the "development"? It's bizarre,' Polly protested.

'The self-same,' Luke asserted. 'Hatched by Mike (Laura's husband) and Joe Hartley, no less.'

'I know you call this a village, but it's more like a hamlet at a cross-roads. All those houses would swamp it.'

'This is the first time I've seen you spirited, my girl. You're recovering,' Marion said.

Polly's eyes gleamed. Though she felt warm and secure in the comfort of the kitchen, she admitted a growing awareness of issues pricking the complacency of Derscott life. 'Will you show me where this is happening? Two fields? How big are they?'

'A lot of hectares.'

'Hectares don't mean much to me,' she laughed, but persisted, 'when this drizzle lifts, show me round there please.'

'The fields are over the lane from Lottie and Ray's.'

'Do they belong to them? I mean do Lottie and Ray need to sell their land?' Polly asked, remembering comments Lottie had made about farming not bringing in much money.

'Lord, no,' Luke said firmly, and with that discussion halted, as his thoughts turned to other things.

Steady rain was falling and more was forecast. Luke spread the kitchen table with his notes about lichens. Between reading chapters of her book, Polly watched as he opened out a map and checked locations where he had seen interesting species on past visits. Noticing her interest, he said, 'If the weather picks up, we'll have an outing to a churchyard in that village.' He pointed to the spot and added, 'As well as good headstones, there's a first class pub.' Polly laughed. 'Don't underestimate the value of a good fire, my girl, when you've got wet feet.'

The kitchen was quiet and the house peaceful. Marion was busy in her study, planning arrangements for her next inspection. Polly was relishing her detective story, but having reached a puzzling part of the plot she paused to mull over possibilities, and then her interest wavered. She picked up her mobile and accessed her messages, hoping there would be one from Haresh. She found she had received three, as well as a batch of photographs. Saving the images until last, she read about the latest stage of his tour, a town he had visited, the craftspeople he had met and the idiosyncrasies of his hire car. By happenchance, waiting for a repair he had come across a sale of local crafts and an auctioneer, Irina was her name, had introduced him to a local clock-maker. Polly was transported into a world where skills were passed down through families and traditions held. As she flicked through the photos she saw benches crowded with carved toys as well as individual items such as musical animals, dancing dolls and boxes which popped up with surprises. Last of all, there was a scene at a local hostelry, with Haresh seated among a crush of people, an attractive woman at his shoulder.

Someone had taken this for him, Polly realised. She looked around the faces, pale in the camera flash, except for Haresh. His brown face was looking straight into the lens, relaxed and apparently happy in his surroundings. The woman adjacent was gazing attentively at Haresh rather than at the camera. Polly replayed the photographs and then ran through the messages again. The mention of Irina was slight. But she wondered should there have been more? She flicked forward to the last photo and zoomed onto Haresh, his crisp white shirt open-necked, the remains of a substantial meal before him and a glass in his hand. A cluster of bottles stood on the table, a generous number, Polly thought, for the five, perhaps six people she could see around his table. The only person paying more attention to Haresh than the camera was the woman with dark hair which fell in waves to her shoulders. Pushed back behind her left ear, a long ear-ring dangled and shone against the dark background of the room. Her jacket, velvet apparently and unbuttoned, showed the low neckline of a thin, revealing blouse. Polly peered at all the detail her mobile would allow. The woman, like Haresh, held a glass and both her hands cupped its bowl. Polly, unable to contain her curiosity, drafted a message in her head. She was being foolish, she knew, and should not react so. Of course Haresh was going to socialise. It was part of his job. He must foster links and cultivate those with novel wares who could supply his growing business, as a specialist provider of traditionally crafted toys. It all seemed so reasonable. In turn, they would mention his commercial interest, involve others and widen his potential. Such notions spun in her mind: the importance of canvassing craft-workers and being hospitable. A meal, a bottle of wine and cheerful company were all part of this.

But could there be more? Could relationships develop – or more personal services be offered by way of inducement? Fears escalated in Polly's imagination as she compared the warmth conveyed by the photograph with the best of times she had enjoyed with Haresh and some gentler times, which she coveted more, of radiant contentment in sharing his company. And then she reflected on recent weeks when, ailing, she had shut herself away and sought no company, just wanting to breathe, to fight infection and to recover. Haresh had been patient and caring. But the invitation he had offered for her to accompany his trip was haunting her. At the time it had seemed too demanding a journey. And the practicalities had seemed overwhelming: the tickets to purchase, packing to organise, the flat to close up and her medical regime to plan. She was still taking one course of tablets and here – well, if necessary, she could return home to the doctor she trusted. But now, she without Haresh and he without her, Polly felt vulnerable and guilty. She switched off her mobile and, in spite of the cosiness in the kitchen, she was wistful.

Luke, noticing her solemn expression, brought her back to reality. 'Just hold that a minute, will you?' And he passed her a bundle of notes on lichens. 'Better get this kit away. Know just how you feel.' The table had served as a work space, enabling Luke to check some lichen records. 'Happens all the time to me, though of course, Marion's job is just trotting round schools. Doing good it's presumed. I wouldn't mind if she brought back musical boxes.' Polly wiped away a tear.

'We could take our walk,' Luke suggested, aware of the dilemma Polly might feel, isolated from Haresh and not completely well herself. He continued, 'Remember, you asked about the fields for our erstwhile development.'

They passed by the shop, now displaying posters protesting about the development, alongside notices of local events and repeat performances of a long-running pantomime. Luke greeted a neighbour and they looked out for a solitary car as they tramped across the road towards the churchyard, by Lottie's nursery. Lights from inside shone through displays of children's work across the windows. Polly smiled as she imagined the activities within. 'We're on our way to the farm, I mean Lottie's farm,' said Polly recognising the route they were taking.

'And Ray's, remember. The Lee's farm's been in the family for generations,' Luke remarked.

'The family's really proud of their home,' Polly said.

Luke nodded in agreement.

'Rob's a nice boy,' Polly continued, 'and's grown to love the animals around the farm. He showed me the litter he's got.'

'Litter?'

'Yes, have you seen them? Lizzie, his dog, has produced six pups. They look adorable and Rob's very protective. He didn't want me to touch them.'

'Six pups has he?' Luke was thoughtful. 'I've sometimes thought of a dog for company.'

They had reached a footpath between a row of cottages, originally housing for farm-workers. In single file they walked the depth of the buildings and to the end of their gardens, before crossing a stile to reach a large field, bordered by trees. This dipped away from the village before rising again towards Great Torrington. A dog barked as they left the gardens behind. A pair of horses, still blanketed for winter and grazing in a far corner, noticed their arrival and slowly made their way towards them. 'All of this is Joe's; you've met him of course,' Luke said.

'Is all of this land for building?'

'Well it hasn't been, 'til now. It's always been farmed,

44

sheep and cows, mostly, as long as we've been here. But it's not only this field, you know. The proposal is for the next field too. Look, you can just see it, the other side of the horses.' A break in the line of trees revealed a gate, but little more was visible from where they stood. 'If it all materialises the land will be covered with little boxes juxtaposed along a regular pattern of roads. It will change the village forever.'

'How much land does Joe own, then?'

'A good amount, though exaggerated by gossip, I 'spect. I know of a large farm near Clovelly, two more near here and supposedly he's got interests in Cornwall; but some may be small. Much has been in the family for generations and they've held onto it. But Joe's progressive; he doesn't just sit on his assets. I've known him trade some fields and buy others. He's got builders involved in this project; he's in earnest.'

'It's the scale of the development that doesn't seem right,' said Polly.

'I know. If you look at old records you'll see this was once old woodland pasture. Not dense, at least not a forest, and farm animals grazed through it. Not long ago there were many more farms around here. They were all small of course, only a fraction of the size of Lee's farm, for instance.'

The horses, now close to them, were curious and nuzzled, hoping for titbits. 'So these are Joe's?'

'More likely to belong to neighbours,' Luke pointed to the row of cottages they had passed. 'Joe's reasonable enough to get on with, and he's probably trying to butter them up. He must be allowing grazing over winter.'

'I'm glad I know the village as it is.' Polly, seeing the rich green of the fields that sloped gently to the village and bordered woodland along their upper boundary, felt a sudden enthusiasm to return with her paints.

'And I wish the village would stay this way,' Luke muttered in agreement. They turned to leave and were soon back at the house, removing muddy boots and outer jackets.

'Luke's taken you to see Joe's fields has he?' Marion asked.

'Well, the two earmarked,' Luke said, tersely.

'It may not bother us much,' Marion commented.

'Rubbish! It makes me angry just to look at those fields and to think of our village. Oh, it's not your doing,' Luke looked at Marion and then to Polly. 'Marion knows how I feel. But she will soft-soap the man, and his lady friend too. I don't know how their cosiness is viewed by Mike.'

Marion, embarrassed, tried to justify her friendship with Laura. 'Her husband's away so much. Don't take it so seriously, Luke. I'm sure there's nothing to it, they're just being neighbourly.'

'You know how I feel. We came to this peaceful village, all minding our own business, the farmers farming, couples making homes where similar have lived for yonks and along comes Joe with I don't know how many acres (or hectares, if you will) with a scheme to build houses. He's no philanthropist. He's looking to the you-know-what. The price goes up every time you read the paper,' and Luke rubbed his fingers together, like a money-lender.

'It'll provide affordable housing, that's worthy enough,' Marion said.

'He's doing it to line his pockets.'

'And he'll create jobs,' Marion squabbled cheerfully.

'For six months. Then what?'

'Darling, mind your blood pressure. Your conscience's too big. We can't live in a museum, and people need houses.'

'We already have houses. Hundreds, thousands, millions of 'em: they need work doing on them, that's all.' Marion tried to cuddle him but Luke responded little. 'Now you're being nice to me. You know you can't win by reason, that's why.' Luke continued muttering to himself so quietly that his words were hardly audible, but among the scraps Polly heard she thought he mentioned 'puppy' and she wondered if Marion had caught this too.

10   The passage

The priest asked questions of Seth about the folks who lived nearby and Derscott's own local priest, who should know of his arrival. But the questions came haphazardly, not in logical order, and between them silence fell in the church. 'It's best we country folks know little,' said Seth, finally. He kept to himself the disappearance of Father Anthony, neither understanding it himself nor wishing to alarm the elderly man. He judged he'd find a better time to recount it all.

Patrick ruminated at the partial tale he'd gleaned, but was too weary to persist and probe. While in his heart he searched the truth, he was willing to acknowledge the shield that ignorance of awkward deeds provided. He realised also that his own life was at Seth's disposal. 'Now, my means of escape, good man?'

'Yes, Father, see this way.' Seth led him to the altar, and folded back the draped cloth edged with narrow lace. 'Trust me,' Seth said, 'and I'll show thee how. Then thou can do it for thyself.' The flagged floor to all appearances stopped short beneath the altar table, beneath which there were boards. Seth ran his fingers down one at the back and felt for a plank which he pulled up, then several more, to make an opening. The hole beneath was carefully fashioned. 'It's narrow here,' Seth said, 'but broadens out and there be air at 'other end. The passage be safe.'

Patrick nodded, understanding.

'There's enough space for 'ee and thy bundle too. Its width'll take myself and I be stout enough. I'll show 'ee.'

The priest looked on and Seth, wishing to dispel his hesitancy, explained, 'The hardest be the first. Once started, thou'll be fine. Just follow me.'

'You'll help me down, good man?'

'Father, trust me,' Seth said. 'But if it happens thou needs return, feel here...' He guided the priest's fingers into a depression beneath the opening. 'Dost thou feel the metal

47

ring?' Seth explained that this marked the plank that if pushed would allow others to be moved.

The priest admired the handiwork. *'Yes, we care for the cause since it be just, and for our own lives too,'* Seth replied.

'Does your local priest know?'

Seth nodded by way of explanation, but did not expand on this.

The priest lowered himself gently down past compacted earth and broken rock, cut away to form crude steps, and steadied himself with the farmer's hand. He felt each step with the toes of his boots. At the base of the short flight, rough planks shored up the wall, about four feet in height. Looking back, the light seemed dazzling, compared with the darkness below.

Satisfied that the priest's footing was secure the farmer gave instructions. *'Keep straight behind this back o'mine. The ground slopes further but there be no more steps. Hold the right, if thou needs steadying.'*

'How steep does it drop?'

'It goes gently enough, near on four paces over forty would be my guess. And it's straight, or near enough, 'til almost the end, where it bends, sharpish. Thou'll know the end, the pigs do tell 'ee. It do smell.' The farmer's laugh echoed in the passage.

'Thank you kindly,' the priest replied. He sensed the farmer was nervous for him, but the elderly man sought the reassurance of knowing he could navigate himself along the tunnel. As the farmer gave instructions from a short way ahead the priest replaced the floor which formed the ceiling of the passage. Each piece fell into place methodically. The task completed, he waited several minutes, giving time to catch any gleam of light around, but he saw none. It was cold, dark and quiet; he could not hear the wind down here. Slowly, he edged forward. He meant to count his steps but knew that, stooped as he was, each pace would be less than the yard it would measure if he were striding out. The air was stale. With his hands he felt the walls and in places as he touched the earth it crumbled, though at other times rocks

48

snagged his habit. He took small steps along the rough earthen floor and stumbled along its unevenness. The farmer gained distance on him that he perceived by the fading exclamations of his guide. The priest grew accustomed to glancing blows across the top of his head where he had not crouched low enough and thought his hood was poor protection. In two places there seemed more space and at one he dared to stand. He wondered at the length he was traversing and believed that in the absence of more planks to support the roof a natural fault of rock must have allowed the building of this passage. Finally, his head, then his feet and hands, met with a facing wall and he saw dim light to his left.

'Father?' He heard hoarse bidding, among animal sounds. 'Don't mind thy nose. Just keep coming on.'

Cracks of daylight fell between the seams of a rough but solid fence which barred his way. He could almost stand upright at this point. From banging and grazing sounds he surmised the farmer was moving obstacles, from just the other side. He also heard more loudly the grunts and squeals of pigs and he realised where he was – in the yard behind the farm. 'Feel a short stake latched across the right? Pull hard on't, I've set it for thee to try.' He listened to the farmer's instructions and obeying them he soon freed himself and squinted into daylight. Nemo ran up to him, followed by Toss, but they stopped their barking, at the farmer's word.

'My good man, that's verily a marvel!' the priest said.

'Aye, it took some doing – but the good start I had aided well.' As the priest had thought, the tunnel had been of ancient use, its construction possible due to the formation of rocks.

'But why start it here?' the priest asked, pointing to the pigs.

'Thou'll never've better cover'n that,' the farmer replied, grinning at the sows, their piglets running and competing for their suckle. 'I'm careful mind, to keep the hog elsewhere!' And he chuckled at the thought of this. 'I'll show 'ee how to start, from this end.' One sow, newly settled down, blocked the movable fence which bordered her pen but with a kick from the farmer she ambled away and freed their path, which

49

sent her sucklings scampering and squealing once more. A loose upright in the fence enabled a hand to reach through and shift the latch, but from the farmyard nothing unusual could be seen. 'We've made good use of 'em swine; there be much I could tell 'ee!'

Sheltered as they were by farm buildings, the farmer knew they could safely talk but, respectful of the age and condition of the priest, he led him within. 'Catherine,' he called to his wife, 'fetch a cloth and, aye, sustenance.' Returned to the hall the priest sank into the settle he'd earlier used. He brushed dirt from his face and felt wetness on his head, which showed red on his fingers. Catherine cleaned the area and wiped his forehead.

'That will heal, soon enough,' said the priest making light of the graze.

'Aye, good Father,' Catherine replied, 'but let me help nature do its work for thee.' She stroked lineament around the broken skin, then moved her attention to his muddied clothing. 'Thou'll be wanting me to tend to this,' she said and he complied willingly. In his long under-robe he looked diminished and she offered him another outer garment and a cloak that Tom had outgrown, knowing it would disguise his religious commitment more securely than the black habit it replaced.

'Go-on wi'er,' the farmer dismissed the priest's embarrassment, 'thou owns that all as well as I and I need not tell 'ee so!'

Catherine gone, the priest relaxed before the warmth of the substantial hearth, with the farmer looking across at him from a wooden chair with broad curved arms, set opposite. In a corner beneath the cream, the cat still lay curled and sleeping on its tail. Patrick looked around to find the other creatures lying in warm crevices around this hall. He wondered about the stray hen, but decided that must have found another perch or become invisible in the gloom.

'There'll be things by rights thou ought to know,' the farmer started to explain. 'Loyalty be strong in these parts and another good man went a'fore 'ee.'

Feelings of sleep ebbed away as the priest caught interest in the farmer's tale.

'Until one month ago, a much younger priest than thee, Father Anthony, were here.'

The priest recalled the name, mentioned earlier by Seth. But Father Patrick, who was not of these parts, had come north from Exeter travelling partway with the King's troops and did not know of him.

'He be 'bout thirty years and born of a good family only a day's ride south-east of here. For several years he looked a'ter our souls and made hi'self welcome with all hereabout. Why he wed my eldest, Jess be 'er name, with Matthew and baptised her young 'uns, when they came along. By rights we were 'specting he'd marry Ellie too, only he's not here to see to that, though the time be near ripe for she and Tom.'

Patrick felt his acquaintance grow with the farmer's brood as he heard more about cousins and the vicinity they resided in, close by. The farmer, glad to have this undemanding audience, elaborated his tale until Patrick reminded him: 'Father Anthony – what became of him?'

'He made plain his 'legiance, he did indeed. Me thinks that were the cause of it all.'

'Tell me, good man,' the priest prodded patiently.

'There's little to tell, though what there be b' bad,' the farmer said. An ember fell over on the fire. Disturbed, the cat caused the hen to show itself by fluttering across to another joist. 'He made his cottage close to us, scarce more'n a mile away but that became too known and 'ee took lodgings 'ere. There's been more'n just thou and 'im passing through. His lodgings – they still be safe, waiting for 'im but thou be most welcome to 'em. I'll show 'ee, when thou art ready, they be the lower part of the wing where young Tom sleeps above and th'entry be from the yard.

'Pardon my ramblings, I be talking of Father Anthony, I be. While we carried on wi' the farm, as oft as not he ate with us, though after dining he'd repair to his own place and his thoughts. He stood for the King as his family a'fore 'im, though he were good to all men. But there be folks hereabouts who don't care that way, 'specially not in a man

51

of God. He knew the passage,' the farmer waved in the direction of the pigs and the church, 'indeed, 'elped to make improvements, refining the hidden parts and strengthening the walls.' The farmer shifted his weight on the chair, moving his legs closer to the fire and the priest. 'As I be telling a while before, the passage be long established. Folks around say the age o'it be a match wi' the church itself. Them two belong.' Father Patrick had heard similar tales before and knew that while the church offered both sanctuary and a place of worship for the priest and others too, the passage gave escape.

Steam and aromas rose from the pots, blackened outside and bubbling within. The farmer added logs to the fire, from the stack drying adjacent in a deep recess. What had befallen Father Anthony, his fellow priest, dwelt on Patrick's mind. The seemingly forthright farmer was slow to answer this. 'Have you been visited recently by Cromwell's men?' Patrick enquired further.

'Aye, that be true,' the farmer replied, 'but men of both sides pass regularly by. Thee be welcome to all I know.' After a moment, the farmer continued. 'He left, Father Anthony did, and by that I mean suddenly, and his whereabouts none of us do know.'

Another moment passed, so the priest intervened. 'Did any suspect he'd been residing here?'

'Local folks would know as much. He'd visited another place, but that was too prominent and he had heard of the safety of priests resting here.'

The priest found matters tangled in his own mind and his silence gave Seth opportunity to continue.

'He left more 'an a full moon ago – and nothing took save his horse, a chestnut mare. The last 'e said were about Ellie and Tom and even 'speculated arrangements when they might be wed. Then 'e were off. I 'spected 'im back in a day or two, but 'e never came.' The farmer moved forward, poked at the fire to loose its ash, then rubbed his thighs and shifted his legs as he settled into his chair and waited for the flames to rise again. 'But at that time, along came Cromwell's men. They looked only broadly 'bout the place *and took my word for emptiness. It were more as if they knew and wanted to be sure of things – which makes me wonder.'*

The priest could read in the farmer's eyes that he held back further thoughts, but he could not tell of what. And he knew that Seth must be guarded, not only for the safety of his own life but also for that of his wife, family and livelihood.

'The next I knew were Jess, with Matthew her good man, coming back from Great Torrington with the Father's token. They asked that it be taken to the seamstress, and that led to thee.'

Light from the small window fell on the priest's face and he was acutely aware of the farmer watching him. 'There's little for me to add, my friend,' he said. 'I travel from Exeter where I've cared for the souls of men standing for the King and, aye, for a good many others too.' The farmer, a trusting man, asked no more and the priest, turning thoughts over in his mind, drifted into sleep.

11   Mike is delayed and snow arrives

News that Mike was delayed was brought by Laura, his wife, though no-one was particularly concerned, except Laura herself. Towards the end of the afternoon she had called round with leaflets, advertising a local pageant to be performed at Great Torrington.

'Come in,' called Marion to the familiar voice, 'we're just about to have some coffee.'

'No we're not. It's a drink I want, a proper drink, not just coffee. I've had enough of this weather,' Luke, in the kitchen, asserted.

'Then open a bottle, Luke, there's a nice red at the left of the wooden rack. How are things, Laura?' Marion turned her attention to the visitor.

'Oh, it'll be another fortnight before Mike's home. There's an extension to his contract. But he should be home in time for the pageant.'

'Where is he this time, Laura?' Luke asked.

'Shanghai.'

'That sounds very civilised for Mike. Isn't it all skyscrapers and technology?'

'Well, the contract's for Lanchow but it's their winter, conditions are holding back construction and he's discussing agreements in Shanghai. He says there's money in it.'

'So it can't be bad,' Marion commented, trying to make light of Mike's continued absence, but Luke was more thoughtful. 'He'll be planning more towns I suppose, Laura?' he wondered.

'Relocating Chinese villages; all tied up with development and infrastructure.'

'I never know what that word means, though I expect we'll need more infrastructure here too, if the Derscott houses go ahead,' Luke said.

'But Derscott's much too small-scale for Mike's professional interest, isn't it, Laura?' Marion asked.

54

Luke was bristling still about developments, Polly thought, and she deflected the conversation further by asking the whereabouts of Lanchow, adding that Haresh, her boyfriend, was in Belarus.

'I've never been there,' Laura replied. 'I don't travel now, at least, not further than Bristol one way and the Eden Project the other.' More lightly, she added, 'I suppose I'm forgetting the trip to Juliet, and Mike once took me to a town near the Black Sea and for a weekend in New York. I liked that. But he does so much globe-trotting he just wants to stay here, once he's home.'

'How is your daughter, Laura, and the new baby?'

Laura's tenseness evaporated at the thought of her Australian family. 'Juliet's fine. She tells me the baby feels the heat, it was 90° last weekend, but she and Bob are making friends and she likes where they're living now.'

'And you have a very nice home here in Derscott,' said Marion.

'Thank you. We came here because I like Devon, it brings back childhood memories and Mike likes the hilly countryside, so different from flat Lincolnshire he knew as a boy.' Laura was quiet for a moment before adding, 'And yes, we've put a lot into making our home.' Changing the subject she asked Polly about Haresh's work and whether he also was with a multinational.

'Heavens, no,' Polly said cheerily. 'He's got his own small company. He imports traditional, hand-made toys and he's away sourcing new ones now.'

'Look, Laura, Polly brought us this, for Anna's new baby. Isn't it delightful?' For several minutes Marion wound and rewound the musical box, with its black and white cows which revolved, watched by sheep and hens.

'All my better-half does is negotiate contracts, finalise deals and spend hours, I mean days, on his laptop. It all seems remote, except when he's here with me.'

Their glasses were emptied and refilled. Together they looked at the evening news on the kitchen TV, as well as the weather forecast, which promised snow. 'We've had similar warnings since Christmas.' Marion dismissed the forecasts.

'What's Joe doing about his stock?' Luke asked their visitor.

'I 'spect most are inside,' Laura replied. 'But he says the Devon Red cope with anything, he just gives them extra feed.'

'I took Polly to look at the development site earlier,' Luke continued. 'Any progress on it, d'you know?'

'Joe hasn't mentioned a problem, but then he wouldn't to me. I expect he and Mike will catch up on progress when Mike's home again.' Laura was cautious and tactful, in spite of Luke's persistence in dropping further queries into the conversation. In the relaxed warm haze, red wine imbued, only Laura seemed strained, Polly noticed, as if her thoughts were thousands of miles away. She noticed Marion linked Laura into the meandering conversation, with promises of seeing the pageant and returning to Laura's. By the time Laura finally left it was well past their usual supper time and lifting books and papers from the kitchen table in preparation for their meal, several pink leaflets protesting about the development stared back at them.

The next morning the landscape was white under a grey overcast sky. Snow covered most things, except where drifts had blown away to show grey slates and the tops of walls. Garden shrubs were completely enveloped although as Polly stood at her bedroom window dollops of snow fell from branches here and there, leaving gaping holes. Yew trees in the churchyard were similarly shrouded. So far as she could tell, the snow had blown in hard, backed by a strong wind. The outlines of two large deciduous trees were clear on their northern side but had snow banked up across their westerly and southerly aspects. A few garden birds fluttered by, looking for lost foliage. Then, from the window, she saw Luke already in the garden, stomping through drifts with a shovel and clearing the drive.

They listened to the national weather forecast as they breakfasted. Reference was made to snow – but not as much as conditions in Derscott seemed to warrant. The Derscott landscape was caught in a snowy veil, though the bad conditions were localised; London was not suffering. Other items captured the headlines – a visit from the U.S. president and an incident in the Middle East. Through the window they could see birds competing for the grain Luke had scattered. As they finished their coffee they heard the sound of post falling onto the mat.

'Goodness, the postman's made it!' Polly commented.

'I'm not sure about that,' Marion replied and unfolded a hand-delivered note.

'That must be really important,' Polly said. Marion spread out several pages of typescript and what looked like a plan. She was silent and concerned as she turned over the sheets describing the proposed housing development. 'Pete's right to alert us all,' Marion said quietly and she handed the bundle of pink papers to Luke.

Conflicting thoughts entered Polly's mind. In a few days' time her visit should end. She planned to return to her flat and felt almost ready for work and for cycling even. Luke guessed her thoughts. 'Enjoy this while you can,' he said, turning to peruse the papers on the building development.

Polly left the warmth of the kitchen to investigate the snowfall in borrowed wellingtons. Everywhere seemed pristine and white with flakes continuing to drizzle and cover the few visible tracks but in places it was verging on the damp and becoming soggy. From the driveway Polly could see the end of the lane and brightly-clad children pushing loose snow into shapes. Undeterred by the melt, they were trying to build a snowman and were distracted by the opportunity of pelting each other with soft balls of snow.

'I've heard the gritting lorry, we'll only be snow-bound a day,' Luke said on her return adding, with a twinkle in his eye, 'even I might be inspired to water-colour – from inside, of course.'

12   *Thinking of the lambs*

Seth gazed upon the priest slumbering on the settle and reflected on the dangers surrounding them in troubled times. The good Father, elderly and weak, needed protection and the farmer's mind ached, thinking of how hazards could be reduced. As Seth sat before the fire, the silence was broken by Ellie, who came to bring out loaves, warm from the oven.

'Father,' she said to the farmer, 'I'm thinking of the lambs soon to come and our old outshut tumbling down.'

'Ay, Ellie.'

'What think thou of 'em being alongside the run, which presently holds thy pigs?'

'Maid, what be thou thinking of? What of the pigs?'

'I wish not to displace them. I know full well, with young ones here and more to come, they need much space. My mind is on the gap from one end of this house, o're to the pigs; there be room enough there for the lambs. How much better it'd be for mother if both lambs, as well as pigs, be close at hand.' She never looked at the priest but other benefits were clear. There'd be shelter between the farmhouse and entry to the passage that led underground into the church. 'And for thou too, father,' she continued, looking directly at Seth. 'Less time would be spent in the fields searching out weakly lambs. I reckon more would live.'

'Let me ponder that,' the farmer said, 'and consider it from all ways.' He mused it could be of wood at first. Later, he'd make it up with cob and straw. He stood, and helped the priest to his feet. Ellie held back the door and they all moved out into the small yard. 'This be what ee' be thinking, then?' he indicated with his arms and several strides how the space alongside the pigs could be covered to make protection for the lambs and joined to the farmhouse door. 'It seems so plain now,' he said, 'though it be quite a way from pasture.'

'It be not just for th' animals, but for thou too, father, when it rains and blows.'

58

'What be Tom saying on this?' the farmer asked, 'Seeing as he'll be sharing with the carrying of sticks and stones with which we'd build?'

A smile crossed Ellie's face, 'I'll ask 'im, shall I, father?'

'Yes, if thou wishes and I'll do so mysel' as well.' The piglets stirred at the sound of his voice. 'Nay, nothing for ye now,' he said to them, 'though ye be coming fine.' He counted the fifteen little ones jostling alongside the two matronly sows. More were due from other sows, so he'd have hams growing enough 'afore long. 'Indeed the lass has sense in what she says,' he conceded to himself, as he watched Ellie's skirt disappear into the barn.

'Tom,' Ellie called. She walked over the compacted earth on which straw was scattered down the centre of the linhay. She knew the cows by name and each its inclination, almost as well as did Tom and her father. The custom had started when she'd been a child, of naming each after a feature of the night sky. So Ellie walked by Venus, Cloud and Comet, while Neptune the bull stood tethered in a separate stall. Still sheltering inside, after months of winter, they had grown used to human company and she enjoyed her evening milking routine. 'Tom,' she looked around with simultaneous surprise and pleasure as his arms wrapped around her and lifted her up, her face close to his.

'Now, 'ow did thou venture 'ere?' he teased.

'Father sent me…and I want to know…' Tom pulled her towards him and held her close to his chest. 'Not now….' Ellie managed to stand apart long enough to explain about the pens. Tom acknowledged the sense in it. 'Come and look, then tell 'im thyself,' Ellie implored.

'But when will thou return?' Tom teased.

'Will milking do?'

'It rightly will,' Tom replied and both retraced their steps to the farmhouse.

13   News from Marion

Marion@Derscott.com, 28 February

Hi Polly

Greetings from Derscott! Luke reminds me you've spent half-term in London with Haresh. We hope you had a great time catching up on all you've both been doing and also had time to enjoy yourselves.

Looking from my window, it's hard to believe that you left in snow. It was sunny yesterday and warm enough to sit under the cherry tree with a mug of coffee. Snowdrops, still abundant in hedgerows and banks, are giving way to primroses and we have a patch of blue crocus by the front door. I love spring, but it's hard work for some. Lambing's in full swing (I think they're aiming for the Easter market). Lottie called the other morning, tired from a long night and I went along to her nursery to help. Their numbers are up and keeping Lottie (and her volunteers) busy. A pair of new infants have joined – twin boys from the house across the road from the shop. On arrival they wore different socks and caps but you can guess these were soon detached from their owners, though good-naturedly each answered to both names!

We are excited about next week. Oliver is visiting (with his parents). Luke and I will do some baby-sitting, to give Anna and David a break. Luke has smartened up the third bedroom with white walls while I've been away and we're hanging blue and white curtains. It'll be lovely to have a baby in the house again. I've saved your musical box as a surprise. It really is delightful and I shall miss it when they take it home! I've written separately to Haresh, but I want you also to know just how much we appreciate your thoughtfulness!

Earlier this week I was in Bristol for two days, visiting a

school you'd find interesting. It specialises in languages and links have developed with a school in Spain. I saw a really good science lesson (Year 9), all in Spanish with a video link to Santander. I've rarely seen students so rapt! I have an inspection the week after Oliver's visit, so will need to make some plans during the family's stay. But I'm sure I can fit that in.

And how are things with you? I hope you're taking good care of yourself and resting, when you can. Luke echoes this! It's easy to underestimate how tiring everything is, what with a full timetable and exam groups as well. I don't mean to sound motherly, but I know I do. I saw Rob yesterday as he was on his way home from school. He wants you to know that he handed his science project in on time and the teacher seems pleased. He's certainly very relieved. He needs his science, he told me (he's still keen on an agricultural course, next year).

Your visit to Lottie's farm has had another consequence. Luke has been to look at Lizzie's pups. I learned about this from Rob. Luke thinks I don't know, which makes me wonder if he's seriously thinking we'll have a puppy. Apparently, Luke meandered round when (I thought) he was checking a lichen on a sycamore tree in failing light. It must have been about quarter past four, because Rob was just back from school. Rob said Luke was surprised that the puppies were all so lively. Of course they've grown since you saw them and I expect they were jostling for the extra food Rob provides. Now I'm waiting for Luke to bring up the subject. I should be happy for him to have company when I'm away. But I do hope he helps train it.

The main topic in Derscott is the building development, which is causing no end of argument. We're set to have a right old village bun-fight about it. I'm sure you'll remember the fields where it's proposed there'll be building? Well, the plan's causing angst among immediate neighbours (as well as among some who are not so close). More say they're against it than for it, but quite a few are sitting on the fence. Have you met Pete? He lives a bit further around the corner from the shop. He's the one mustering support for an action group.

When you were here he was distributing the pink leaflets (and we've had more since then). He's angry with those who don't care, because he feels they should. He and some others have been on local TV. It really is so damaging for the community and hurtful, too.

Luke makes no bones about it and sides with Pete. He's all for barricades and saving rural England. But I don't like to join picket lines, myself. It's partly because I know we can't live in a time warp and also because of Laura. It's not easy for her, Mike's away so much of the time and I don't like to see her isolated. Quite a few say nothing rather than speak out. Ron, the car mechanic, can see more business coming his way and Vanessa, too (she's the hairdresser). It has its lighter moments, though. In church on Sunday we prayed for peace in the world and for peace in our local community. The rector's words about neighbourliness raised a giggle here and there along the pews.

On a more cheerful note, the Torrington 1646 pageant was very successful. I went to two performances last weekend (once with Luke and again with Laura, as Mike wasn't home). It's been a real box-office success with sell-out performances. I think in part it's because so many local people are involved and also because of the casting (or type-casting). The costumes and scenery were very good, too. Audience participation was lively with the vast majority siding for the Royalist Cavaliers though enough cheered the Roundheads to make a proper hullabaloo, which continued later, in the streets. The curtain-calls went on for ages. It was a damp and dark February night but the atmosphere was carnival-like. It was good to see people of all ages and whole families really enjoying themselves.

Polly, both Luke and I enjoyed having you here and hope it's not too long before you visit us again. Everything's coming to life, spring's almost with us and North Devon is changing daily. You're most welcome to bring Haresh over the Easter break. We'd enjoy catching up on your news and Haresh's travels. There may not be musical boxes to be found at Devon sales, but there'll be a very warm welcome for you both, and you can relax in peace.

Forgive me for rambling on. It's just nice to send news, as well as our very best wishes, and love, from Marion

Marion@Derscott.com, 12 March

Hi Polly

Couldn't wait to let you know! We have a musical grandson. The musical box has been a great hit! Oliver smiles and even gurgles with the tune. While he can't focus yet, his parents certainly can – they are entranced by the cows revolving around the sheep and hens. Anna and David feel you've given something really special for their new baby and they'll treasure it.

Oliver is adorable and sleeps well. We're smitten grandparents and enjoy any opportunity we can to baby-sit, which is what I'm doing right now while the new parents take a stroll with Luke. I'm visiting a school in Cornwall tomorrow, after Oliver and parents leave. So in spare moments I'm gathering papers for that visit.

Hope all goes well and look forward to hearing from you. When will you be able to bring Haresh to see us? Best wishes from everyone here and love, Marion

Polly@Pollychalk.com, 21 March

Hello Marion

Many thanks for all your messages. Woosh! it's been a busy week and an almighty rush, but I'm switching off now for the weekend and then it's nearly the end of term. As well as all the usual happenings at school, we've had a concert and it's been more successful than we dared hope. While it's taken a lot of rehearsal time, a good number of parents have come along. Some of my best students were playing instruments and I've been giving catch-up lessons so they don't fall behind. It's lovely, though, to see them supporting each other. The steel band was applauded loudly and a girl in my Year 10 form is a gifted violinist. I'm sure no more than a handful would usually listen to classics, but they raved at her playing a Bach solo-violin piece. You should have seen her smile! I felt really proud of them all, but there just aren't enough hours in the week!

I'm so glad Oliver and his parents are enjoying the musical box. Yes, some of the new toys Haresh brought back from his last trip are fascinating. He flew to Riga where he found some soft toys made out of fabric – they're for very young children. Then he went on to Estonia. Their traditional items are mostly crafted in wood but he's also found some very nice ducks woven out of reed! Now he's becoming interested in a few of their modern pieces, not all of them are for children. His collection is becoming more diverse and he's spending the next few days photographing and expanding his web-catalogue. All of this is eating into his time and prevents his doing other things, but I like having him around.

We had a very happy and relaxed half-term. On the spur of the moment I went with Haresh to Edinburgh, via his parents in Northumbria. It was the first time we'd met. His father's a retired doctor and his mother part owns an antique book-shop, but her background's in nursing. She's English, from the Midlands, and I think met his father when he was studying in Birmingham, just qualified from Banaras. As you might guess, they have a lot of books around their house. She showed me some of the volumes she has for sale, with really lovely colour plates. They asked about my parents, which was kind of them. They even suggested that one day they may all meet! Haresh was a little embarrassed at that! I suppose I should think about taking Haresh to see mum and dad, they hear so much about him. It's not so easy to drop by, though, now they're living in Chicago and they seem a bit cautious about him. But they have mentioned a possible visit home, to escape the hot and humid mid-west summer, so before long we may have a get-together.

After a day with Haresh's parents, we made our way north to Edinburgh. Do you know the city? I found the stone uniformly grey but I loved the symmetry of the architecture and streets. It's very compact and our hotel was part of a handsome terrace. Haresh had some people to see (toy importers and distributors). While he was busy I sketched around where we stayed, just behind Princes Street. There's so much history in the area, you can almost feel it. We visited some places with Mary Queen of Scots connections. They're very atmospheric, what with the castle of Holyrood and we came across another, on a drive to St Andrews. It was quite drizzly that day and one castle I remember was gaunt and intimidating, very evocative. We returned from St Andrews along a coast road back to Edinburgh and villages appeared out of the sea mist, just a few houses facing a harbour and sea. I'd like to return sometime in better weather. There's much more to explore.

As usual, though, once back at school, life simply revolves around that! Half-term seems ages gone. The guy in the flat upstairs is absent and I think must have let out his flat. I have noisy neighbours! I wouldn't mind early risers (a bit of a prompt would be very welcome, most mornings), but they stay up at the other end of the day, which bothers me. The trouble is, they're so nice. I have been to see them about the noise and they listen most politely. Perhaps they're selectively deaf. I hope Herbert (the owner) comes back soon.

I'm interested to catch up on news of your village development. Is this near to being resolved? I quite understand about your being considerate of Laura, though on balance I side with Luke about the building plans. From this bit of north London it seems like sacrilege to cover the green fields on the edge of your village with bricks. The houses will be overwhelming!

On quite a different matter, I wonder about Lizzie's puppies? Is Rob keeping them with their mother or has one found its way into your home yet? Thanks for your invitation to make another visit. I would love to enjoy the peace and pleasures of Derscott again and I know Haresh would like to meet you, too.

All the very best, from a dusty and noisy flat in north London, love Polly

Greetings Polly

It's been great to have your news, many thanks. And I'm so glad you enjoyed your trip north.

Yes, you've guessed right, we now have a four-legged friend! Janus, our adorable puppy, is temporarily asleep at my feet. Luke exercises him in the garden (no walks beyond that just yet, the vet says) and I feed him. Not that he's fussy about food! He seems capable of digesting anything he can get his mouth around – socks, doormats and, of course, puppy biscuits. To admit that he's currently sleeping is an admission that occasionally he needs sleep. While overnight he slumbers, the daytime is a very different story. You can be assured of a loving, licking welcome. He's used to being outside at the farm and Luke intended to have a kennel for him here, but of course here he'd be lonely (no Lizzie and siblings), so we softened and he's indoors and sometimes allowed in the conservatory. But he's being good (on the whole) and is very winsome. I can't believe you won't fall in love with him, too.

News of the 'development' is slow to come. Pete thinks that a formal proposal is wending its way through council corridors, but we haven't heard anything. Mike (Laura's husband – remember it was the sale of their land that's led to this) has been home for a week and is off again tomorrow. Laura is immersing herself in another drama production in Torrington. This time, she actually has a part. Anyhow, the play is keeping her busy and her mind off Mike. She seems more anxious about him as each trip comes along. (Luke says that's because of how Mike himself feels, which would worry me, in her shoes.) But Mike will be back, in a few weeks.

We're hoping you'll visit us soon (bring your sketching things) and Haresh too, if he can make it. The countryside is at its best. Hedgerows are lined with scurvy grass, primroses are everywhere, red campion is out and violets in damp places. In the garden Janus sniffs the flowers and tries to catch birds. They must think him very silly!

Hope we'll be seeing you soon, love, Marion

14   Fairfax's men

'Jess!' The farmer, catching sight of his elder daughter on her sturdy roan, the babe secured within her long cloak and the infant boy riding astride the saddle, called, 'Be everything a'right?' He lifted Adam down and then helped Jess with the young one, still asleep against her shoulder.

'I've come as fast as possible for me,' she said, embracing her father and then Ellie. 'Fairfax's men be on their way.'

'Art thou sure, daughter?' the farmer said. While he had just reason to be wary of Parliamentarians he did not wish to be overcautious and cause alarm among his family.

'My Matt says they be visible from clear over Chittleham'on and I should come an' tell 'ee.'

''Ow many ar't be seen?'

'Ten, no more, but they be cutting this way, it seems, not going direct to Great Torrington, and we thought for 'ee.'

'Good daughter – and y'selves?'

'We be fine.'

Catherine, aware of her daughter's entrance, told her to rest, while she caressed the young boy and promised him some bread. Five years older than Ellie, Jess was broader, in part through rearing children, and also through her appetite. But the same dark eyes and curling hair of sisters showed.

The farmer, aware of Catherine's indulgence of her grandchildren, curbed her fussing. 'Nay, wife,' he said, 'Jess must soon be back again. The sun be slipping down, she can't delay.' Seth pondered at the Parliamentarians going so far into the countryside, unless they had real reason, and he shared his suspicions with Catherine.

Meanwhile, the priest hung back, leaning against one side on the settle. He observed the warmth of the greetings the farmer's family exchanged and saw they were appreciative of each other and the dangers they might face. He though, felt independent of their kinship and instead believed the church was his family. Raising himself forwards from his seat, he *slipped out of the hall and around the house to where he would find his own lodgings and rest from the day.*

'It be nightfall soon,' the farmer again warned his daughter Jess, concerned for her safe return. He helped her back on her horse, and she said goodbye to Ellie. Adam was seated at her very front and clung onto the horse's chestnut mane, pummeling its neck with his tiny fist, but the horse stood firm. 'Let Tom go wi' thee,' the farmer said.

'Aye, gladly,' Tom said good-naturedly. They set off around the edge of the farm, keeping to a gentle track bordered by hedges. They needed an easy way, as Jess still carried both Adam and the babe. Once or twice, Tom cleared a branch and went on ahead in the dimming light. Tom took her to the door of her cottage and led the roan to safe grazing. Jess was greeted by Matt who lifted the babe from her and took Adam indoors. Their home was on land that once had been Seth's, but been given on his daughter's marriage. Now Jess's closest neighbours were her husband's kin who, like her own family, supported the King.

Tom asked Matt for news of the soldiers' progress, but he had no more. 'They must be bedded down by now,' he surmised, 'have sympathy for their hosts!' After bidding farewell Tom turned his horse around, took short cuts, and returned in half the time.

The farm and its people were near slumbering by the time he was back. Catherine had laid out for him a thick slice of bread and some cheese, which he washed down with cider, before he sought his bed. As farm-hand his quarters were in the roof of the wing that abutted the hall from where, through a tiny peep-window, he was granted a view of the barn. The space below him Seth had bestowed to the priest and so Tom did his best to minimise the sound his own footsteps made on the flagged floor as he walked by. He heard the elderly man's deep breathing, irregular as if he was restless in his cot. Tom reached his own bed by a ladder and as he lay beneath the thick, coarse blanket his thoughts dwelt on Ellie and how she looked, sleeping. He knew he should be up at daybreak and that gave hardly enough time to cover all the tasks waiting to be done. A hedge to be mended, then the animals to be watched and fed, made more than enough for the farmer and him. And now Ellie suggested a new shed, close at hand, for sucklings and lambs. As if he had not guessed her intentions – to provide cover for escape. It worried him that she kept conjecturing these ideas. She meant well for the Royalist cause, that he knew. But she felt things so strongly. His mind lingering on Ellie, he fell asleep.

At the first touch of light in the sky, Tom was up. He pulled his thick jerkin over his undershirt and fastened his leggings. Mud, splashed on his clothes, had dried while he slept and fell off in flakes as he readied himself. Rain had fallen since last night, though the air seemed dry and cold now. He stepped down to the next floor as quietly as he knew how. He heard no sound from the priest and looked towards his cot. The covers were turned back and it was empty. He knew the space well; there was no place for concealment and he puzzled where the priest might be. He reached the door and noticed the latch had been cushioned with a rag. The priest had intended to leave quietly, as well as early. He resolved to search later, after tending the cows.

15   A disappointment for Polly

'Polly, is that you?'

Polly was peering at the screen of her computer when her mobile rang. 'Haresh, darling, 'course it is. Where are you?'

'In my flat. How about coming round?'

'Great! But I thought you were going to Germany today?'

'The website's taken so much time I've had to postpone. My plans are all behind. But I'll show you what I've done. It's looking good.'

'I might be slightly ravenous. Are we eating? D'you have any food?'

'Oh, you know me. Let me take you around the corner, to Raj's. Term's over? I am right about that?'

'Well we have a staff meeting tomorrow, but for the kids, yes.'

'You sound tired. I'll cheer you up.'

'Give me an hour, I'll be there.'

Polly braked her cycle to a slow halt at the railings outside Haresh's flat and secured it safely within the basement enclosure. She was a few minutes early and would enjoy lingering with her thoughts, anticipating the pleasure of his company. Her helmet removed, she shook her hair free and paused to check her appearance. The exercise had felt good: was she finally recovered? It had been a long haul from her chest infection. Leaves were not yet out on the trees that formed an avenue along this residential road, so visibility was good in spite of fading light. A few children were about, cycling on the pavements. People on their way home, some with briefcases and shopping bags, scurried up the raised entrance steps of the row of Victorian terraced houses, now nearly all subdivided into flats. She noticed one couple, against the flow, leave a house and walk away together. They looked happy. And then she saw Haresh. He checked his watch and walked towards her. As always, his timing was impeccable. His dark hair gleamed and his easy strides brought him closer by the second. Tall, his bearing was good and he looked so fit, benefiting from the regular lengths he did in the local pool. His skin was light Indian, paler than his father's and darker than his English mother's. He was wearing his well-cut fawn jacket, her favourite. She ran into the warmth of his arms.

'I've missed you!' he said, enclosing her tightly and kissing her on her lips.

'And I you.'

Arms entwined, they walked to the small neighbourhood restaurant that was cheerful and busy. As they waited for their main dishes they munched pitta bread and hummous. 'The website's almost done. I'll show you later.'

'I've tried looking for it.'

'It's not live yet.'

Their dishes arrived on heated trays and with garnishes suspended on a candelabra stand. Polly watched as Haresh turned this in his fingers, analysing its movement and balance as bowls of dips rotated. It might have been one of his hand-made toys, which were his way of reaching children, she thought, and their families too. An engineer by training, he liked contact with people as much as perfecting mechanical pieces. The gamble he had taken a couple of years ago was paying off. Frustrated by the distance between his job in the design of prosthetics and the patients who would benefit, he had walked away from the relative security of a bionics firm. Now he was investing and trading in hand-crafted toys, virtually all from small foreign workshops. But he might need to expand his organisation to support the growth of his business. Haresh caught Polly looking at him. His large brown eyes, warm and trusting, met hers.

'Smile for me, darling. It takes the tiredness away.' He paused for a moment. 'If only I could take time off but I'm so busy. And I need to go to Germany or I'll miss that opportunity. I wish you could come with me over the Easter break but it isn't that sort of trip.'

Polly tried to hide her disappointment, but it showed. Haresh leaned across the table. 'You know I do wish you could come. And you can, if you'd put up with business meetings, sandwiched between trade fairs and flights. But it will be rushed; it isn't a scenic journey and small-town sales. You'll end up exhausted and you've been so ill. To be honest, you would have more space and time to relax with Marion, and she's always inviting you. Would it be a good thing to visit Derscott again?'

'But you and I: we might have a little break together?' Doubts she feared started to nag her imagination.

'I really feel guilty about that. I'm sorry, my love, but there's just not enough time right now. I'm sure we will soon, I promise.'

16   Preoccupied with interests of their own

Polly awoke to a slight scratching at the door. Bright spring sunshine diffused through the light curtains of her room. As she lay, contemplating the hours ahead, the scratching resumed. Curious and ready to start the day, she pushed aside the duvet and opened the door. An enthusiastic puppy charged into the folds of her nightdress.

'He's not meant to be up there!' Marion called.

'He means no harm,' Luke replied.

Janus jumped eagerly about the room, tugging at the hem of her duvet and licking her ankles and feet. Frisky, he was renewing the friendship forged the previous evening. Not wishing to endanger his (reasonably) good record of behaviour, she scooped him up and started on the downward walk to the kitchen. He lay quieted in her arms, his fur black and white in patches contrasted across his eyes that sparkled with ingenuity. She lowered him gently at the bottom step but quick as lightning he bounded straight back into her room. Recaptured from the duvet he again lay docile, his head resting in the crook of her arm. This time she closed the door firmly behind her as she carried him downstairs.

'He knows how to get the better of us all.' Marion spoke as she took him from Polly's arms and returned him to his basket in the kitchen. 'Now you're down, take a mug of tea to enjoy while you're dressing. How d'you feel about an outing to the coast? Janus will have to stay in the car; we'll give him some exercise in the garden before we go.'

Janus had a collection of rubber balls, bones and squeaky toys of which any dog might feel justly proud. For safe-keeping these were stored in the conservatory out of easy reach.

'I'm sure he thinks they're alive,' Marion observed as she and Polly played catch with two balls so that Janus could run between moving targets. Once captured, he gripped a ball between his front paws, a second moving object being the only distraction that would cause him to relax his hold.

'Well they do bounce,' Polly replied.

'That's true, at first.' No longer heeding them, Janus's attention was centred on chewing to bits the ball he held. Sharp, needle-like teeth had pierced the outer shell of rubber that was rapidly pocked with holes.

'He's probably amused by our antics and decided to concentrate on better things.'

'He's just a puppy, aren't you, Janus?' Marion looked down at the patches being worn in the lawn. She continued, 'I'm not sure what we're going to do about this. Soon though, we'll be able to take him for runs outside.' Polly noticed trampling across a border and a few bedraggled plants.

'It's time we were on our way. The car's ready,' called Luke. He lifted Janus into the back of the car where he settled quickly.

Polly recognised the beginning of their route but soon they turned off the main road, into the lane leading to Hartland. The view was screened by hedges as they drove along the high, flat peninsula. The village, extended by peripheral building, was hardly big enough to constitute a town. At its hub, small white painted cottages with slate roofs were gathered, as if keeping secrets unto themselves. The lane wound further, past St Nectan's church with its landmark tower and then they followed signs to the quay and the carpark. Suddenly, before them the land dropped, the slate cliffs plunged and there lay the sea. 'How stunning!' Polly exclaimed.

'We thought you'd like it,' Marion said.

'It seems like the end of the world,' Luke observed, adding, as he contemplated a procession of oncoming traffic, 'and bear a thought for the driver.' The narrow lane wound steeply following the sharp incline of the cliffs. The view to the south was the precipitous profile of the Cornish coast, detail lost in shadowy distance. On the Devon side the grassy bank fell with almost as much urgency. Ahead of them lay the sea interrupted by parallel rows of steep, jagged slate. It was a clear bright day and, though not sunny, visibility was good. Luke steered the car left into a level field used as a parking area, but almost empty of vehicles. 'Janus will like the view from the car,' Luke said thoughtfully, 'let's stretch our legs and enjoy the air.'

They walked down the track to the small harbour. Light reflected from watery surfaces; close to them a reef of rockpools stretched, carrying the eye to the edge of the sea. The tide seemed at its lowest ebb, about to turn and make its six-hour journey inwards. It was fringed white, but beyond that it appeared calm, a wide band of grey-blue. An island stood on the horizon.

'What's that?' asked Polly.

'Lundy,' replied Marion. 'We visited once. It's a small island with a certain grandeur, all granite, windswept and wild. It used to be the haunt of pirates.'

'I think Haresh would like that.'

'It is a bit of an adventure, with magnificent cliffs especially on the west – you can tell that, even from here. Bird watchers and climbers go,' Luke said. 'I can recommend its lichens too, at least one in particular – it's called the golden-hair lichen.'

'Luke, you don't need to bore Polly with lichens,' his wife observed.

But Polly's thoughts were far from here; they were with Haresh in Germany. She wished he were here and could share this day, this place and the view. The sea in its continuity reached out far beyond the north Devon shores, out to the west with waves travelling across the Atlantic. Haresh was in quite the opposite direction, and that thought troubled her. It would be his lunchtime now. She thought of him in a bustling trade centre, enjoying bier and a sandwich. But with whom, she wondered? She turned away from her friends so they did not see her frown. The margin of the shore looked as complicated as her thoughts. Undulating folds of rock wound up the cliffs in exaggerated loops.

'*Built of land and sea*, it's a spectacular coastline,' Luke said, knowingly, 'among the best in England they say.'

'Polly might enjoy the flowers,' Marion suggested.

'Well you know I like those too,' agreed Luke good-naturedly, leading the way and pointing out features as they walked south along the coastal path. They rounded headlands, looked at rock formations and enjoyed seeing drifts of white sea-campion, its nodding heads contrasting with the bright, clear colour of sea pink, erect in crevices between slate outcrops and here and there the tiny blue flowers of spring squill were dotted. In the direction of Cornwall the sun emerged and on cliff tops a light breeze rippled through lush grass, carrying the scent of early gorse. 'Who said *the ghost of a garden fronts the sea*?' asked Luke.

'My poetic husband, I suspect,' smiled Marion and clasped his hand to lead him on. But he could not relinquish his interest in observing things. His eyes picked out the miniature world of mosses and tiny flowers, hidden among rock and turf. A little further along primroses lined the edge of a stream that they crossed and further still they gasped at the steep, almost vertical, cliffs that plummeted to rocks below, bordering the sea. 'We sometimes see people climbing those scary slopes,' observed Marion but instead of lingering further she asked, 'should we leave Janus so long?'

They retraced their steps. 'The tide's turned,' Polly said, noticing the waves were enlivened, dancing and retracting more strongly.

'Has a nasty habit of doing that,' Luke teased. 'Anyone feeling peckish?'

'Your mother said on our wedding day, as long as you're fed…,' Marion recalled.

'It's alright, I'll check Janus,' Luke added, quickly.

Polly took their comfortable, reciprocal teasing as opportunity to escape into a world of her own. Now the sky appeared a huge blue dome, its vastness emphasised by the slow moving of white clouds, across which gulls glided and flew out to the deep blue sea. She'd like to return here, to sketch and paint. Hedgerows, about to show the white blossom of sloe and wild pear crossed their path in their procession inland. Their return, mostly downhill, was speedy and the inn on the quay provided shelter and food. Polly and Marion amused themselves looking at the maps of shipwrecks displayed around its walls, until Luke joined them. As they finished their soup, wiping its creamy residue from their bowls with remnants of bread, Luke commented on the tiring effect of sea, air and exercise.

'And soon there'll be Janus, he'll love this walk,' Marion said and Luke returned a smile.

'Perhaps we should be going,' he added.

On making their way from the inn they were greeted heartily, as if by a friend. 'And what might Derscott people be doing here?'

In the shade of the porch Marion was the first to recognise him. 'Why, hello, it's Joe, Mr Hartley. Well, we've been for a walk, enjoyed the scenery and felt we deserved a bite to eat. And how are you?'

'Just walked over my boundary, so to speak,' he replied warmly.

'You're alone?' asked Luke.

'Not quite,' and Joe pointed to his two black labradors, their eyes watching his every movement as they lay quiet, beside the door.

'Of course, we're forgetting, your farm's close by,' Marion said.

'I come down often to give the dogs a change and see what the weather'll bring. There's warning of a westerly tonight.'

Luke, not wishing to seem unfriendly, suggested Joe might like to join them, they could all return to the bar for a drink, but Joe brushed the offer aside. 'That's kind of you, but I'll say how d'you do to the landlord and be on my way. My daughter's with my wife and I must get back so she can be off. Heather's good to us both, you know, couldn't manage without her.'

'Your wife?' Marion enquired kindly.

'Much as usual and better than a week ago.' Joe was pensive. 'It's patient work keeping her that way.'

They bade him farewell and with a wave he passed through the inn door. Luke, Marion and Polly climbed the short, steep slope to the car.

But not for long was Janus asleep in his basket. It was his

turn for a short run in the garden immediately on return to Derscott. Polly, eager to text Haresh, had slipped upstairs to her room and Marion felt the need to check her emails. Though no sooner were they embarked on their respective tasks than they heard the front-door bell.

'Polly!' Marion raised her voice above the hum of her computer. 'Come and join us. My neighbour Laura's called by.'

Laura's attractiveness and customary good grooming did not mask the tension she was feeling. She sat on a couch that enveloped most people in comfort though she, all angles and elbows, looked ill at ease. Her pale hair outlined her face gracefully but she was frowning, her eyes were pink and cheeks shiny.

'We're having some tea, want to join us?' Marion asked considerately, recognising her friend had been crying, and she disappeared to bring in Luke to join them. Surely Janus could play by himself, Marion thought, in light of Laura's distress. Left alone for only a few moments with Polly, a stranger, Laura stumbled over an explanation. 'Mike's out of touch, that's why I've come.' Then, collecting herself she recounted snatches of her childhood experiences of Devon, random at first until they converged on her reasons for being in Derscott. 'I've always loved this part of the West Country,' Laura admitted, 'when I was just a girl we holidayed near here. My parents would visit a friend of my Mum's called Betty – they'd known each other since childhood. I used to play in the garden and afterwards would sit by the fire in her thatched cottage, listening to Betty and Mum telling tales of their own school days ...The fire was always lighted, even in mid-summer; but these are just memories now. ...After I married Mike we came down here because I felt it was where I could make a home. He's abroad much of the time, you know.'

Luke on joining them mentioned their earlier encounter with Joe, but Laura was disinterested. So they digressed onto general things over the mugs of tea that Marion handed round, but the discussion was never relaxed and Laura declined to have her tea replenished. 'Oh no, I must go, I'm expecting a call. I can't reach Mike on his mobile. I worry about him; it's silly I know.' Laura excused herself and departed. While they hoped Laura felt better for unburdening some worries they thought little more about her, being preoccupied with thoughts and activities of their own.

17   An excursion to Dartmoor

Polly, interested in an excursion to the edge of Dartmoor, welcomed Luke's invitation to accompany him and Malcolm, a lichen enthusiast, to visit a moorland churchyard, but little did her friends anticipate that the day would end with a visit by the police.

'Oh, Malcolm'll be prompt. Wouldn't expect anything less from a local authority planning officer.' Luke brushed aside his wife's concern about his friend's possible lateness and ribbed, 'Don't think I don't realise. You're looking forward to our being gone, so you can work on that computer of yours and think about inspections.'

Marion smiled, acknowledging some truth in Luke's comments but not wishing to offend Polly. 'I just want you to have a useful day in a churchyard and I know Polly will enjoy a trip in that direction.'

'We'll need a big flask for elevenses; can I take one from the cupboard?'

'Make sure you give Polly a decent lunch.'

'You needn't worry about that, I've already checked out possibilities.' Luke realised Marion knew the village they were heading for was little more than a hamlet. But he wasn't letting on that a few miles down the road was a hostelry of which all Devon, let alone Dartmoor, could be proud.

Malcolm, as Luke anticipated, arrived on time, neither early nor late. A tall man, with a shock of greying, light brown hair, he was an imposing figure despite his weathered anorak and mud-stained trainers. Reassuring Marion with his genial manner, he cheerfully welcomed Polly, a beginner, as an addition to their small team. As they set off, he explained his enthusiasm for lichens on Dartmoor granite, the local stone of which the churches themselves and many of the memorials in the churchyards had been constructed. Luke had lent Polly a magnifier and once in the churchyard the two men pointed out easily-recognised examples of common lichens. Malcolm conferred with Luke as they continued their scrutiny of the church walls, its stones rough-hewn and gaps filled with mortar. Quite soon, they had counted and recorded forty species on their walk clockwise around its exterior.

Having become familiar with some lichens, Polly was happy to search at her own pace, and she became curious about the walls of the porch and then the west tower. Pausing as she discerned minute differences, she noted the absence of usual traffic sounds in this isolated spot. Blackbirds scurried around paths and through bushes that had sprung up between memorials. A small flock of goldfinches fluttered from tree to hedgerow and then out of view. Polly's interest wandered as she circumambulated the church around the shaded north towards its east end, a brighter, more open aspect. Beyond the church there were several stone cottages and a few of cob with thatched roofs, and then no more dwellings. Built into the side of a hill, the churchyard fell away to the south-east, across land put to grazing and through which a line of trees, bent and twisted by the wind, led the eye on to Dartmoor.

Mist rolled and drifted across the landscape so that tors seemingly erupted then disappeared. Polly's contemplation was interrupted by another visitor, a good deal more local than her friends. An elderly woman was negotiating the steep slate steps of the lych-gate carrying buckets of spring flowers. 'Tis for a christening cum Sunday,' the woman spoke with a Devon burr, her blue eyes sharp behind rimless spectacles. 'You be a visitor here?' Polly explained about the lichens and the woman chortled, 'Oh, we all be interested in different things! Is that they all bent down over there?' She had noticed Luke and Malcolm.

'Your family lives nearby I expect?' Polly asked.

'Course we be, that is, nearly all,' she said. 'We all comes and we all goes from hereabouts. We be on the stones, if 'ee looks around. Look at 'm names – I be a Pengelly on my family's side, married a Down and 'is mother's a Leigh. They say there's a Pearce married long-ago to a cousin and that wouldn't surprise me, neither! We're all 'ere as I will be too, someday.' She spoke with pride in her voice.

'So whose is the christening?' Polly asked.

The woman's face broke into smiles as her glasses bobbed up and down on her nose. 'It's a boy, my Liza's youngest and they've called 'im Z - A - C, Zac. I reckon I'll get used to it!'

'It sounds straight out of the Bible to me,' Polly smiled.

'Afore I go, let me tell 'ee summat. 'Taint something many others than uz locals know, but the Pearce was a Widecombe man, married – oh, I 'taint be knowing how many gen'rations back – to an aunt o'mine. A Pearce, you know, of that Widecombe song. And misty times, days like we 'ave right now, but at night-time 'specially, you 'ear the horse, echoes of Widecombe, all the way 'ere. Eerie, 'tiz, the groanin.'

Polly was baffled. She made a guess: 'Widecombe Fair, Uncle Tom Cobley – was that the song?' she asked.

'It be, right enough, just look 'ee on. All uz 'as knows be gone early from 'ere on days like we 'ave. I'm not saying it would harm ye, but 'taint pleasant, hearing 'em groans. I know, since I've 'eard 'em.' And she turned, to enter the church.

Polly, puzzled about the veracity of what she'd heard, felt uncomfortable. Luke, thinking she was overwhelmed by the variety of lichens to be seen, called her over. He was perusing headstones around the eastern side of the churchyard while Malcolm surveyed those at the south. 'Want to record-keep for us?' Malcolm suggested.

'I'll try,' Polly replied.

Malcolm handed her a clipboard and pencil and explained how to tick off the species. 'The headstones are all granite and slate here,' he commented. They lifted the hoods on their jackets as they continued through a light shower. 'We just need to tackle the trees now,' Malcolm said as their list of lichens lengthened, but Polly's capacity to keep records waned as the shower intensified into steady, heavy rain and the recording sheet became sodden. They found temporary refuge under the boughs of an old yew tree and watched horses passing by, the riders visible above the hedgerow around the churchyard. As the clip-clop of hooves faded, they still remained beneath the tree and inevitably the incessant rain found routes through the foliage and fell in even heavier drips upon them. 'Let's go inside,' Malcolm suggested, as he could see no sign of the weather easing.

Luke remembered Marion's warning to look after Polly and his conscience pricked. 'It's time for lunch... we could dry off somewhere warmer than the church,' he suggested. Polly felt relieved. Rivulets of raindrops leaked down her neck and squelched between her toes. She was starting to shiver.

Luke drove Polly, with Malcolm following in his own car. They travelled slowly along a single-track lane in poor visibility. Though the heater was turned up to maximum, seated in wet clothes they all felt uncomfortable and the windows misted over. Polly was silent but, snatching quick side-glances, Luke noticed her eyes followed Malcolm's progress through reflections in the wing mirror, as both cars splashed a muddy route between steep hedgerow banks. Ahead, a huddle of granite buildings appeared, dwarfed by a church that had a proud crenellated tower. The local inn looked hugely popular. They pushed open the oak door and found themselves in a vestibule off which various rooms opened, all heated by open fires.

'There must be another way of getting here,' Polly responded as she saw the crowded interior. Other people looked dry and some were smartly dressed for a business lunch in the dining room, not enveloped in garments saturated and heavy with rain.

'Exeter isn't far along the main road,' Luke admitted.

Wet through, drops of water ran from their outer jackets and traced their steps across the slate floor that had been polished by generations of use. They made directly for a hearth and shed their outer garments around chairs grouped by a vacant table. While Malcolm and Polly warmed their fingers and feet and recovered before the heat of the fire, Luke ordered food at the bar. Before long, piping hot soup was brought, soon followed by sandwiches and the edge was taken off their hunger; they realised they were starting to recover. They dallied, until brightness showed through the windows.

'Where now?' asked Malcolm, adding, 'if you would both like to, that is.'

'I have old records of the church here,' Luke replied carefully, 'only thirty species were found – it shouldn't be difficult to exceed that.'

'How d'you feel about it?' Malcolm asked Polly. A considerate man, his kindness melted any reservations she felt and cheered by sunlight that was breaking through, she agreed. But they lingered a little longer in the comfort of the inn while Luke and Malcolm checked descriptions in a book on lichens. Finally, they retrieved their outer clothing that was now mostly dry and warm and they emerged into sunshine.

The village church was just a stone's throw from the inn. Polly, hardly optimistic about remembering many of the lichens she had seen earlier that day, had to view them dampened now. But encouraged by recognising a few, she realised that some new species were growing here, including circular orange patches that she mentioned to Luke.

'Good of you! That one likes limestone and it's telling us what the memorial's made of.'

But in spite of their efforts they were not to exceed seventy species as before long the light started to fall, so they called it a day. 'See you again soon, I hope,' said Malcolm and he retrieved from the depths of his glove compartment a bar of fruit and nut that they split among themselves, before starting on their separate ways home.

Intrepid still, Luke steered a course down further narrow lanes confined by high hedges. He conceded they were on little more than farm tracks and muttered lines of poetry with rhythmic emphasis while Polly hoped silently that they would not meet on-coming traffic. Shadows lengthened and the light dimmed further. Luke, using the headlights as harbingers of their passage, picked out the pale faces of flowers in their beams: primroses and flashes of purple in hedgerow banks.

'Could they be orchids?' Polly asked.

'Early purples,' replied Luke, 'they remind me how glad I am to be here.'

The glow of windows at farmhouses marked their progress. Their route cut around Okehampton, through hamlets and villages until the tower of Derscott appeared. Daylight had completely gone by the time Luke slipped the car into the driveway and they lifted out their spare clothes, bags and boots. 'Come this way, Marion'll prefer it.' Luke guided Polly around the side and like a bolt Janus shot towards them and jumped around their legs and their belongings. 'Did you think I'd forgotten you?' Luke rubbed Janus's fur and the puppy lifted his paws in playful boxing. Polly watched, but was glad when Marion opened the back door. Then she could sink into a chair and gaze at the Aga.

Changed into dry clothes, they sipped sherry and basked in aromas of good cooking. Marion had spent her time well, at her desk and in the kitchen. While they waited for their meal to be completed, Luke pondered over the day's findings, though Polly listened to music and turned the pages of her novel. Their leisure was interrupted by the sound of a car drawing up and a sharp ring at the door bell. 'I'll go,' said Luke. He returned a minute later and asked Marion to join him.

From her armchair Polly overheard the conversation. The police were at the door. They asked Luke and Marion to confirm their identities and then enquired about Laura's husband, giving his full name and address, so there could be no ambiguity. Did they recollect when they had last seen him? Was he often away? Would they say he had seemed himself? Marion and Luke readily told them all that they knew – but the fact was, they knew little. Polly looked questioningly, as they returned to the kitchen. Perhaps Laura was right to be worried after all.

18   Peace of mind

Grey morning light turned to colours through the patterns in the east window of the church. Tracery, several hundred years old, topped the three window sections. Silently, the priest recited the prayers, confessional and preparation for communion. He had come to this place at others' bidding. Thoughts had flitted through his mind, doubts that he might see out this day, or the morrow to come and he sought peace. He felt sure he had disturbed no-one as he had made his way to the church. Through the kindness of the farmer's wife, Catherine, he had slept in clean linen. This morning he had donned his cleric's stole over the rough wool of borrowed garments. As the family lay abed he had walked 'neath their windows, down the lane and around the edge of the churchyard to the porch on the south. He had turned the key of the massive lock and let himself in. Initially in gloomy dawn, he had been barely able to pick his way around the church, but as light had broken it had transformed the interior. In following the familiar order of the communion service he had pushed aside the questions that were troubling him: why he was here, the fate of the farm, what had become of the young priest before him. He held the consecrated bread and wine and instead sought truth. He stayed, kneeling at the altar, saying prayers he knew well and which comforted him.

The sun rose higher as he rested, praying. Though he heard no voices the church was not quiet, with the wind blowing around its walls, jackdaws in the tower and what was probably the occasional scratching of a mouse as it scurried nearby, although his eyes were no longer as sharp as his ears. Time was marked by the pools of light which flickered brightly across the floor and walls when the sun came out, tracing its orbit as the hours moved on. His mind was deep in thought as he knelt, though he became aware of the creaking of hinges which could only signal the swinging of the heavy church door. He stayed kneeling, hardly noticing the interruption, as a bundle of fresh snowdrops, carried by the maid, moved towards him down the aisle. Ellie had been worried that the priest's soul might have been transferred to his maker. He knelt so quietly and looked so calm, that she was still unsure. She walked over to him, her light step making barely any sound. She realised how attentive he was in prayer, entranced in his observance. Ellie lowered the snowdrops on their slender stems and knelt beside him. Slowly, he acknowledged her presence. Patient, she was silent until he glanced over to her. 'Ellie?' he said, kindly.

'I've brought flowers, Father – for the Sabbath, of course.'

He realised she had found him out, and was touched by her concern. 'How knew you to come my child?'

'My father – he...' the little she said revealed Seth's concern at the priest's absence and his confidence in his daughter.

'I understand,' the priest replied.

'Though I know thou hast broken thy fast, Father,' she meant by taking communion, 'I have brought thee this.' She held thick slices of bread, buttered yellow.

'We're at God's table,' the priest explained and temporarily rejected the food Ellie had brought. She placed the flowers in a small bowl on the altar while he lovingly wiped the communion vessels, placing them in soft linen which protected them in their wooden case, then he wrapped the whole in rags so it looked like a common bundle. Finally, he retired to the back of the church; Ellie followed him and again tendered the bread.

'All your life you have been here, child?' the priest asked. He lifted a slice of this morning's bread and sucked on every morsel.

'Oh yes, Father. Jess and I both were born on the farm and there were two others, alas, that now lie by the church. Jem I recollect – he being five years younger than mysel', but he only grew to four, then one winter we all were sickly and he did not live. The other, Joe,' and she looked at the priest,

'was older 'an I and I've heard mother say he was a perfect child. But he died afore I was born.'

'So you and your sister have grown to help on the farm?' Now content, he watched beams of light through the windows dance on Ellie as she spoke and he listened to her tale.

''Afore Jess was wed she did a lot. And when the season's right we have others in to help. We be well placed here, for things to grow.'

The priest had in mind to rest in the church all day; he appreciated the sanctuary it offered. Travelling had tired him and while he was content to serve the Lord at the farmhouse, as in any place, he wished his time to be spent talking with God and being in His place. He lapsed into silence and Ellie, without the prompts he provided, became quiet also. After a time, his need for peace partly answered, he again paid attention to her presence at his side. 'Your father will wonder. You should return and be with your family.'

'Nay, he knows I'm safe and, besides, he sent me here.'

The priest said nothing more and immersed himself again in prayer. Ellie enjoyed the continued quiet but in the stillness of the church increasingly she felt chill through her bodice and asked herself if she might not be of greater use, returned home. She would ordinarily have visited the market in Great Torrington today but her mother, Catherine, found reason that her daughter should stay and instead herself had gone with a widow who lived close by, who also had goods to sell. Ellie thought it likely that during this time she had spent in church her father and Tom would have begun the new shelter over the sty. She watched the priest in his meditation with the Lord. He was still, save for his lips, which moved occasionally. She thought she could surely slip out now he had properly broken his fast and return, if she had news to give, and bring him to the farmhouse for warmth and food for the night.

19   Local man missing

Polly's day was destined to be tranquil but a visit to Great Torrington alerted her to a puzzle that seemed faintly amusing at first. Luke's plan was to visit the town so that he and Polly could visit their banks and Marion was taking parcels to the post.

As usual, Polly, from her bedroom window, had noticed the small group of children waiting for their transport to school, but they had reached their destination well before Luke slipped the car out of the drive. A left turn to Torrington, a slow drive through the cross roads, then negotiating tractors moving hay and animal feed to fields and he was on his way. Polly lost count of the fields harbouring very young lambs that played among older sheep. Buzzards kept watch from telegraph poles and gulls, scavenging among newly-ploughed fields, were highlighted in sunshine that splashed over the landscape between the passing of clouds. In the distance, slopes were brushed yellow: the first of the early rape was opening. Traffic increased as they approached Torrington. Other cars were coming in from villages for the businesses and shops and yet others were travelling further afield, following routes to Okehampton, Holsworthy or Bideford. Luke found a place in the car park he favoured that was set back from one of the main streets in the centre of Torrington, South Street; Polly recollected this high vantage point.

Luke walked over to the edge of the steep hill. 'I always enjoy the vista,' he said. The scene was dramatic, down a steep slope to the river below and then across rolling landscape, eventually to Cornwall. Today, clouds of white mist hung above the river, like an enormously long and rolled-up eiderdown, nestling between green coverlets. Turning to face the town, Luke led their way through its streets still confined by the old houses that lined them, as they walked in single file to avoid other pedestrians, several baby-buggies and an occasional invalid car. Most of the buildings were three storeys, many were gabled or had decorative pediments and were painted bright colours below their slate roofs. Marion pointed out *The Black Horse*, which Polly recognised from her earlier visit, and also the location of her bank. As Polly made her way towards this, she spied a hoarding for the local newspaper, which showed *LOCAL MAN MISSING* and she smiled at the headline, thinking it incongruous and doubtless the invention of a journalist. Did people often go missing hereabouts? 'We'll have our own copy when we're back,' Luke said, at Polly's elbow. 'Living where we do, it always comes late.'

20   Market day

Eggs, carrots, parsnips, hams; at every turn in the small market, produce brought in from farms was displayed. Farmers' wives, cheeks flushed with anticipation of selling their goods were watchful and bargained over prices. They greeted friends and jostled with them. Small reunions, some weekly, allowed news of both family and local importance to travel. Catherine looked over the cheeses brought in from Chittleton but decided she had as good at home and considered turnips would be more use.

The earth was heavy at Derscott. Her Seth had enough to do without raising 'em. She had harboured the thought – more than that, she had spoken of it outloud – of a possible garden for the kitchen's use, sited near the scullery door. This was the very place her husband had in mind for shelter for pigs and lambs. She had once conjectured at an area for vegetables that the orchard might afford, as this be where she raised her herbs, but Seth contested there would be no telling what damage the horses would do, when they were allowed in to graze fallen, damaged fruit. Good-naturedly, she praised Eliza from Methercombe for the handsome job her husband made with turnips and she picked out a number, well shaped and compact. Her neighbour, the widow Loft, had brought in her baking with twenty saffron cakes and they were half gone.

As Catherine sat she watched passers-by and drove off children, at least until it was time to go, when there could be broken cakes to give.

Tales were exchanged of the King's soldiers, seen last in Taddiport below the town. Patrols marched up Mill Street and kept watch from Castle Hill. They caused no bother and little alarm though many wished they had deeper pockets and would oblige by buying wares. Some favoured the Parliamentarians. While fewer of these were lodged near the town there was much talk of their growth in numbers and *their presence across the countryside, with visits to farms and pillaging of food.*

'It seems like our old ways are no good, no more.' Amos, Catherine's aged cousin, never moved from Torrington, paused to talk with her. 'It don't make sense to me,' he continued. The cousin, known in the family for his willingness to converse, was short of words, for once.

'Amos!' Catherine exclaimed, 'thou be looking smart today – and it be good to see 'ee.'

He seated himself next to her in a corner of the Shambles, where the market was held. Customarily, on market days, the more elderly rested there. Many had accompanied younger family members and they were used to meeting friends, or more distant family, who had likewise made the journey. The mistress from Priestacott told her cousin from Downcombe of the wedding at Leaford and her sister from Yarnscott exchanged news with the wife of the herdsman who had left their employ and now helped out at a farm down the Torridge valley. 'I don't rightly know where God has gone!' Amos said.

Catherine looked at him with surprise. 'Why, Amos, that be very serious for 'ee.'

'And so should be!' Having found his tongue, Catherine's cousin expanded his concerns. The God he believed in, had believed in all his life, was being turned aside by soldiers of the Crown in favour of fighting to defend the King; Cavaliers was the name the Royalists called themselves. The rest were soldiers who stood for Parliament and inclined to a simpler God: Roundheads they had become.

'Less noise, hush, cousin,' Catherine chided him gently, wishing to avoid a bother in this public place, 'others may differ in their view.' She looked about to see if any paid attention to her cousin, or were disturbed by his opinion. Satisfied, she added as an afterthought, 'Reckon we be all the same a'fore this started, and thou be right to wonder what good'll come of it.'

But Amos persisted, as if ideas had been dwelling in his mind and now he had an audience with whom they could be shared. Catherine was conveniently near and had polite ears.

He had no regard for others, roundabout. 'Can thou tell me how they know what is more right than we be 'customed to?' After a pause for breath he continued, 'They be behaving as if they be God, themselves!'

'Amos, feelings run high. It be not our place to question such,' Catherine gently rebuked.

''Tis a 'right for thou,' he continued, 'right by the church, thou knows where right is. But where I be there be different ideas. Do 'ee know of Baptists, and of Abram Dark? 'E be a good man but 'e's not God, yet there 'e be, setting up worship on 'is own! And folks be go 'in, too.'

'If they be praying and find comfort in 't, can it be bad, Amos?'

'It ain't that easy,' Amos fought back with his words. 'If we don't agree which God is right, then we don't know what is right!'

Catherine kept quiet about existing divisions – the Catholics who looked to Rome and the Church she was loyal to herself, which she had thought belonged with the country, but was now divided by the conflict of Parliament with the King. 'Come 'long, Amos,' Catherine tried to humour him, 'thou be knowing well enough where 'ee stands and thou hast always been ready enough to guide me right.'

'That time be gone,' Amos protested, 'I knew 'cause there was God: one God. But 'ow do I know now? There's too many Gods for folks to know.'

The discussion ended as the widow Loft returned with a quart of cider. Having sold her cakes and bought some essentials she had been persuaded to purchase a good quantity of local brew. She offered a cup to Catherine and Amos, saved the rest and, after talking some more, agreed with Catherine they should be on their way to reach Derscott by nightfall.

21   St Michael's Church

Polly explored Great Torrington and realised its past was very near the surface.

'You be staying with someone?' The girl behind the counter at the bank realised Polly was not from local parts and her face lighted with welcome. 'Enjoy your stay, there be history here.' Polly recollected Marion's comments about a pannier market and St Michael's church and being the only customer she enquired of their location. 'Look for the pink archway to your left, beyond our town hall, the Pannier be just under there,' the girl explained, 'but St Michael's be at your right.' When she stepped outside Polly saw the market entrance immediately, its arcade lined with small shops and stalls. There, people gossiped over wares, eyed home-made jams and cakes alongside kitchen goods at budget prices, and cotton underwear of generous proportions. She passed by pickled onions to buy local cheese, a golden slab wrapped in waxed paper, and surveyed bunches of early flowers from local gardens, as well as pots of cuttings for borders and seedlings for vegetable patches. *Why's this called the Pannier market?* Polly wondered. It was another question to take back to Marion and Luke.

Polly found St Michael's church across the High Street and walked into the shade of its grounds. Footpaths surrounding the raked earth of empty flower beds were covered with cobbles, just like the passage in the local inn. The church's presence was immediate, its spire rising proudly above this hill-top market town. Once inside the church she found a leaflet on its history and as she read these lines she recollected, with sudden vividness, the tale Marion had told of firey Civil War battles, with Royalists on the side loyal to the King fighting the Roundheads who supported Parliament. And she also remembered, from her last visit, the period costumes: woollen garments, leather jerkins, felt hats and bonnets of the people that had gathered to re-enact events at Torrington. A significant conflict, Marion had said, and prominently displayed on the leaflet she was holding was its date: 1646.

This was the church that had been devastated by gun powder, Polly learned. On rereading the account she marvelled that Guy Fawkes had become legendary for a non-event while here, in a small north Devon town, a catastrophic explosion had actually occurred. She read on about this tragic event and envisaged the hundreds of Royalist troops trapped within the church walls, unable to escape the fire, smoke and fumes. Following the conflagration the soldiers' remains had been heaped into a mass grave, the spot allegedly marked by a raised and cobbled ridge. She felt disquieted and, true enough, on her return this ridge became obvious and she hurried by. Probably thousands of times each day local townsfolk and their children passed over it. But below the cobbles she realised, lay the bones of hundreds of their forebears.

She reminded herself of her rendezvous. The library, next to the large car park at the top of Castle Hill, was where she was to meet Marion. The staff were well prepared for queries such as Polly's: a display, a shelf and a table were reserved for local history. Overwhelmingly, the main topic was the Civil War and Polly's amazement grew at the climactic scale of activities in Great Torrington, a small but busy town even then. Immersed as she was, she did not notice that Marion had joined her until a file of press-cuttings of recent battle-enactments appeared alongside her. 'History's still with us,' Marion said.

'I didn't realise the extent of Civil War connections.'

'And not just here – in the surrounding villages too.' Marion recalled hamlets where cottages, still named *The Barracks*, had housed Royalist troops or some of the other side, and a local grand house that had been the residence of General Monk. Their conversation, becoming animated, was starting to attract the attention of others and sensing this they replaced some books and left, with several borrowed volumes. Polly's curiosity had been whetted.

'We must be on our way,' Marion said kindly. 'Luke's

bumped into an old friend and has gone with him to the Common: I told him we'd meet there. It's not far and we'll enjoy the walk.'

Marion suggested they use a high path, a local look-out, and they found the mist along the river below had not only persisted but had expanded and billowed up towards the town. A lone dog sauntered between parked cars, disappearing into greyness along the network of paths that led down to the water's edge. Keeping an even height, at times a shaft of sunlight broke through to reveal the opposite slope across the valley, showing remnants of a medieval narrow-field system. Suddenly the path cut downwards and they walked between wild shrubs, at one point alongside a vertical rock outcrop. The mist, drifting in swathes, betrayed any sense of distance. They might have been on a mountain ledge, or near a cutting for the river.

'Let's climb up again; my memory must be playing tricks. We don't have much of a view today and this drop is steep,' Marion admitted.

'The books in your library give a true enough description,' Polly commented, 'the hill is an awesome defence.' In these misty conditions her ears were more use than her eyes and she listened hard. A light breeze rustled through overhanging branches. Low voices became apparent; both she and Marion stood to one side of the path, in anticipation. The hazy outlines of a couple became more obvious, grey and steadily approaching with plodding steps marked by the tapping of a stick. They were walking a dog, arthritic in its old age and panting as it tried hard to keep up, even with their elderly steps.

'Are we on the right path for the Common?' Marion asked.

'This be the Common where ye be now,' the man asserted, and started to explain how it circled in an arc around much of the town.

'The old bowling green car park, that's where we're meeting my husband…'

'Then thou be a'right,' and he confirmed the way for them to take. In only a short time they emerged at a main road, which ran along one side of their destination.

As Marion had mentioned, Luke was not alone. With him was a tall man holding the reins of two retrievers, alert beside him. 'Marion, you'll remember George, my ex-colleague,' Luke said.

'Heard a lot about you!' George interjected, 'I envy you living down here. Molly hasn't been well, we're just here for a break and the dogs have taken me for a walk.' He brushed his thinning hair away from his eyes and smiled pleasantly at the two women through large, horn-rimmed spectacles. He wore a thick sweater of bright colours and bold patterns, with the frayed collar of a check shirt just visible around his neck. While it was impossible to tell what his girth might be, his height was clearly evident, and amounted to at least six and a half feet. Alongside Marion he looked gigantic, but she elevated her gaze and greeted him warmly.

'This is my friend, Polly. We've come from the town, along the crest of the hill. The walk's been good for us and I expect these two would lap it up,' Marion said admiring the placid obedience of the two dogs. 'Has Luke told you, we've got a puppy of our own at home?' They chatted for a few moments about the ways of young dogs and ex-colleagues and soon George said he should be going, but not before asking their advice on nearby places that Molly would enjoy. The conversation turned to another of George's interests – local history. 'You'll have to ask Polly about that. Visitors always know more than we do ourselves!' Marion said, 'she's just been to the local library.'

'And it's really very good. They've got a lot of books, on the Civil War especially.'

'I had wondered. The mist over the river in the last few days has been very suggestive. You can imagine horsemen rounding the bend and taking a village or two by surprise.'

'George, that's very poetic for a finance man,' commented Luke.

'Perhaps because I'm in finance I need the romantic,' George said amiably. 'We're staying downstream, in an old cottage at the edge of the river. A bit different from our usual view, suburbia,' he admitted, wryly. 'Molly's brought her paints. That's what I've left her doing now. The light's different all the time and she loves it.'

George turned to go. As soon as the dogs sensed his intention they strained at their leads, almost frisky at first before they settled to an even walk, looking left and right, as George paced back towards his car.

'Time for us to be getting home,' said Luke. 'I've always had a soft spot for George. And his wife's a painter, Polly.'

'Let's show Polly the view from here; she may want to come back.'

'It's another of my favourites,' Luke said, leading the way across the plateau at the top of the hill to a carriage path with an outlook south and west where the mist was clearing. 'See the scrap of mist in that direction? It's hiding the way to Frithelstock. And that's an old place, if ever there was one. There's an ancient priory there.' Polly shielded her eyes as she looked into the light, a landscape with sharp curves and rising hills was unfolding, contours shaping land and villages. She mused over the snippets of information Luke told her. 'I never tire of looking out from here. It's about man and his environment.' Luke went on to mention farms and local big houses, some converted now to accommodate groups of young people, others reigning, dignified or decrepit, at the end of long driveways. Over the scar of an old clay quarry, in a shaft of light, they caught sight of buzzards circling high and searching across the hilltops. 'They've got young. A sure sign, if they're hunting at this time of day.' The interruption reminded him of the need to return. 'I'm forgetting, Janus'll be missing us,' he said.

Luke eased the car into the driveway at the front of the house, which was shaded by day. They left the car and waited by the bushes, expecting to hear Janus, excited and yelping. But he was quiet. Luke frowned and also stayed silent. 'Here are my keys,' Marion passed them to him. The house was quiet still. Without pausing to take off his jacket Luke walked through the hallway and into the kitchen. There, dozing on his bed was Janus, lying with a paw on a well-chewed rag. His ears twitched, and an eye opened, as he shook off his dreams and bounced at them, welcoming them home.

22   Speculation about Mike

Replete at the end of their meal, Luke's thoughts returned to the newsboard they'd spotted in Torrington, '*LOCAL MAN MISSING*'. Marion and Polly still toyed with the remains of apple crumble and strong coffee. 'No, don't feed him,' Marion chided her husband, 'this is human food.' Janus settled quickly enough, when he realised no treats would be forthcoming and Luke's unease abated with Marion's reassurance that Janus's bowl was still half-full.

Luke lifted the most recent edition of the local paper onto the table. 'See, it's so full of advertisements: cars, houses, carpets… you name it. And places to eat. You'd think home-cooking had gone out of fashion.'

'I thought you had an item to look for, you know, the headline we spotted in Torrington,' Marion reminded him.

'That's right, now what was it? I remember…about a local man who's missing. Well I never. It's only an inside paragraph, but listen to this….' Luke read out the first few lines and reached for his glasses to continue through the smaller print. He settled, square before the table, to the task. 'It's Mike they're talking about, there's no doubt it's him. And there's quite a bit. Isn't it odd, he's only late by a few days and it's not the first time it's happened?' He fell quiet, ruminating to himself, while Marion picked up the newspaper sections Luke had shared with Polly.

'Well I never!' Marion echoed Luke's words on reading for herself the opening lines.

'It certainly gives us something to think about,' Luke reflected.

'How much more do they tell us?' Marion asked.

'All sorts, I don't know where they find the stuff. And this is just a local paper.'

'What d'you mean?'

'They give such detail of Mike's movements over more than two weeks, it's mind-boggling. That's about when he was home last isn't it? There are statements from his company and his contacts in the Far East, a photograph of Mike and even mention of Laura – but no official statement from the police and nothing from Laura herself. She's described as the grieving wife, though that seems strange and, at the very least, presumptuous. If I were Laura I'd be upset and angry, very angry.'

'Do they know something that we don't ourselves?' Marion speculated.

'Concocting a story, that's what they're doing. Trying to bump up their readership. It's dangerous. The article's very careful to state that anyone with news of Mike's whereabouts should contact the police.'

Luke passed the pages across to Marion who recognised the sections of the text that Luke had mentioned. And as she read it she herself felt injured, on account of the feelings of the family involved, most crucially Mike and his wife, Laura.

'I don't like this. You're right, it's intrusive and suggestive but couched in words which avoid responsibility,' Marion said with feeling. 'It's astonishing that they can find so much to write about for a person who's been missing just a few days. They even have a quote from a fellow passenger who says Mike seemed sleepy on the plane coming into Heathrow. That particular statement doesn't surprise me, does it you?'

'Perhaps we should feel reassured that we can all be traced in this way,' suggested Polly, mindful she had thought the story amusing at first.

Luke was thoughtful. 'You'll be calling Laura, I expect,' he spoke to Marion. 'She might be in need of a friendly word having to cope with this publicity: it's scurrilous.'

Polly, meanwhile, was turning the pages of the property section.

'You're hoping to persuade Haresh to come down this way?' Luke teased, attempting to divert attention.

Polly blushed. 'It seems a fair number of people around here want to live abroad,' she parried. 'The adverts for overseas places cover quite a few pages.'

'You think there are a lot, do you?'

'Perhaps I don't look at them often enough. But there are houses for sale in eastern Europe, the Middle East, USA and some in countries I'm not sure exactly where they are on the map.'

'Not everyone down here's as impoverished as us you know,' Luke spoke dryly and added, 'but I expect the prices abroad are much lower than ours.'

'I'm sure you're right about that. But is it sunshine people want, or investment?'

'Now you're talking, Polly. Just look at our weather; perhaps they want both.'

Unwashed dishes before them, they tossed ideas around the table and fabricated possibilities about Mike, exceeding even the imagination of the local paper. Marion asserted a stopover was most likely and then, perhaps confused and overtired, Mike had missed a connection. Luke, however, thought there was more to his absence, perhaps a secret rendezvous, an entanglement that had taken time, a lover in a far-off country or a speculative venture.

'You're a rogue, darling,' Marion commented.

'Now don't misunderstand me,' Luke said. 'A chap's allowed a bit of exaggeration and innuendo. I just think he may have his fingers in another pie.'

'What about property?' Polly suggested.

'Could be,' replied Luke. 'Though why he can't be satisfied with what he's got beats me.'

Janus, awakened during their conversation, had stretched his limbs and quietly ambled under the table. Finding trouser legs appealing he nibbled here and there, undetected at first because the recipients of his attention merely changed their leg position or apologised to each other, imagining they had kicked or been kicked, inadvertently. But a pronounced tugging at Luke's corduroy turn-up could not be mistaken as anything but suspicious. Luke moved his leg, looked down and saw Janus hanging on, his jaws clenched around the fabric. 'Off,' Luke roared. The volume of his shout and the brisk and sudden movement had the desired effect.

'He's just playful.' Marion defended Janus.

'I was beginning to think he was too docile. But look what he's done to my trousers!' Luke protested.

'Time for a game, isn't it, Janus!' The dog responded to their attention by wriggling and jumping excitedly. 'None of that, little imp,' Marion said as she lifted him from the floor and cosseted him. He quickly became still and rested his head on her forearm.

'You're falling for his charms,' Luke ribbed her. 'C'mon, I'll take you out,' he added, transferring the puppy into the crook of his own arm.

It was starting to drizzle and Polly watched from the kitchen window as Janus jumped and chased after the rubber toys which Luke threw and bounced to encourage the dog to exercise. 'Beware: wanting one of these is catching you know,' Marion smiled. But Polly dismissed the idea, at least for the present.

'I'll take myself off for a walk, if you don't mind,' Polly said.

'Are you sure? You'll get wet,' Luke observed.

'Borrow the spare waterproof,' suggested Marion, 'and how about wellies? Mind where you go – it's easy to lose track of where you are with this mist around.'

Stepping outside, the cool air stripped away the cosiness of the kitchen, the cheerful friendliness of Marion and Luke and all the welcome distractions they provided. In spite of its relative isolation, in many ways this tiny village harboured all the complexities of a much larger place. But she was here for a rest, she knew that, and for space. She cogitated on that word. What did it mean? She puzzled. A nothingness, yet it could have dimensions, she thought. What take would her Year 10's have on space, she wondered? Would it be the planets, a film, exploration or the name of a pop group? As she walked out of the driveway she lifted her face upwards and felt light rain, cold on her cheeks. Hastily, her fingers struggled with the hood that unfolded from her borrowed jacket and she pulled this open to cover her hair as she walked towards the road junction, the public's perception of the village. Lights illuminated the interior of the shop: it would be open for several hours more. She waited for a car to pass, before turning down the lane that led to Lottie and Ray's farm. She had constructed in her mind a short circular walk. The route was merely a hunch but she looked forward to exploring, by herself, the environment around the village. Her starting point was one of Joe's fields, the site of the building proposals.

She tried to dismiss from her mind the implications of a housing development as she squelched through the mud around the stile and picked her way over to firmer ground. She strode towards a footpath sign she had noticed about a hundred yards further down on the left-hand side, staying parallel with the hedge which was gloomy in grey light. She looked for the horses normally grazing here but there was no sign of them so, undeterred, she crossed another stile and the path broadened into a small track, obviously little used and overgrown, with long grass and dead thistles reaching over her knees. While so far her walk was going according to plan she was now faced with confusing choices.

Contemplating the lines where hedges met across the slopes of the fields she noted two gates, one to the left and another on the right. She chose to walk left, since she knew that at worst she would return too quickly to Derscott and at best the way would lead along the edge of woodland and then back to the village. This field had been ploughed and was muddy underfoot but, keeping to its perimeter, she followed a faint path and soon came to another stile and then a sign pointing the way along a clump of stout and upright beech trees, which heralded the edge of a copse.

While Polly's face was freshened by misty rain, inside the jacket she felt warm, dry and a certain contentment. Could she describe the countryside as quiet, she wondered? It was certainly not silent. Her jacket creaked and her steps in wellingtons were marked by the snapping of twigs as she strode across dry patches and by squelching sounds as she made her way through damp earth and mud. A robin sang nearby, blackbirds rustled between bushes, rooks called across high tree branches and pheasants, disturbed by her presence, clattered clumsily away. She listened for the cry of a raptor. In the distance she heard a dog and sheep grazed on nearby fields. She thought she picked up the rumble of a tractor but there was no sound of road traffic. If not quiet, this setting was peaceful.

The trees overhead cast shade, even on this dull day, from their network of smooth grey branches through which ivy trailed. She followed the path by the side of the copse that was defined by a steep bank studded with tree roots and ferns to her left. Here and there she noticed deep holes with bare patches in front, running down between the roots, entrances to homes she realised, for small animals. Janus would love this, she anticipated, as soon as he could take walks through the local countryside. The trail of scents would excite any dog. She smiled as she thought of the half-grown puppy, and reminded herself to ask where the rest of that litter had gone.

Soon, Polly realised, she would leave the protection of the wood and she felt reluctant to terminate her walk. Spying a fallen tree trunk lying across the path, she could overlook one aspect of the village from the seat it provided, padded with moss and lichen. She had been walking thirty minutes or so and might be back in another ten. She was coming to love this place and the texture of its life. In London, for all its history, the present was so busy there was little scope for reflection; here she was constantly reminded of its past, its potential and vulnerability to change. But the current development plan seemed an immediate threat.

Polly caught the sound of wind stirring through branches, glanced at her watch and then the darkening sky and knew she should return speedily. She cut down a steep slope onto a well-used track, just in time to glimpse the lights of a local bus pass by where the track joined the lane. She realised it would have brought home from Barnstaple a few people who had been shopping and also teenagers from the local sixth form college. As she neared the gravelled lane she recognised the entrance to Laura's home. Gate-posts of brick with carved stone pineapples on top, marked the ends of neatly clipped yew hedges. She paused, the proximity of the house surprising her. It was right on the edge of her walk, surrounded by woodland, fields and land owned by Joe. Laura might wander over the paths she had followed, Polly thought. And what of Mike? It was Mike that was missing. Could he possibly have taken a walk, followed a path and fallen, injured and unknown? This was ridiculous she knew, as he was not even home. Though perhaps, and she shivered at her own imaginings as she gazed on a pile of stout and broken branches, some rotten, that lay at one side. She reasoned these had probably been brought down to avoid tree damage due to high winds. Their shapes were suggestive. Could Mike Townley, she wondered, lie dead and unseen near this very path?

She stared, concerned, and did not see beyond the tall wrought-iron gates that were drawn open. Then, collecting her thoughts, she stepped forwards. Joe's car was parked on Laura's circular driveway: there was no mistaking it. Polly had spotted the car a few times about the village and Marion had confirmed it was his, and well known locally by its colour and the stickers it displayed for the farmers' union, this year's agricultural show and home-produced goods. It was also muddy, unlike Laura's limousine which somehow shrugged off the dirt from the lanes and hedgerows and stayed immaculate. Lights were switched on inside the house. Embarrassed by her fears, Polly felt she should hurry. She did not wish Marion and Luke to be concerned about her. And Marion had been right. It was certainly possible to take the wrong path and to lose your way across the fields.

'So where've you been?' Luke took Polly's jacket and spread it out to dry. Noticing her quiet demeanour he added, 'Walked a bit far, did you?'

Polly tried to be cheerful but her own words sounded stilted, even to her own ears.

Marion asked, 'So how did you say you'd returned? I mean just the end stretch.'

'By Laura's. I recognised the gates. I didn't realise her – I mean their – house was so near the footpath. And Joe's car – I'm sure it was his – was in the drive.'

'What might that mean?' Marion commented.

'My love, you're lost to inspection,' Luke said.

'Well, it's all detective work.'

As Polly changed out of her trousers, streaked with mud along the inside knees, she recalled her walk. She remembered the puddles and dung in the churned-up earth where cattle had gathered around gates and stiles. She had been glad to recognise the outskirts of the village on her return to Derscott. Laura's house had been a real signpost. Already, she realised, she thought of it as Laura's, but ideas about Mike would not leave her. She wondered about him, the sort of person he was. She would find a chance later of asking Marion and Luke.

'Urbane, but you'd expect that, with the amount of travelling he does,' said Marion.

'Considerate enough to Laura,' Luke offered, 'but he's always a bit short of time and some might find him a bit brusque, especially if crossed. I admit he seems to know the business he's working in. No-one's ever asked me to go to China,' he finished ruefully.

'You make him sound mysterious,' Marion rebuffed, but Luke shrugged his shoulders, so she continued, 'and remember, we've usually seen him when he's just back from abroad. He's probably been jet-lagged, feeling jaded.'

'How long have they been here?' asked Polly.

'Not long. And no sooner do they come than they start tearing down old gate-posts and a plain farm gate of seasoned wood. They weren't good enough! Now they have that eight foot monstrosity of gilt and fleur-de-lys. It can be operated by remote, like a TV, you know.'

'Luke, you're not in the least bit sympathetic,' Marion said.

'Well, people come and live in the country and no sooner are they here than they behave like they're in the suburbs of Leeds, or Birmingham.' Luke paused for a moment before elaborating. 'He didn't stop at the gate, you know. The house was perfectly good before he started on it. Old Miss Willett lived there. Now, she was a character and a half, and she wasn't short of a bob or two. But they had to improve it. The front's all new, a downstairs extension and the garage is huge – you could play football in it. The plumber says they've got six bathrooms – just for the two of them!'

'Luke, he said six toilets.'

'Did he? Well, it amounts to the same thing.'

'So they've spent a lot of money on it?' Polly asked.

'A packet. Makes you wonder where they've got it from,' Luke said.

After Luke's comment there was silence, interrupted by Polly, 'I expect his job's well paid?'

'It may be, but he's moving in another world. Not one I know a jot about,' he replied.

'D'you mean he takes up opportunities which come his way when he's abroad?' persisted Polly, growing curious.

'Marion knows what I think; you can call it opportunistic, if you like. Mike's into deals and sails close to the wind, for my money.'

Marion noticed Polly's puzzled expression and tried to reassure her. 'I don't think he's into anything illegal. Globe-trotting the way he does he finds out about things we never know of.'

'But there's no smoke without fire, that's all I say,' interrupted Luke and then, with a touch of sarcasm, 'remember all the fuss and bother when he bought Miss Willett's.'

'I think we're extrapolating, cruelly,' Marion replied sharply, before adding more thoughtfully, 'but he could be speculating in property, I suppose.'

'I knew you'd come round to my way of thinking,' Luke's tone was more amenable, 'you never know, that's all I say.'

Later, at the end of the day, this exchange drifted back to Polly's mind when, alone in her room, she was preparing for bed. Half-dressed, she searched on her mobile for messages from Haresh. She was trusting of him and did not wish the spell to break. Occasional thoughts pierced the utter reliance she felt. But could he be misleading her on his travels she wondered? When he was near she felt so happy, so confident. Newly arrived there was a text, an update on news and an image of some new clockwork toys. He planned to add them to his Christmas catalogue, he said. She scrolled the message for more and found he wished she were with him; he sent tender wishes for the night. He loved her, she was reassured, and warmth spread through her as she slipped beneath the duvet.

23   Shelter for the lambs

All day, Tom and the farmer had laboured, clearing stones from the earth and dragging them together to bridge the house and the boundary wall behind the pig-sty, to extend the base of the outshut. It was heavy work but they had kept a good pace, stopping at noon for simple sustainance which Ellie prepared – soup, bread and cheese. Warmed by the fire, they talked of the priest. 'Did 'ee say owt?' the farmer enquired.

'Just praying,' Ellie said, "except when 'e ate mother's bread, then we sat at the back where the sun throws light.'

'It ain't right 'e spends so much time in there!' The farmer thought of the priest's bones and slight frame, battling the wind to spend the day praying in church. Seth knew that with Tom he would be busy that afternoon to get nearly done, providing a shelter for the lambs. He planned to top the makeshift walls with a cover of branches laid across that would be weighted with stones. When the days were warmer then he'd make the walls more solid, face them with mud and dry out the cob. 'Ellie, tell him we'll be ready for 'im when nightfall comes, so 'e should complete 'is prayers by then! I'll walk up mysel' to find 'im, if 'e be not down!'

With that, Seth and Tom returned to their task, leaving the hall-room to the cats that settled in their corners while the hens were chased outdoors by the women. The farmer and his lad worked briskly through the afternoon and kept their vigour until light fell. They had much progress to show for their efforts, but with all their other tasks, realised it would be another day before they were ready to lay branches overhead to keep the weather off the lambs.

Tom made his rounds, as was his custom. Glimmers of remaining light sank behind the farm, the church threw long shadows and further west a few shafts of light streamed behind clouds, over the sea. Nemo ran alongside him, followed by Toss; they knew his circuit as well as he himself.

First, the cows. They'd been tended earlier, Ellie had returned to the farm with pails of milk, now he checked all was well and they had fodder for the night. Satisfied each beast was in its rightful place he pulled the door across and slipped the beam into its home, securing the door. The fastenings moved and creaked, then were silent. At first the sounds of lowing cattle lingered in his ears. As he made his way down the slope their noises ebbed and it was quiet all around. He snapped odd twigs as he trod the edge of the fields, which made him all the more aware of stillness. The dogs sniffed around his ankles and led him down by the copse to where the sheep settled, as was their custom. Already they were huddled down. Here and there an early lamb nestled against its mother, but most lambs were still to arrive. He paused and listened for owls but this evening none were hunting hereabouts. As he completed his rounds he felt light rain on his face. He listened intently and thought he heard the sounds of Seth, with the priest, returning for the night.

24   Growing ideas

The day started with fragile sunshine. Polly had woken early with the call of a thrush, followed by the song of blackbirds in a tree bordering the front garden. She stretched her limbs, before wriggling free of sleepy warmth to greet the day. The front door closed quietly and she heard movements downstairs. She guessed Luke had walked the short distance to the village shop to collect an extra paper. She visualised him in front of the Aga, turning over the pages to digest the latest stories and challenging the journal's interpretation of events. By the time they were eating breakfast he would throw out a contentious comment, just to tease Marion and herself, hoping for a rejoiner. *What would it be today*, she wondered? As she walked to the bathroom she caught his voice raised in rebuke and imagined Janus had found news-sheets to be playful things. Then it was quiet again and she supposed that a compromise had been reached.

'I gave him the business section, my love,' Luke was explaining to Marion, 'he can make better use of it than me.'

'I,' his wife corrected.

Luke lifted the pages to cover his face while Janus kept a paw across his scrumpled, half-chewed sheets.

'Is this a truce?' Marion asked.

'Not at all, just a gentleman's agreement.'

Apparently dozing, Janus was quiet as they breakfasted. 'So, what would you like to do today?' Luke addressed both Marion and Polly. Without waiting for a reply, he continued, 'Remind me, when can I take Janus for walks?'

Marion consulted a calendar. 'Not much more than a week from now.'

'Thank god. That's what we think, isn't it, my boy?'

'Well, don't you want to come with Polly and me?'

'Is that I?'

'No.'

'Oh, I give up.'

'Luke, love. Don't you want to come with us? Here, have another slice of toast, and think about it.' Marion cajoled her husband into willing co-operation and caught sight of him eyeing Janus and the lost business section. Perhaps Luke worried that next time it could be politics, international, news, arts commentary, or even sports.

'I know I'm getting crusty,' Luke said. He looked out of the window. 'The world's waking up. We're into spring, you're not buried in inspection papers - I mean software – and Polly's here. We could have a little trip out.'

'Anything that's captured your curiosity that you'd like to see, Polly?' Marion looked at her friend across the table.

Instinctively, Polly gazed through the window. Flower buds, showing pink, were about to burst on a cherry tree that was growing close to the house and decorated with bird-feeders, around which two blue tits darted. A drift of hellebores led the eye to an early azalea providing a gaudy focus of purple-red at the end of a side border. Morning light picked out young leaves on clusters of low bushes. Early crocuses had gone, but some daffodils were still in flower and the stout green leaves of later bulbs gave promise of more colour to come. 'A garden,' she said, 'is that a possibility?'

'You don't get many of those in north London, do you?' Luke was droll.

'Don't take any notice of him,' Marion said good-naturedly. 'I think that's a splendid idea,' she said. 'In fact, we could go somewhere that grows their own plants. Luke, let's take Polly to *Deepest Devon*.'

'Oh, a shopping trip!'

'No, I didn't say that. It's just for a look.' Turning to Polly, Marion added, 'I'll pack a little rucksac. We'll take a flask and some fruit.'

'Deepest Devon,' Polly reflected on the words, 'and I thought I was already there!'

As they laughed Janus jumped up, the plates and mugs rattled on the breakfast table and Luke retrieved the derelict business pages. Thoughts were awakening in him of cultivating any talent the puppy had inherited as a sheepdog.

Outside the sunshine was strengthening and the lawn was reasonably dry so he took Janus to practise walking to heel. Marion stole a glimpse of Luke's well-intentioned efforts, with Janus a willing-enough learner. She concluded it was a matter of perseverance and might require more patience from the owner than the dog.

Janus returned to the kitchen with Luke following behind. 'Don't fuss him,' Luke said and changed the subject, talking as much to himself as to Polly. 'We're going to one of my wife's favourite places. I'm never sure whether the attraction is the plants or the gardener, if truth be told. But I'm happy to drive in that direction, we cross two rivers – good for fishing, they are – and within sight of six churches too.'

Polly sat quietly in the back of the car, looking first one way and then the other. The previous day's mist had gone, the warmth of the sun had lifted the temperature and Luke was right, it was truly spring. Place names she had noticed on signposts were coming to life. As they drove through Bickleigh they were reminded by Luke about the quality of its architecture and the ample portions served at the local inn, and then the narrow lane gradually became steeper and the surroundings more wooded as it descended into a road busy with local traffic. 'The river Taw,' Luke referred to the river that flowed alongside. 'It's good for trout along here. Does Haresh fish?'

'He hasn't mentioned catching them,' Polly replied, 'but he's certainly partial to them on a plate.'

'Then he'd soon learn; it's a useful skill.' Luke slowed as he negotiated bends in the road and an occasional lorry. 'We'll cross this before long,' he said, meaning the river, 'and be on a quieter stretch.' But quieter also meant narrower as the car climbed steeply up the opposite side of the valley. 'This is a decent place to live. If we weren't in Derscott, I'd opt for here,' Luke said as they arrived at Nympton. 'They've even got a Palladian villa, at least, some chap has. The stately pile's along the river.'

'That somebody might be female,' Marion said.

'Aye, it might be a chapess.'

And so they continued, with Luke's jesting and exchanges

with Marion providing a relaxed, jocular ambience. Polly's attention was diverted by the detail and variety of the cob cottages they passed, many being thatched, and also by the rolling green hills surrounding them. As the lane followed the rise of a hill it narrowed further, woodland and undergrowth closing in. Among the ferns, Polly spotted tracks running between trees and she wondered where they might lead. Now and again they were confronted with a pheasant. Stately and colourful a bird would stand its ground as Luke slowed the car and the instant they believed it might end up as feathers it would rise, wings clacking, in shallow ascent over the hedge. When the car reached a ridge, with lanes apparently falling off on each side, they spied a placard bearing the name of a local farm that was next to a sign painted with the words *Deepest Devon* and an arrow pointing right. Just as Polly thought that this lane could not contract further, it did. Luke drove carefully along well-used tyre tracks, avoiding erosion and dips in the gravelled driveway where he could. Still bordered by woodland, leaf-litter, sodden after winter, lay over weeds along the verge. 'You do direct me to some places,' Luke muttered.

'I'll take over if you like,' Marion said.

'I don't think you'd like it down here, thank you,' Luke replied and Marion was silent.

The sign had indicated a mile to go, but it seemed much further than that to Polly as she searched for possible passing places. She supposed that, if necessary, the entrance to a field could be used to circumvent another vehicle, but the earth was muddy and that option seemed a last resort. Finally, they came to a cattle grid and a plaque bearing the name *Deepest Devon*: they had arrived. Beech hedges, neatly trimmed, bordered the drive and an arrow directed visitors onwards. 'Here we are, girls,' Luke said, watching several hens scurry away as he turned the car into the spacious yard in which a commercial van and a few cars were parked.

They crossed into the forecourt surfaced with grey cobbles, worn and polished, before an imposing farmhouse. Mostly rendered, the house had a handsome stone porch supported on granite pillars at ground floor level. The porch extended the full height of the building to accommodate a room on its upper storey and at least three twisted brick chimneys rose from the old thatched roof. 'It's quite something, isn't it?' Luke said, as he saw the look of surprise on Polly's face. 'A significant house in its day and what period of building could it be, d'you think?' Their consensus was staunchly Jacobean fronting an older dwelling. Within the porch, pairs of shoes stood along one side and on a blackboard, propped against the front door, were the words: *In the garden.*

Undeterred, they trooped after Marion as she strode towards a spacious greenhouse, its windows were open and many seedlings and small pots of plants ranged inside. Another visitor, a pretty woman, younger than Marion but older than Polly felt herself to be, was weighing the merits of plants for her rockery. From her side a tall, lanky man wearing a green apron turned to face them. 'Well, hullo,' he said and, looking at Marion, added, 'you know your way around, d'you mind taking care of yourselves? We're a bit busy at the moment.'

'If that's alright with you?' Puzzled, Marion added, 'It's always a treat to see your plants.'

'There'll be someone to help you when you're ready.' He pointed to the open door of a large wood-framed barn through which they caught sight of several workers, assisting with the packaging and delivery of plants. Encircling the farmyard, the sunny side of the wall was festooned with early *Clematis* and petals were breaking loose on buds of fruit trees, espalier-trained. Beyond this area the garden fanned out across a rolling hillside.

'This is beautiful a lovely spot,' Polly said appreciatively, heading for an undulating lawn around which they walked, commenting on the shrubs and borders that graced its natural curves, before returning to the greenhouse. There they perused individual plants, well-tended and healthy, that were labelled for sale or as stock for cuttings. The other visitor made way for them to pass further down the shelves of pots.

'If you want to take anything back, let us know,' Marion told Polly.

'I was wondering about the north-east. I mean Haresh's parents – what d'you think?'

'Let's ask,' Marion said, but the nursery-man, who had reappeared with a tray of colourful alpines to supplement the rockery plants already on display, was fully occupied. Luke showed particular interest in prickly plants and Marion, to Polly's eyes, seemed a trifle disconcerted. 'Need a spot of help?' Luke asked and quietly listened while Marion justified the several herbaceous perennials that she favoured, and Polly chose a healthy young *Clematis* with its prize-winning pedigree described on its label. Unable to catch the attention of the nursery-man, they were helped by one of the temporary staff who carried their purchases to the car for Luke to store carefully in its boot.

'I'm no nursery-man,' Luke said mischievously.

'Will you help me plant them?' Marion asked quietly and giggled.

Luke was negotiating their return down the driveway with care and was mindful of the welfare of the plants they had purchased. While Marion chatted about where she would like to see them in flower, particularly the anemones and Jacob's ladders, Luke was non-committal, aware that Janus might become an avid digger and this was a predilection hard to restrain. Polly could foresee a conflict of interests and chose to admire the view, rather than interrupt.

'It looks different, travelling in reverse,' she commented after a while.

'That's because it is. I'm taking us a different way, so we can enjoy some other villages,' Luke replied and with a twinkle in his eye he added, 'you can spot an interesting church on the right, if you look through the trees and down the hill. It has a lovely tower.' He slowed the car and found a convenient spot in which to draw to a halt. 'Let's stretch our legs,' he said.

Marion opened her vacuum flask and poured coffee into mugs she had brought. They sipped hot drinks as they strolled along the wooded verge, seeking views through the branches and undergrowth of the village and nearby countryside. Polly, however, noticed glimpses of white;

perhaps sheep or cattle, she thought, before realising a small development of uniform houses was neatly defining lines and curves spread across fields, towards the village they had passed.

'That's recent, since we last came this way,' Marion broke Polly's silent comment.

'Who lives there?'

'Well they may be locals – you know, in starter-homes. And in mellow moments I think why worry?' Luke replied, resignedly, 'plus ça change.'

'But are they? I mean are things more the same, with the more change we have?' Polly said.

'Philosophy, does it help?' asked Luke. '*Change and loss in the heavens, swift moons make up again*? I've a feeling those words have been around a long time.' And then, wanting to brush aside uncomfortable thoughts, he added, 'C'mon, let's be going.'

Soon the houses were forgotten. The lane bore its way down a steep hill, branches on each side brushing against the car and, looking ahead, they seemed almost to meet. Marion stayed silent; she thought driving this route required concentration and Luke should keep his mind on the road. Polly mused over their conversation. The landscape was verdant, so much looked incorruptible. But was it, she wondered? And change: the only thing you can be sure of is there'll be more, they told students at school, so be prepared. This idea worried her but she was prompted back to the present by Luke.

'Know where we are now, Polly?' he asked.

'The wood I came by on my recent walk?'

'That's right. In a few minutes we'll be passing Laura's. Want to call in, Marion?'

Conflicting thoughts crossed Marion's mind. Overwhelmingly, she wanted to support her friend who would be confused and worried by her husband's absence. And Laura had to cope not only with that, but also with publicity and the item in the local paper about Mike, because he was missing. How did they know this had not spread further, into the nationals, she wondered? But it hadn't been reported in the daily that was delivered to their home and Luke had bought an extra paper this morning without seeing Mike's absence mentioned. She hoped her friend remained confident and would allow them to give what support they could offer.

'We only need to stay a moment.' Luke was tentative. 'If you want to, that is.'

'Oh, I do.'

Polly caught Luke's look of consternation in the rear-view mirror. She could empathise with his and Marion's wish to keep up Laura's spirits. But what of herself? She was no more than an acquaintance and would feel superfluous. She might even dilute the rapport that her friends shared with their neighbour. And she also realised that if she joined them Janus would be alone for longer still. 'How about my returning now and I'll check on Janus?'

Luke was edging the car into Laura's drive. 'Would you really?' he said, with a touch of eagerness in his voice. 'Do you know where we keep his toys? He can have a few biscuits. You'll find those ...'

'No, he mustn't,' said Marion sharply. 'We'll be back in no time at all; certainly within an hour, and we don't want Janus getting fat. But Polly, make yourself a mug of coffee – it's almost lunchtime – and you know where to find biscuits for yourself.'

25   Visit to Laura

Luke and Marion stood before Laura's entrance door. In a room at one side, where Marion would leave her coat on wet days, a table lamp glowed but the house was still, the only sound being of birds fluttering in shrubs that screened the lane. 'Go on, you push,' said Luke, urging Marion to press the doorbell to the left of the substantial doorway. He stood behind her, imagining their impromptu visit was entirely justified by Marion's friendship with Laura. Marion, in turn, chided herself. She could so easily have shared the cake, half-eaten yesterday and, with a little foresight she could have bought flowers or locally made biscuits on their way.

'Perhaps she's out?' Marion queried.

'Try again,' Luke encouraged. 'My guess is she's hanging onto the 'phone.'

A light went on in a passage that led off the hall, a sudden shaft of brightness showed the opening of a door and the shadow of a figure appeared behind the upper windows of the heavy entrance door. It was opened and Joe stood before them.

'We've come to see Laura. We thought…we thought she might need a little company,' blurted out Marion.

A hint of a smile crossed Joe's face that had looked stony at first. His expression softened as he drew them both in. 'Come on in, you weren't to know. I've drawn my car around the side.'

They stood on an expensive doormat, as large as the entrance door itself. 'We can't keep on meeting like this!' said Luke, surprised at Joe's solemn manner which prompted these banalities. 'We live just round the corner. My wife and Laura they're, I mean we're, neighbours so we thought we'd come round and see how she is, see if we can help.'

'Let me take your jackets,' Joe said, still without smiling. Disconcerted by Joe's quiet attentiveness, Marion and Luke fumbled with the fastenings. In contrast, Joe scooped up their garments with accustomed briskness and hung them on a coat stand, adjacent to their left. Marion eyed the expanse of the polished wooden floor and remembered her shoes in which, until a short time ago, she had been walking across a garden. Joe noticed her twist her ankle to view the sole of one of her trainers.

'Don't worry, just come through,' he said. But Marion, uncomfortable with the thought of treading mud on impeccable surfaces, untied her laces and eased off her shoes. Luke did likewise. 'I do as I'm told indoors,' he commented lightly to Joe. As they lined up their shoes they noted a small pile of business correspondence, today's junk mail and a few envelopes that looked more personal, lying on a mahogany side table, below one of Laura's arrangements of spring flowers in a heavy glass bowl.

'I should have switched another light on,' Joe said apologetically, 'I'm really not being much help at all.'

They followed Joe across the hall, along a short passage and paused beside double doors. 'She's taken it very badly,' he whispered. Luke had avoided going inside the house since Miss Willett had left. In part this was because he wanted to keep intact the memory of the local worthy in her antiquated rustic grandeur. But he had never quite felt at ease with Laura and Mike and was happier meeting them on his own territory or over, but not through, their new gateway. He remembered this as an old cross-passage sixteenth century farm house, worthy of being a manor house, but he caught a whiff of its being enfeebled, adulterated even, by interior design. He liked clean lines as much as the next man, he readily admitted. He accepted the wish to cover the old flagged floor in the hall with suspended timber, at least that's what he thought they'd done, but a scattering of thick rugs had suited Miss Willett alright and was a hundred times more colourful. And now, facing double mahogany doors that bore fancy brass handles, he wondered where common sense had gone. The hairs on the nape of his neck bristled. He felt his face redden and his muscles stiffen. Instead of farm dogs rising inquisitively from their warm corner, you were greeted with flower displays and porcelain what-nots on tables and window ledges. A fat, long-haired cat eyed him suspiciously. Joe, noticing Luke's change of humour mumbled, 'You're ready?' and Luke shamefacedly glanced at Marion. She had gone very white. 'Marion, you're alright?' he whispered and nudged her gently.

'I think so,' she replied.

Luke jerked back to reality and asked Joe, 'Sorry, I didn't catch what you said.'

'She's taken it very badly,' he repeated.

'I'm so sorry,' Marion said in a little voice.

Luke, confused by his memories and circumstances was slow to grasp the reality that Marion was coming to terms with. Joe turned one of the twin brass handles slowly and bright beams of sunlight fell towards them, across the shade of the hallway. He pushed open first one half-door and then the second. Initially, all Luke noticed was the carpet. It was no longer red, patterned with flowers and scrolls with worn patches leading across to the fire, but had been replaced with wall-to-wall deep and creamy pile. They must have had a mint to pay for all of this and now, to keep it going, Luke believed. He nodded to his wife, 'Please, you first.' Marion hesitantly trod on the luxurious floor covering, preceding her companions into harsh daylight.

The room had changed beyond all recognition, Luke felt, as he followed Marion. She silently walked towards Laura who was seated curled against cushions at one end of a long, brocade-covered couch, dwarfed by its size and pale opulence. She stared at them, looking drained and wide-eyed, her blonde hair brushed back from her face and her customary light-coloured knitwear adding to the impression of desolation. Her hands though, with her long fingers and painted nails, surrounded a squat tumbler holding a small pool of amber liquid. Force of habit or determination had driven her to apply make-up with her usual diligence. Luke noticed that her mascara was smudged down across the upper part of her left cheek. Close to her now, Marion said again, 'I'm so sorry, Laura,' and her friend nodded, averted her gaze and sank her head into her shoulders.

Joe pulled two chairs at angles before the couch and

motioned to Marion and Luke to be seated while he lowered himself alongside Laura. Marion held back from embracing her friend, sensing that if approached too closely Laura might curl further into herself and become yet more inaccessible. However, the distance Laura created was not just in her stance, it was also in the hollowness of her gaze. Marion thought how true it was that one could be so near, yet interminably far. 'I should have come sooner,' she said.

Laura, turning her shoulders towards them and looking in their direction, spoke in a scarcely audible tone, 'But there was nothing, nothing you could do.' She put her glass down with careful deliberation, centrally on a small table at her side. Not wanting to disturb the stillness, they stayed quiet for a moment that stretched to a dozen in the imagination of both Luke and Marion. They heard birds outside in the garden and the quiet operation of the radiators supplying the pleasant, uniform warmth across the room; Joe also seemed reluctant to interrupt. Luke noted a second glass, presumably Joe's, on another small table, not far from where he sat. 'At least they're not pretending,' Luke thought to himself, slowly acknowledging that if Mike was seriously absent there was really no reason to pretend at all.

'He was missing,' Laura stared vacantly ahead, not looking at anyone in particular, as if she were alone and recalling thoughts to herself and the others were just witnesses. 'I didn't know where he was. He called – and then, nothing.' She lowered her eyes onto her lap, where her fingers lay, each hand clasping the other. Joe spoke quietly, 'She called me, didn't you, Laura.' He put his hand over hers, but she showed no response, her shoulders remaining stooped and her head bowed. 'You know all the rest; it'll be in the news, if it isn't already.' The quiet, measured tone of his voice betrayed a hint of bitterness. 'I called the police. It's what anyone would do.' His great, worn, generous hand lifted from hers and he slipped back into his chair. Marion started to speak but a clock struck a silvery antique chime. They listened to its flourish for twelve noon, but it was later than that now and the song-like interruption seemed at odds with the climate within the room.

'He said he'd have that fixed for my birthday,' Laura spoke quietly and added, 'but it will always be slow now.' She looked at Joe. 'Tell them,' she said, 'I don't think they really understand.'

Joe looked at each of them in turn and, speaking slowly, explained, 'I'm sorry, you can't have known. Sadly, very sadly, Mike has died. It's been a dreadful shock to us all,' he added, noticing the dismayed expressions of Luke and Marion. Laura, though, remained still, as if all emotion was frozen. Before either Luke or Marion had time to respond Joe continued, 'Mike came home last evening, strangely delayed. He was four days late. He said he was 'phoning from Heathrow. And that was odd because recently he'd been using Bristol. He gave me a ring and Laura, naturally. She'd been desperately worried. And then, when he reached home, and he was slow doing that, Laura says he had looked absolutely exhausted.' Joe weighed his words carefully as he spoke, Luke thought, and waited for him to say more. 'Laura 'phoned to let me know he'd reached home. I'd asked her to because I wanted to know he was alright and, in any case, Mike and I had some business to talk over. The next morning she 'phoned again.'

Laura raised her head just slightly but enough to catch Joe's eyes and turned to face Marion. 'He was dead.'

A confusion of thoughts ran through Marion's mind: how could Mike be home, but dead? They waited for Laura to continue. 'He'd just wanted to go to bed. He said he felt *so, so tired*. I've never heard him say that so vehemently before. He didn't talk.' Laura looked directly at Marion and said meaningfully, 'The funny little greetings we'd adopted, just special to each other, you know, the few words that mean so much....' And she broke off her explanation. 'There was nothing. He said nothing. So I thought that talking could wait. I thought a good night's rest and all would be well. He just wanted to rest and he took some painkillers. It was about eight o'clock last night. I switched on – oh, something I'd recorded, the end of a group final for the world cup that he'd texted and mentioned about a week ago. But he wasn't interested.'

'Monday night's draw with Russia?' Luke asked quietly.

Laura looked at Luke, as if for the first time recognising his presence alongside Marion. 'That's right, but Mike didn't want to know. He didn't want to eat either. I'd made a meal and he couldn't face it. He picked at some cheese and crackers I brought upstairs, but all he really wanted was a drink of tea. He went to bed so I closed the house and joined him. I lay there next to him, unaware until this morning that he'd gone. I mean, that he was dead.'

'Oh, my dear, Laura.' Marion moved forward as if to reassure Laura with a hug, but her friend was immobile and awkwardly Marion returned to her seat.

Luke watched Laura, pale and enveloped in shock. 'He died in his sleep then? I'm really so very sorry. And if I feel shocked you must be stunned.' His blunt statement reached Laura more directly than sympathy. But silently he wondered how she could have slept alongside him, and not known.

'He was next to me and I didn't realise. Until I woke, that is, and he was cold, too cold – and I couldn't make him warm.' Laura hid her eyes, but no tears fell.

'What an awful thing to happen.' Marion spoke her thoughts out loud. And then they all slipped into silence again, not liking to ask more.

Joe picked up Laura's glass. 'Like another?' he asked, and she nodded. 'Forgive me,' he said to Luke and Marion, 'I've not been very hospitable. You both look like you could use a drink. We're just having scotch.'

'That'll do fine,' Luke said and Marion agreed.

When Joe left the room Luke thought Laura looked further diminished. And that was not usually the case, he conjectured, of a person in her own home. But her fine bone structure, pale natural colouring and drained appearance from the shock of recent events emphasised her frailty. So did her clothes. He wasn't one to notice what women wore, but those insipid and soft garments faded into nothing against the pastel furnishings, still very new. Some might say the room was tastefully decorated, with a touch of glamour in the gilt, he conceded.

This was the only time he'd been in here since – no, he

shouldn't keep reminding himself that it had been different (and better) in Miss Willett's day. The building had been altered when these folks moved in. And they had certainly changed the furnishings. Then you could sit comfortably while the fire spluttered and Miss Willett talked about sheep prices and how the calves were coming on. But the grazing had been taken, some of the land bought by Joe. Luke pondered that. Yes, of course, when Miss Willett died Joe had bought some fields. They'd all thought he'd extend a bit of his own farming to Derscott, and so he did, at first. But then the new development was proposed. He realised now, Mike and Laura bought the house and tarted it up and Joe had not been averse to making extra profit on the land, by planning to build on it. Luke pulled himself back to the present. No-one had spoken in Joe's absence. Laura remained in still-life but Marion was making small helpful rearrangements of the furniture, placing yet more small tables near their chairs. 'Is there anything I can get you?' she asked Laura, but the offer was declined and the tinkling of ice in glasses heralded Joe's return.

The whisky relaxed the tension Marion had felt. 'Joe, let us know if there's anything we can do,' she said, continuing, 'there may be people to 'phone, or notify.'

Laura stiffened. 'Not yet,' she interjected, 'not until I feel I can myself.'

Marion, considering how she might summon company and support for her friend, found her intention expressed by Luke. Very carefully and gently, he said, 'But your family might wish to be with you, I think that's all we mean.' As he spoke he realised he knew little of the personal lives of Mike and Laura and their backgrounds. Families and connections were no longer simple, of course. But at a very basic level, it was plain that Laura needed support. And family usually rallied round to provide that.

Sitting there, Luke's thoughts wandered. The room had a very feminine feel, with little he'd choose for himself and he couldn't imagine Mike selecting these colours and pieces of furniture either. He came back to thinking of Miss Willett. Now she'd inherited family stuff. It had certainly put up with wear and tear and even he had recognised scuff marks, but it had been clean and polished by the strong arms of the daily help, overseen by the mistress's sharp eyes. A body felt comfortable in the deep arm chairs and in cabinets and shelves there were books to whet the imagination. That's what was missing, he concluded: books.

Laura, through all his imaginative rambling, had remained silent. Her stillness was broken only by slight movements, a turn of her head or crossing of her feet. Luke took another sip from his glass and Laura followed, sipping hers and replacing it, precisely in the place from which she had lifted it. Was this a deliberate mannerism, he asked himself, to convince herself she was in control? 'You know we're here, Laura, only a few yards down the lane, and we'll come anytime. Just give us a ring, or come round yourself.' His voice was gentle and considerate.

'And practical things, Laura,' Marion added, 'messages about the next few days – we'll give apologies, if that would be helpful. And there's food.' Marion glanced at her watch, 'It's lunchtime, near enough – would you like some soup, for example?'

Joe smiled. 'That's about my level of cooking, if Laura can put up with my kitchen skills.'

Marion thought she detected faint gratitude around Laura's lips as she replied, 'Thank you. I won't forget to eat.'

People say that when they will, Luke thought.

Joe realised that too. 'Later, I'll go through tasks with Laura,' he said, and looking directly at her, added, 'if you'll let me, that is.'

'You can't do anything,' she said resignedly, 'he's gone. I feel he's taken me too. I can't believe it.'

'I understand,' Joe said softly.

'You've got worries enough of your own.'

'Aye, but the carers come in. She's alright, on an even keel at the moment. This, here, your news – it's the most pressing and immediate. I want to help, as do Luke and Marion.'

'We were making this our home,' Laura said, for the first time moving her eyes around the room and apparently looking at the carpet, chairs and pictures. 'He didn't want to carry on much longer, you know. He told me it was tiring and there were so many agendas. That's the word he used, *agendas*, as if he attended meetings, joined discussions, met people who had motives of their own.'

'And he had all those changes of time zones and resulting jet lag.' Marion did not lose sight of the ordinary pressures of constant travelling.

Luke though, reflected on Laura's reminiscences. Interesting words she was using, apparently Mike's words, relayed second hand: *so many agendas*. Whom had he met, or what circumstance had he tumbled into? However, were such fancies out of character for Mike? Were they allowing imagination to take over reality? With a start, Luke realised Laura could be aware of more than she wanted or was ready to share.

Joe tried to recall Laura's attention. 'It's your home, of course, Laura. Just remember you have friends you can call on.'

'We've been here three, going on four, years,' Laura said flatly, 'and this is what it's led to. He's gone. They took him this morning.' As if stuck at that moment and unable to move on, she stared down at the pale, anaemic carpet.

Marion was starting to feel awkward about her continued presence. Joe was clearly at home in these surroundings and knew his way around. While she believed in the value of human company, she felt inadequate to provide the help Laura needed. With the passage of time, Marion was sure she could assist more. Laura needed a period of adjustment to come to terms with an immense shock and loss. They had been here – oh, she wasn't sure, perhaps forty minutes – and Laura was still frozen in grief and seemed unreachable. She turned first to Laura. 'I'm so very sorry,' and then to Luke, 'd'you think perhaps we should make our way back?'

For all his usual bluster, Luke was sensitive to the dilemma that faced Laura, Joe and even Marion and himself. If he had been able to exchange thoughts with Marion he would have agreed wholeheartedly that Laura needed help. But he and Marion had other considerations and demands on their time, as also had Joe. It seemed to him that if it was time Laura needed, it would take a generous amount to heal this wound. He knew Joe had an invalid wife, let alone the business of farming and entanglement with building developments to manage. Luke did not wish to probe, or appear inquisitive.

Joe again tried to reach through to the woman at the centre of this tragedy, the person who needed help, 'Laura, you're shocked, of course. It must be terrible for you – and we feel the shock too.' His concern showed as he looked across to her, her fingers now slowly crossing and uncrossing, each hand tightly gripping the other in turn.

'Thank you for coming, I am grateful,' she said, her voice tapering to a whisper.

'With the shock of all this, her husband going,' Joe shook his head, 'a good neighbour is appreciated.'

'Joe, we should slip away now, but we'll call round again tomorrow. Let us know how we can help. There are bound to be things we can do.' Luke turned to Marion, 'Should we leave our 'phone number?'

'Laura has it, of course, but just to be sure.' Marion, without success, fumbled in her pockets for a scrap of paper, so Luke tore the front off an envelope he was carrying and wrote their 'phone number above the address.

6   Detectives at the door

Joe took the number and also their empty glasses and led them back into the entrance hall. He was starting to say more but halted at the blurred images of persons, visible through the upper windows of the door. Then the bell rang. He turned the lock and they faced two serious-looking people, male and female, each carrying a slim, black document case.

'Mrs Laura –,' said the older figure, a man.

They were conscious of being scrutinised carefully.

'May we come in? I'm Detective Inspector Marland, from Devon and Cornwall Constabulary, and this is Detective Constable Dewar.' The two officers held out their identity cards.

Later, Luke admitted to being surprised, even taken aback by Joe's scrutiny of their IDs, but realised it was justified because both were in plain clothes and a sleek dark green saloon, not the usual marked police car, was parked outside. And they were not the two officers who had recently called at his own home.

'We've travelled from south Devon; this is all one patch,' the detective inspector said considerately. He was a man of fifty, Luke guessed, and his younger colleague about thirty. They stepped confidently over the threshold and then all stood awkwardly on the polished floor. 'I don't think we've met: you are?' the detective inspector enquired.

'Our name's Everett, Luke and Marion Everett.' The woman officer glanced up at Luke as he spoke with some haste, and she asked him to spell their surname.

Luke was the first to volunteer information. He supposed that information was the response the officers sought and they would be used to people behaving oddly, shocked by circumstance or police presence that could be ominous. 'We, my wife and I, we're neighbours. We came round to offer support. We didn't realise until we got here what had happened. But we're only from a few yards away, down the lane in Derscott. My wife's been Laura's friend.'

The officers both nodded courteously. 'Of course, so you're neighbours,' the detective inspector said, who then turned to Joe, 'and you, sir?'

'Joe Hartley, a friend of both Mike and Laura. She 'phoned me this morning and I came as fast as I could.'

'You were the first here?'

'Yes, yes, that must be so. I wanted to help. Laura's very shocked and so am I.'

'And you reported the death, 8.03, I believe.'

'That sounds about right.'

The constable was still taking notes. Luke felt embarrassed. 'My wife and I, were just leaving. It's a coincidence – it just happened that we came to the door as you –,' Luke stumbled over his words.

'Yes, I do see, sir, and these will be your shoes?' The detective inspector looked down at Luke's worn loafers and Marion's trainers neatly paired at one side of the large doormat, and their owners' stockinged feet.

Marion explained, 'We called just on the off-chance. We had no idea Mike had died. Earlier we had visited a garden – I mean, we didn't want to tramp mud all over Laura's polished floor.'

'If you just leave your details with my colleague then you can go. We'll know where to find you if we need to get in touch.'

A few minutes later Luke and Marion returned to their car, which looked ordinary and splattered with mud from local lanes, alongside the smart saloon. 'That could travel sharpish along any road,' Luke said, as he snapped his seat belt into place.

'I feel a bit sick,' Marion replied.

'I know, love,' Luke said, 'dreadful news, and poor Laura.'

On return home, Luke summarised for Polly the turn of events. Mike had flown back from a business trip to the Far East but four whole days after landing, more or less, were unaccounted for. Oddly, he'd returned to Heathrow, not

Bristol. Yet Mike had arrived at the door of his own house and in his own car, apparently by himself. But he had been further delayed, as well as exhausted and just wanted to sleep. He didn't wake up: the next morning he was dead. 'And now the police,' Marion said. Even Janus was subdued and retreated to the back of his basket. 'It all sounds trite, recounted to the police,' admitted Luke, 'I don't understand.'

'Whisky doesn't suit me midday,' Marion said.

'I'm hungry,' Luke grumbled.

Marion, eager to regain normality, picked over the day's post. She recollected the stack of mail she had noticed at Laura's as she separated out the junk and the advertisements from her own correspondence. One letter, in a brown envelope, seemed hand-delivered. She tore it open with her fingers and pulled out several pieces of typescript and a plan, all copied on pink paper. 'This is some coincidence,' she said. 'Just look, it shows the plan of the development on Joe's land and it's from our village activist, Pete. He's keeping up the pressure, alright.' As she read the pages she passed them on to Luke. 'It's still Joe he's fighting. We didn't mention, Polly, Joe was there with Laura when we arrived.'

'Food, my love. That's what we want.'

Polly was grateful for the halt that Luke summoned in these elaborations. 'And we're forgetting our purchases – I mean the plants. I'll see to them.' He returned to the car and with Polly's help transferred the pots from the carboot to sheltered spots in the garden where the young plants would be in good light yet protected from sharp winds. 'I always think you can never be sure what you've got until you get home. It's like buying shoes.' Luke gazed with particular affection on a hellebore. 'I've got a soft spot for these,' he said. 'My aunt, she had one near her garden shed and I'll always remember it. Of course, there are more varieties now. And here's yours.' He handed Polly a plastic pot about six inches across with a few stems and trifoliate leaves showing at the top. 'And what did you say that is?' Luke was inquisitive.

'A clematis called *Niobe*. Haresh's mother, she likes them

and when I was up there she mentioned she was looking for one that's not too sprawling, for near the kitchen door. This will be brilliant, it has claret-red flowers, the gardener says.'

'Humph. It'll be alright then. You can't go wrong with a good claret. But I don't go in for climbers myself. You never know where they're going or when they'll stop. We've enough trouble with the ivy in the hedge at the bottom of the garden.'

Polly smiled.

'Well, I dare say she'll be pleased. Don't want to put you off, you know. But how're you going to travel with this?'

'Luke, you are denting her enthusiasm, and mine too. I've been craving a clematis myself, for years,' Marion peered around the door.

'You never mentioned it!'

'Come and eat. Only a moment ago you said you needed food.'

Hastily, Luke handed Polly a small cardboard box and some packing paper. 'I reckon it will be safe enough in this,' he said and Polly thanked him.

As soon as the meal was over, Luke's teasing recommenced, interspersed with conjecture about Mike's death and curiosity about the building development plans. The cheerfulness was a reaction, Polly thought, to cover the confusion he and Marion felt and also some raw feelings. As they settled into a discussion about Laura, Polly slipped away. She planned to telephone or text Haresh so she found a warm corner in the conservatory. It was a place Janus had already discovered and he was there, playing with a rubber toy, its squeak now punctured but he jumped every time it bounced, his surprise undiminished. Polly looked at her watch. In Derscott, it was early afternoon. Where Haresh was it would be later and, with luck, he would be in his hotel room taking stock of the day.

She was speaking to him soon. He could have been in this room with her, she felt, and yet he was hundreds – no, over a thousand – miles away. What had he found, she asked, and then listened to accounts of his explorations. He described the villages he'd been through, the range of goods he'd looked at and the offers craftsmen made of more to come. As he spoke she was transported into his world of crisp mornings, storks' nests on church towers and meeting rooms warmed by enamelled stoves. 'Tell me about Devon,' he asked. And she tried her best to recount in a few words what she had been doing and local events. She hedged about Laura and simplified the story. She wasn't sure she could explain about Mike's return without revealing her own concerns which she managed to ignore most of the time, about Haresh himself and his own travelling.

'What an enormous shock,' Haresh said, 'I'm sorry for your friends. Your visit to Devon is complicated and more difficult than we had hoped.'

'But I'll soon be with you,' she said, 'it's only a few days now, and I'll be home, and so will you.'

'I must explain,' Haresh said, seeming to measure his words carefully.

Polly had come to recognise a catch in his breath, the slight inflection and she anticipated his explanation. He had been invited to another town with its market. It would only be two extra days and he had managed to delay his flight, at little extra cost. The visit offered more finds, he was sure of that. 'I'll miss you, Haresh,' Polly said.

'And I need you,' he replied. 'My love, do be with me next time.'

As their conversation came to an end Haresh said he'd 'phone the following morning and, already, she was looking forward to that and calculating the time she should expect his call. Polly sank back in the cushioned garden chair. It all seemed so worthwhile. His trips enabled him to develop his business with ever better and more varied merchandise. But she thought of their relationship and how she missed him and knew he felt the same. How much longer could she – they – cope with his travelling and their staying apart? They might find a flat together but that alone wasn't what she craved. It was something more permanent, more binding and was called marriage, she recognised. At this point she pictured her parents and recalled an incident that occurred the only time that they'd all met. While trivial in itself, her parents had hesitated, been guarded in their warmth, quite unlike their usual open sociability. And afterwards her mother had been tight-lipped and her father unwilling to discuss it. She had reached a turning point in her thoughts; a line she did not wish to pursue right now and this brought her back to reality. She considered Derscott and admitted she liked it here. On this trip she had again brought her water-colours but they were still in her case. Perhaps now was the time to bring them out. She could take a walk; the light was still good and she'd find one of the views she admired. In the background, through the door that was barely ajar, she heard Luke and Marion still talking about Laura, the report they'd seen in the local paper and the arrival of the police. They were anticipating a visit by the police at their own home, to confirm how they'd come to be at Laura's that morning, and they'd probably have to answer further questions, as well. By Polly's feet Janus still played with the rubber toy; but thoughts of Haresh flooded her mind. She wished she were in his arms and now would have to wait five full days before she could hear the softness of his voice, feel the warmth of his breath and his mouth on her lips, wanting to move closer. First, though, she had to return to London. It seemed unwelcoming without Haresh's presence. Perhaps she could stay a little longer in Derscott.

27   *Abed*

Tom ran his finger down Ellie's neck, her skin felt silky and warm beneath his roughened hands. Her dress, secured at the neck with small worked buttons, fell open inch by inch, as he slipped each button through its fabric loop. He lowered his mouth to the hollow at the base of her neck. He shifted his weight and moved over her, Ellie's arms around him as she kissed his shoulders and his mouth. He felt her warm beneath him, her legs slightly apart and then he pulled more at her skirts. He woke suddenly. Beneath him was only the straw mattress. The pillow had slipped. He pulled it back into place and wondered at his dream, the same on many nights. Did Ellie conjure similar thoughts as she slept, he mused? He had felt as if he were close to her, his body feeling her skin, hair and breath, the warmth of her arms, curve of her back and softness of her breasts. Night had not yet fled, the dark remained: had he called out in his sleep? This thought embarrassed him. Below him Father Patrick was silent, still. Tom wondered at the ancient man, who seemed isolated and vulnerable. How familiar was he with the current unrest; how far had he travelled; where was he heading for? For a moment Tom wondered if the family should question the priest's loyalty or connections, but quickly he dismissed that notion. The farmer had led the old man back after nightfall. Seth had remarked at the chill of the church and how unaware the priest had seemed of this. However, as soon as he had been seated in the farmhouse the priest's relief had shown. His pallor went and his cheeks glowed in the warmth before the fire, as he gratefully accepted the nourishment Catherine provided.

Tom listened to the wind, gusting around the house, sharpened with showers of rain which glanced off the small window. He blamed the wintry sounds for interrupting the pleasure of his dream. But he had more sense than to know his dreams would suffice. His thoughts drifted. He lay under his cover, trying to gauge when light would show in the sky. He might have long moments yet, in which to doze and lose himself in hopes which amounted to nothing in reality. He thought he knew how Ellie felt and wished they could be properly together and wed. But he worried about her ready willingness to risk herself, as for this unknown priest. He also worried about her parents and her father in particular. Seth might find him not worthy enough. Tom knew he brought no land with him and Ellie might win a better match. He'd caught Seth's eyes on him several times and could only guess at his mind. Tom had nothing to offer except himself. He drifted between uneasy thoughts, light sleep and the sounds of squally weather around the farm. Gradually night waned and it was time to rise.

Out of habit, he was quiet as he straightened his bed and fastened his clothes. He trod carefully down the flight of steps in order to lessen their creaks. His glance caught the priest, a small figure beneath the bedclothes, as he walked by. Tom was impressed that a man could sustain a day spent in prayer and be assuaged by it so that he minded not the wintry church with its damp, cold draughts. Last night he had seemed perished through entire flesh and bone. Tom walked a few steps further then he lifted his boots left last night by the door, raised the latch and let himself out. The routine was familiar. First, he made for the cows, to see to the milking. They were restless in their stalls and welcomed him, giving their milk and receiving more fodder. One, into her second year and called Moon on account of the time of her arrival, had no milk to give but this would soon be different, when her calf was born. He saw to her last. She nuzzled him and turned her head, watching his movements as he raked straw and threw fresh upon the floor. Ellie, a little later than usual, had slipped into the cow shed. He was busy as she lifted the pails, as well as embarrassed by the notions he'd had while asleep, though he was thankful she knew none of this.

'Same as yesterday!' she commented on the volume of warm, creamy milk and with a smile carried full buckets and was gone, to the dairy at the back of the farm.

'By rights, it should be properly daytime now,' Tom

thought as he closed the shippon door. Usually, he made his way straight back to the farm to break his fast, but today he was concerned about the sheep and ignored the gloomy rain to check their well-being, before returning to eat. He pulled the hood of his coat over his head. The coarse fabric, woven from the wool of sheep he had shorn himself, served him well almost the whole year through. He put it aside only in the heat of summer and that now seemed a long way off. Mostly, it was chill or damp, he admitted to himself. This morning it was both: hardly rain, more like heavy dew that verged on drizzle and fed the cold that seeped into bones and lingered. He crossed the track that led from the farm and made for a hedge. He usually cut across the first field, skirted the crest of the hill and thus returned to the farm, but this morning he was more careful in case lambs had come or a sheep was troubled. Going around the hedges reminded him of the damage winter had caused and repairs to be done before spring. Tom heard a bleating and in a hollow, under an old blackthorn, he noticed the stumbling of a new-born lamb, its feet testing the ground and its legs giving under its weight. The ewe was attentive, nuzzling the infant and sharing its scent. All was well there, Tom thought, and he continued his circuit. He had welcome news for the farmer, but not all arrived so easily, Tom feared. The lambing shed was Ellie's idea and, he conceded, would be put to good use.

'One new and two to worry over,' Tom reported when he was back inside the kitchen. He shook his coat and spread it over a pile of wood near the fire, disturbing the cats, still not up and about, but continuing their night's doze in the comfort of the hearth.

'What's that thou be saying?' asked the farmer and he listened to Tom's account. 'Well, the time be right, but the weather ain't.' He noticed Tom's wet features and how he rubbed his hands in front of the fire. 'Here, make good with this.' He helped Tom to a bowl of porridge, thick with oats, and saw the lad look around the room. 'Thou be searching for Ellie?' the farmer observed. 'She be concerned for the cream, and for the butter too.' The farmer was working leather in the dim light, rubbing in oil to soften it. He could

do this and feel the warmth of the fire in his joints before venturing out. 'I be feeding the saddle that one of our recent visitors left.' He glanced at Tom but saw no need for further justification. The lad's mind was elsewhere.

'The Father was abed when I left my own,' Tom said, to deflect the farmer's attention from further reference to Ellie.

'I thought not to disturb him,' the farmer said, 'thinking the rest'd be good for 'im. But thou be right, it be time he's up, while there's breakfast to be had.' He left the leather piece he was working on and gave the porridge a stir. 'Tom, when thou be ready, bring 'im down.' Tom ran his spoon around the inside of his bowl, scraping it clean of porridge.

'Thou be ready for more, agin?'

'Gladly; I'll have it wi' the priest,' Tom replied.

The farmer nodded. He liked the lad and saw in him shades of his own youth. He knew the feelings were keen enough between the boy and Ellie but considered how they might last. Tom was a good worker, willing and considerate. But he remembered what Catherine's father had said to him, in similar circumstances. 'It's not a girl thou be marrying, it's a family thou be getting – be thou up to us?' As he saw Tom now, he believed the lad well fit enough. 'When thou's ready, go look on 'im.'

A few moments later, Tom returned. 'He be not there!' Flushed at the disappearance, Tom recounted that he'd looked in every corner of the space in which the priest might be, that the bed had been turned back neatly and, so far as he could see, the priest had taken with him all he'd brought. The farmer ran his fingers slowly over the leather he was working. 'I reckon we know where he's gone,' he said, and put aside the fastenings he was working on. 'Come with me, lad.' They left the warmth of the farmhouse, wrapped their wool outer garments around them and made for the church.

A cat stretched and curled back into its place by the fire. Another ambled out from under the table and found a corner beneath the cream oven. The stray hen, grown used to the warmth of the hall, preened itself, high in the rafters. The hall room was their own again.

28   A 'phone call

The moon had been full and its cold light through the open curtains had played across the ceiling of Laura's bedroom, from time to time interrupted by shadows of low hanging branches on the large horse chestnut tree outside. It was dawn, yet in spite of sleeping little Laura was restless to leave her bed, as if relinquishing this and embarking on the day might restore some measure of order to her thoughts. All night she had lain on her back and almost immobile, with the vacant space belonging to Mike beside her. But they had taken him. Attempts to sleep by closing her eyes, remembering the exhaustion she felt and the last tot of whisky before putting out her bedside lamp had been scantily rewarded. Her memories of the night were like dried leaves hanging on twigs, separate, lifeless, not amounting to anything at all but they rustled, disjointed, stirring partial memories and more persistent unease. How long would they keep him: and then what? All they had was his body, as the Mike she had known was cold, so cold and he'd gone. What were they finding and where would all this lead? Her fear was growing. She was scared by the gaps in her knowledge. It was as if the unknowns about Mike had become tangible. The comfortable space alongside she had stretched over when Mike was away and its soft depression that marked his occupancy were now forbidden territory, his resting place was abhorrent. Her mind was numbed by shock and apprehension and her body behaved likewise; in pretence of sleep she had confined herself to a narrow strip and been still. True, she had shifted an arm to pull a cover closer around and turned an ankle a few degrees, maybe. But as the day was throwing grey light on familiar shapes she realised she had hardly shifted from where she had lain last night, when she had sought comfort and recuperation in sleep.

She heard the first birdsong of the day, turned back the quilted bedspread, left the warmth of the mattress and stepped towards the window. This room faced west so early light was directed onto the view ahead with its stream and copse, rather than onto this face of the house. With sudden vividness she remembered Mike's arms around her, greeting her with caresses as he had when they had made this house their own. But now, no more. The last touch had been so cold. This is where they used to stand, with their wide prospect before them, valued because it was shared and had been found by them. She ached in fear of what had gone. There had never been reason to draw the blinds and they had slept with them open. She and Mike used to laugh about their neighbours: trees, birds and sky in this rural location with its church, pub and a few houses. But today she sought the comfort of a small space; she wished to cordon off the outside and find peace that was secure. She walked around the bed, keeping her eyes on the ground and she sank into the cushioned chair by the chest of drawers. Perhaps tonight she could doze here, she thought, but her mind remained confused and in front of her was the bed with its memories. She would walk through the other rooms, she thought, before deciding where to sleep this coming night. She picked up a robe, wrapped it tight around her, collected her glass from the previous night and went downstairs.

Was there anyone she should 'phone, she asked herself? People queried her about calls she had received and whom she'd like to call, herself. No 'arrangements' (was that the word, she asked herself) could be made until Mike was back, released. It was Joe she wanted to speak with, Joe who understood Mike and had a rapport with him. He had been able to dispel Mike's worries, and hers too. But the police had put a stop to her reaching him with their request for Joe to accompany them for questioning. Was this 'custody', she wondered?

She'd felt an urgency to 'phone her daughter, her only daughter and indeed her only child. But everything had happened so quickly. Without thinking she'd dialled the number in Australia and spoken to her son-in-law, who'd been characteristically and unfailingly courteous. Probably he too was shocked by the news. It hadn't been an easy conversation. Juliet was out. He would break the news to her he said. And an hour later Juliet had returned her call. At the end of a fumbled, shocked dialogue, her daughter said she would 'phone again. And she did: she said she was coming over as soon as she could make arrangements and she had also offered to contact Mike's son, Manuel, but Laura wished to make that call herself.

The police. She had never had any reason to bother them, or to think about them particularly, until now. Well, she recollected and almost smiled, hardly any reason to think of them would be more truthful. She had assisted with a production of the *Pirates of Penzance*, by making costumes for the bumbling sergeant and his corps. At that time, in quite another place, she had sought the help of a neighbour, a police constable. But the detective inspector and his detective constable who had called on her the previous day bore no resemblance to light operetta. She almost shivered at the comparison. True, they had been polite, even considerate, but their questions, which had a veneer of being straightforward, hid a clinical, analytical precision. Over and over, it seemed to her now, they had asked about Mike's usual movements, his routines and habits. They had started with this last trip and dwelt on his returning to Heathrow, not Bristol: had she known of any reason for this switch? His gentleness catching her unawares, Detective Inspector Marland had enquired if she knew of any enemies Mike had. Shocked that he would wish to consider this she was dumbed and stared back into eyes that while not unkind, were appraising and objective. 'Let me know if any come to mind,' he said, 'and we may come back to the question later.'

Other information they sought was more general but mostly matter-of-fact: the company he worked for, his reasons for travelling, contacts abroad, destinations of trips he had made and also about his wider family. And then they asked how she knew these things and what she had been doing herself, these last few weeks. She had recounted 'phone calls and explained the difficulties of maintaining contact during his travels with inevitable time-changes, meetings and other commitments. But now they had his mobile 'phone and hers too. They had taken his travel things, still in his suitcase, as well as the clothes he'd arrived in and the briefcase for his laptop. She'd been even more surprised than the police at the contents of this: just a bottle of whisky but no laptop. They wanted to know if he took any medication and she had handed over his blood-pressure pills. So far as she gathered, half the male population over fifty took them. They had asked her to gather any papers she thought relevant. They would be back, they said, with a computer technician and that was because she'd agreed they could access Mike's desktop – in fact anything they wanted, she would willingly provide. But they couldn't bring back Mike, not now. All they had was a shell.

She went into Mike's study. Alongside the desk was a filing cabinet. They would empty that, she was certain, though all they'd find would be papers, the sort any householder kept: bills, small transactions, policies, guarantees and car documents. Mike did most things electronically. The desktop would be more significant and this she hardly ever used. Mike had encouraged her to attend a course to learn about computing, but she had not persisted and what bits of knowledge she had gained were rapidly forgotten. He had shown her how to order goods on-line and she knew she could buy almost anything she wished this way. But she liked to see her purchases, to try on new clothes and to squeeze tomatoes and smell fruit at the local greengrocer's. She liked to use her mobile 'phone, she valued it for its flexibility, but the computer – that, they were welcome to scrutinise. She expected they would remove, copy or download (that was the term, she remembered) anything they found interesting, and then they might leave her alone. She wondered if that was how Joe felt now: alone. With a sudden recognition, she reflected on whether there was anything she should be doing for Joe. His wife, pitifully, might not comprehend this turn of events and any change in routine could be a great worry to her. Should she be enquiring about Joe? Contact his solicitor even? Had she been remiss, she wondered. She checked her watch. It was still far too early to contact anyone.

Why had the police been so serious about interviewing Joe, she worried? Would they take her next? The absurdity of this, she thought. And yet, she had slept next to Mike and the worst nightmare she could ever have imagined had become reality: alongside her, in the same bed, he lay dead. Her fears escalated as she thought back to what had prompted their arrival. Everything was happening so fast. The coldness of Mike and in panic her 'phone call to Joe. An hour later he'd arrived and, quickly summing up the situation, had dialled the emergency number. A doctor, an ambulance and another policeman had followed in succession. She had watched the young policeman make a 'phone call from outside the house as he'd left and then, before lunchtime, the two detectives arrived. The senior one, he was called Mr Marland, asked questions and the woman took notes. She knew they'd be back. They would consider her role; it was their job to do this she realised, to suspect her actions, motives, and even her state of mind.

Laura grasped the arm of the swivel chair in front of Mike's desk and it slipped from her, rotating slowly. There was a small couch in this room, a cast-off which had come from her previous home and with which she had been reluctant to part. Mike had never minded accommodating her past but most of her furniture had seemed out of place. They'd kept the couch in here so she could join him, if she wished, and sitting upon this now she viewed pictures – souvenirs of their travels together and separately. But none, yet, of China. She had hoped Mike would bring a flower painting, or calligraphy. This gap would mark the end. She turned to view another wall. Then she returned to a nagging question: why did they want to question Joe?

He had always been so helpful; ever since he had offered to buy part of the farm land from Miss Willett's estate that they had bought with this house. Friendship had just developed. Laura wondered if the police would question her about this. Sifting through her thoughts – the chronology, she could call it – might stand her in good stead. Make her seem less foolish, less forgetful, less shocked. Mike and she had been here three (going on four) years: simple facts and easily checked. Before they moved in, while improvements were being done, Joe had tendered to purchase several large fields. At the time, little other interest had been shown in them, she had to admit. He had offered a fair price and had smoothed arrangements by always knowing where to go for information which was outside their usual experience, making concessions about odd details, working with a knowledgeable solicitor and being consistent. A forgotten saying came to mind: *his deed's as good as his word*. She could see nothing wrong in all of this. Lately, Mike had spent an evening with Joe, while he'd been home and she was tied up with local dramatics. Occasionally, Mike would bring a souvenir from his travels to thank Joe for a leg of lamb or a brace of pheasants which had appeared. And Mike had always been considerate of Joe's invalid wife and would travel over to the farm, if Joe needed to be there.

Almost bursting with the conflicts of protest and despair, she asked herself what friends were for, if not for companionship and diversion? Laura knew that she, Mike and Joe viewed things differently at times, but what was wrong with that? Joe's head was full of meat prices, subsidies and yields. Mike was glad to have relief from constant travelling and to listen to Joe's relaxed style of cataloguing local news and his own plans. She had only seen Joe stressed-out once, and that was recently. He'd become really uptight about foreign exchange rates: just something they had been chatting about casually and he'd really blown up. But it was over in a wink. Joe was a great one for plans and they always seemed to work out well. She expected that was what worried people about his proposed developments at Derscott. Mike had said he could not have put forward those plans without Joe's purchase of the land that traditionally had belonged to the house she and Mike had purchased. The proposal hadn't pleased the locals.

Laura shuddered at the way people had stared and whispered when she went into the local shop and she'd persuaded Mike to stop visiting *The Stag Inn*. There'd been a time when they'd gone to church together. She remembered Mike commenting on the age of the stonework and how it linked generations. He wasn't usually reflective in that way, but she had loved sharing such moments with him. Sometimes he'd take a walk, just to the top of the lane, into the churchyard and back. He'd tell her of small things he'd noticed: a different bird, flowers newly out and even inscriptions on some of the memorials. One particular epitaph had captured his imagination and become a salutation they used for each other, *We be with thee* he'd say on arrival home, or when leaving on his travels. It was on just such a local walk that he'd recognised Marion and acquainted himself with Luke. They'd been the only people nearby who'd been friendly and Marion was the more outgoing, although Luke had been kind, yesterday. It was probably out of pity. *I must look ghastly*, thought Laura as she considered her own appearance. But the last twenty-four hours had been horrible and before that she'd been worried and felt uneasy, almost like a premonition.

Time was slipping by. She knew she should breakfast and dress. She'd dress first she decided, so she retraced her steps, straightened the bed and quickly had a shower. She put on a light blue sweater and pants. The sweater was one Mike particularly liked, soft to touch and warm. Then she returned to the kitchen, pulled a stool to the bench and tried listing everything she needed to do. But ideas would not come. Mike had gone, Joe was absent and she felt a huge hole. She pushed the kitchen notepad away and instead toyed with a bowl of cereal. She had never liked the stuff but had taken to eating it because the mixture she bought was good for you, so they said. Perhaps she should have a glass of juice or make some coffee. The 'phone rang. It was not yet eight o'clock. 'Hello,' Laura said quietly.

'Mrs Townley, my name's Angie,' the voice sounded sympathetic. 'I'm from Mike's firm. We're all so sorry to hear about Mike.'

'Angie... Angie who? Who are you? Why do you – I mean, how d' you know?'

'My name's Angie...' And now the line went fuzzy. To Laura it sounded like Angie Smeeth, but the voice continued. 'I'm so sorry this comes out of the blue. I'm from human resources in Mike's firm, the global development division. Mike has been such an asset. We want you to know that.'

'He's gone. How d'you know?'

'We were contacted last night, by the police in England.'

'I'm sorry, I'm not myself.' The receiver slipped in Laura's hands and she was cut off.

A moment later the 'phone rang again.

'Laura; may I call you that? It's Angie again. I'll give you my direct-line number.'

Laura was just collected enough to write it down and read it back at Angie's request.

'I'm available to help in any way I can. I'll come down, if you'd like that.'

'Oh, there's no need, really no need.'

'D'you have family with you?'

'Good friends are close by. They're very kind. I just need time to understand all of this.' Laura recoiled both from sharing confidences with someone unknown and also did not wish to invite further complications.

'We have received a call we thought you might wish to know about.'

'Yes?'

'From eastern Europe, Montenegro.'

'It would be business, something connected with Mike. He went all over the place. But you know that. He was working for you,' and Laura's voice trailed off. She realised her comments were disjointed and she must sound upset.

There was a pause and then Angie asked, 'No personal friends in that region?'

'None of Mike's that I know of.' No sooner had she said this than an ugly doubt wormed into her imagination. Shadowy thoughts about Mike's previous marriage grew more distinct in her mind. His son. Now he could be travelling a lot. As if to push such thoughts out of her mind she said, too quickly, but the words rushed out before she could stop herself, 'I have an aunt with a house in Greece, isn't that nearby? Mike has met her...but why am I telling you this? She would contact me, not Mike, if she was ill or in trouble out there. Can you deal with the call? Or just forget it? It doesn't seem important right now. You could help me by looking after it.' Laura hoped this would satisfy the inquisitive Angie, give her something to do.

The warm, kind voice continued, 'Keep my number near you. Remember I'll do anything I can to help.'

'Thank you.'

'And I'll ring you again, in a few days' time, just to keep in touch.'

Resenting intrusion into her private grief, Laura returned to Mike's study and wiped tears from her face. She mustn't allow things to get in the way of sorting papers for the police. She wanted to do her best for Mike, and keep the house calm, a sanctuary for herself and where he'd been, free of interference.

29   A born farmer

Polly found it easier to sleep late than to sleep well. As the day brightened she remembered she was still here, with Marion and Luke, in Devon. But the house was quiet. She wondered if her friends were up – or if she had slept through their activity. She shook herself free of the duvet and glanced at her watch. Already, it was eight o'clock. In recent days, by this time they had breakfasted and decided the shape of the day. Hastily, she went to the bathroom and dressed. Still, she was not aware of others around the house. With deliberate noise, she went downstairs and looked in the kitchen. It was empty. Not even Janus could be seen. As usual, the door to the small square room once used for dining was closed but she heard the rustle of papers within, pushed open the door and found Marion.

'Come in,' Marion said.

'Am I intruding on inspections?' Polly asked, 'you've got down to work quickly.'

'Oh, bless you, Polly; if it was inspection stuff I'd have sorted it by now. I'm teasing out the truth behind the development.' With calculator and pencil Marion was analysing information Pete had given her.

'You're taking this so very seriously.'

'So would you!' Marion rejoined, 'I'm testing the theory there's a mint of money to be made!'

'You mean by Joe?'

'No, it's not that simple. If the costs supplied by Pete are accurate, it will be the building contractor who comes off well.'

'D'you think Joe realises that?'

Marion was absorbed. 'There's hot water in the kettle,' she said, 'make yourself a drink.' Polly retreated to the kitchen, leaving Marion to her calculations, and she admired a large bowl of porridge, warm and molten on the Aga. Looking through the window she saw Luke. Already, he was bouncing balls for Janus who had mastered the art of a mid-air catch. Polly made herself a mug of coffee and picked up the daily newspaper that Luke had folded on the table, to be enjoyed at breakfast time. As she turned its pages she felt that the news locally around Derscott seethed with interest compared with that reported in national papers. Perhaps it was because of the personal involvement, she admitted, whereas all these international issues were so remote. Nevertheless, some items intrigued her and she welcomed one about extra funding for schools, while cynically speculating what would be cut, to balance the books of the nation. She heard Marion's mobile ring, but only briefly. It seemed to Polly that Marion's response had been eager but the piercing jingle of the 'phone had reminded Luke of breakfast and he brought Janus inside to enjoy his own bowl of puppy food.

'Tell me what's happening in the world,' Luke greeted Polly cheerfully.

Polly mentioned a book review she had read.

'D'you believe him? I mean the reviewer. I bet if you look in the *Guardian* you'll have quite a different take.'

Polly smiled and replaced the paper, properly folded, next to Luke's porridge plate.

'Where's Marion? I'm ready for breakfast.'

'She's very busy, I'd say, in the dining room,' responded Polly.

'Not eating though.'

'No, she's doing paper work and there's been a 'phone call. That will be keeping her.'

Before Luke had time to retrieve his wife, the door into the kitchen was opened by Marion herself. Polly thought how like a stage set they were, of disparate characters, suddenly coming together. Never happier than when juggling too many interests, Marion beaming.

'I've been busy,' she said, 'not just throwing balls for Janus.' Marion winked at Polly as she teased her husband.

'Umph,' he said, concentrating now on the newspaper.

'Which crisis d'you want to hear about first?' asked Marion as her husband continued lifting spoonfuls of porridge to his mouth.

'The last call was from Lottie – and for you, Polly.' Marion relayed the message. 'Would you like to pop over and look at Rob's course work? He's really proud of it and I think Lottie would be glad of any comments you have.'

'Of course I'll go. Shall I meet other members of Janus's family, as well?' At the mention of his name, Janus cocked his ear, but they ignored him so he remained recumbent, guarding his empty food bowl.

'That boy's a born farmer. There'll be more to look at now than when you were last around, I'll be bound. Ask how the calves are faring,' Luke said.

For a few moments they tackled their breakfast in silence, each was thinking of the opportunities the morning might bring. The only sound was of Janus, who was now apparently slumbering and dreaming judging from the little yelps he made. 'So what have you been up to? Inspections?' Luke asked Marion.

'No, the briefing's not come through yet, but it's due.'

'Well don't keep me in suspense.'

'I must 'phone Pete.'

'Oh, so you'll tell the other man, but keep me in the dark!'

Marion smiled happily. Polly wondered whether one day she herself would sit at her own kitchen table and similarly rail with Haresh.

'We're too busy, you know that. We've got the pale widow and her mystery down the road; Janus to be exercised at home; your inspections; the development looming; Polly going to see Rob – and Malcolm's coming today.'

'Oh, I didn't know about Malcolm. You'll have to take care of him yourself.'

'He 'phoned while you were in the bathroom. I didn't see any harm in his coming. He gave such a good reason it was hard to ignore. We'll be out, won't be under your feet in any way. Like to join us, Polly?'

'Of course, if you'll put up with me.'

'You can talk with all the old ladies who do flowers for christenings.'

'Shut up, Luke,' Marion said, 'she's a power-house of

149

biological information. The question is will she put up with your eccentricities?'

'I'll buy you lunch, Polly.'

'That's more like it,' Marion said, 'how about it, Polly?'

So Polly's day was arranged and Marion was freed to look after paperwork and make 'phone calls, as well as to keep an eye on Janus.

Polly sought extra warmth and reached in the chest of drawers for a sweater in a raspberry shade, with cabling down the front. Spring had taken a step backwards, there was a nip in the air and she anticipated churchyards would be chilly. A woollen hat, that would be useful too, she felt. While she knew Marion might have one to lend, she thought she would try the village shop. That sold most things and was on the way to Rob's. 'Will Lottie mind my just turning up?' she asked Luke.

'Give her a ring, she may still be there, if she's not looking after her babes.'

A minute later Polly let herself out of the house. At the shop, the bell rang noisily as she pushed open the door to step inside. She had deduced from earlier visits that the loud ring was triggered by a home-made device fitted under the door-mat. A row of eyes looked her over as she walked alongside shelves and scanned the ranks of tins, groceries and magazines displayed neatly on fitments, alongside painting sets, pencils and indoor games for children. As she searched for clothing, whispered gossip was exchanged in the depths of the interior and she caught the sound of Joe Hartley's name. 'Taken 'im in, they surely have.' 'But what of her 'usband?' 'Used ter be such a virtuous 'ouse, 'an all.' 'Never credit it, an' in Derscott too.' 'Do she ever cum in 'ere?' 'I sees 'er in church occasionally.' 'But the 'usband seemed to wander the surrounding more'n within.' 'Reckon things be on 'is mind do 'ee?'

Polly looked towards the cluster of people kindling speculation about Laura, her husband and Joe. Their attention was broken by the shopkeeper, Mr Tripp, as he asked, 'Can I 'elp you, m'love? Are you looking for something partic'lar?'

'A woollen hat,' Polly said.

150

'Won't find one back there: clothing's around this end.'

The small group dispersed, some drifted to the postoffice counter reigned over by buxom Mrs Tripp with her permed grey hair and others wandered out of the shop, the doormat bell signalling each time it was stepped upon. Polly was presented with a straightforward choice: a plain black machine-knit with a turn-back band like a cuff around the face, or a thicker knit in Plymouth Argyle Green. She chose the latter, on the grounds of warmth. 'Won't miss 'ee in 'em!' the shopkeeper commented, going on to explain, 'Mrs Ridger do 'em. I'd normally 'ave a wider choice on offer, with Manchester United as well, but this side of the year the rest're gone.' Polly paid happily and after causing further ringing to resound through the shop she set off to see Rob, not doubting that the villagers' supposition would continue and be elaborated, both in the post office and also elsewhere.

'Hi, Rob!' Polly called, spying him bottle-feeding a lamb, by the back door of the farm. He had grown since her last visit, even in the space of just a few weeks and the down was thickening around his cheeks. 'How old is this one?' Polly asked.

'A week. I've helped a good number onto their legs this time.'

'You must be proud of them all,' Polly replied, thinking how capable the boy was becoming.

'They've been coming through the holidays and I've earned £40 in all.'

'Wow.'

Tenderly, he helped the lamb to finish the bottle and then lifted it into its pen. 'And I've another two need feeding. Want to help?'

'Sure.'

'But Mum says you'd like to look at my coursework.'

'There's time for that too.'

Later, Rob removed his boots and Polly her outdoor shoes and they went through into the house. Just as last time, his files were set out in the dining room.

'You've spent a lot of time on this. Your presentation's very good.'

Rob glowed with pride but was embarrassed to say much. 'I worked really hard, I did.'

Polly turned over the pages, noting the organisation and detail of his work. It was nearly all handwritten in neat black script, with photographs and graphs included. 'What does your teacher say?' she asked.

'She thinks it's good. At least a B.'

'You must be really glad about that?'

'And I'm going to get an upgrade on my computer. Dad's promised me that. If I'd ave 'ad one I'd 'ave got an A*,' she said.

'I can understand,' Polly said, 'your work is really promising. I'd be glad to be your teacher.'

'You 'elped a lot!' Rob said, handing her another file for scrutiny.

30   Casserole in the Aga

Malcolm was seated in the kitchen by the time Polly returned. A mug of coffee was in his hand and next to him a mound of belongings: several notebooks, a field-guide about lichens, a well-worn canvas bag that held his camera together with other bits and pieces, and his waterproof jacket. Having spotted a cluster of villages on his road map, he had looked up old lichen records and realised they were worth checking. Several interesting species had been found on past visits and now others, newly recognised, might be found. 'Look at this.' He showed Polly a specimen he had brought from his collection. 'If you see anything like that, let me know. It'd be a first for the south-west!'

Luke had set up, on a cabinet by the window, a viewer that magnified and they went over to take a much closer look at the specimen Malcolm had brought. 'You think we may find that where we're going today?' Luke asked enthusiastically. 'Then let's be off.' They said their farewells to Marion. Polly travelled with Luke who knew the way to their destination, with Malcolm in his own car, tailing them. 'I'm not really sure we'll find that rarity,' said Luke cautiously, 'but he's got keen eyes and you never know what may turn up.' They spoke little for a few moments, as Luke negotiated the pot-holes in the lanes and checked in the mirror that Malcolm was still behind. 'So how did you get on with Rob?' he asked.

Polly described her visit, the progress Rob had made with his project and the lambs she had helped to bottle-feed. 'Aye, he's a good boy is Rob,' Luke responded, 'should do well, while there's land to farm.'

Malcolm had no need to consult maps, as long as the two cars travelled in consort. But at times his car lagged behind and Luke worried about losing him, or both cars having to stray onto the verge to allow another to pass. As they drove on through a copse they noticed large twigs brought down in recent winds had been thrown across the hedge, keeping stray debris clear of the road. Suddenly, though, they arrived.

Parking was a conundrum in the small, compact village. After several minutes of reversing, negotiating tight corners and avoiding a tractor, the car was eased into a slot close to the churchyard that was neatly maintained; parishioners were attentive. Luke and Malcolm wasted no time in starting their survey and Polly practised her skills of record-keeping. Soon, however, their activity attracted interest, even in this quiet setting. A man of grey complexion and clothes of muted colours that matched the headstones, announced himself as churchwarden. Rubbing his hands together and sporadically parting them, he leaned against one sturdy memorial after another and showed pointed interest in their activity, with a proprietorial air that belied his faded appearance.

'Damage? Don't they damage the stone? Should we be scrubbing them off? There's stuff you can buy to do that, you know.'

'No need.' Polly explained, 'the lichens just use it as support.'

The churchwarden remained vigilant, scanning them each in turn but Luke, Malcolm and Polly became less conscious of his presence and unaware of his departure as, with their quiet persistence, their records of lichens accumulated. It was almost one o'clock when Luke announced, 'You've both earned your lunches. Let's take a break, shall we?'

But hopes were daunted. The local inn did not serve food midday. 'No matter,' Malcolm said, 'peanuts and bitter will do me fine.' The warmth of burning logs in the grate enticed them. They relaxed and chatted but Malcolm kept his eye on his watch and before long suggested they resumed their survey.

After two further hours in the churchyard they were ready to call it a day. Polly's records were extensive and needed checking before Malcolm returned. 'Home calls,' Luke said decisively, 'Marion's bound to have a casserole in the Aga.' However, on return to the house they were greeted by a message. Behind the front door, propped against the telephone, stood a large piece of card: *Janus fed and exercised. Find me at The Stag, with Pete.*

'What the –,' Luke said.

'C'mon, old man,' Malcolm said, 'I'll be on my way.'

'The least I can do is buy you something to eat. You need a meal, I want a meal and I promised to look after Polly. One thing I can be sure of, *The Stag* serves all day – we're hungry folk in Derscott.' Luke was emphatic and bustled the other two into joining him on the short walk to the local inn. 'You'll drive all the better when you're fed and Marion will never forgive me if I allow Polly to starve. We can go through the checklist. My, I wish we'd found the species you showed us earlier. And if only Marion would let me bring Janus. They don't mind dogs in *The Stag*, you know. They'd lose half their customers if they turned them away.'

Malcolm, who was not familiar with dogs and the rearing of puppies, kept silent. It looked to him as if Janus had a will of his own and a certain guile. But in the kitchen, in the warmth of the Aga, the dog slept. No bad thing, Malcolm thought.

Marion had been riled at first by Pete's assumption that she was acting as a go-between with Mike, and thus Joe. She had suspected for some time that other discussions had been held – cabals she called them – plotting action against the development plans. Awkwardly, Pete justified the discussions which had taken place but found it hard to explain the exclusion of Marion and Luke, especially since it was so obvious, meeting with her now, that she was both committed and capable in resisting plans. He had 'phoned her at lunchtime but she had wanted to meet at a later time and at a rendezvous outside her home. She had thought this would free space for Luke and their guests, whom she assumed would have consumed a hearty meal in the village close to their churchyard. Luke had set off exulting fulsomely on food enjoyed with friends on similar occasions. On arrival at *The Stag*, Marion ordered a drink and sandwich for herself, a belated lunch. Pete was there already, sipping a pint of local ale.

He pressed for information before they started talking about development plans. How was Laura? Was it true Joe had been questioned by the police? What did he have to do with Mike's death? Marion was politely evasive. When Pete persisted she told him they should leave aside these diversions if they were to make good use of their time. The written proposal, submitted to the council and circulated to householders in the village, was fact and merited scrutiny.

'You know I copied everything they sent,' Peter said.

'All on pink paper?' Marion smiled. Pete was no match for Marion's determination and intellect, but had the ear of a large proportion of the villagers who objected to the extent of farmland being covered with houses. Amenable and friendly, he cultivated interest in his initiatives by suggestion, innuendo and gossip. While not denouncing the value of data and hard evidence, he found many people ready to join his side in response to plausible explanations, encouragement and, best of all, a touch of scandal. In height he towered over her, but was bent around the shoulders. However, seated on padded benches by a table at *The Stag* their eyes met and he had to face Marion's direct approach. He and his wife Cherry had been in the village for as long as Marion could remember, but Marion did not think he was local. He ran a peculiar little shop in a corner of the nearby metropolis, Barnstaple. The front of the shop was little bigger than her pantry, but the premises had labyrinthine depth with passages, staircases and a back door that led to outbuildings and a loft. While ostensibly he traded in second-hand music records (and this is how she had come across him first, searching for an historic recording of a 1950's popular record for Anna) she marvelled that this alone would even pay the rates. In moments of kindness she thought he must be trading on the internet. If the small fliers he distributed around the village were measure of his computer skills then he probably had sufficient knowledge and he could be buying and selling records worldwide. More cynically, and allowing her imagination full rein, she had speculated whether other more lucrative goods were being exchanged and vinyls and, older still, 78s were merely the cover, allowing people making purchases to meet. It was easy to forget, just these few miles inland, the many opportunities the extensive coastline and inlets provided for importing, and then trading, substances with high street-value.

'Now, what d'you make of the plans?' Marion asked, brushing these thoughts aside and taking a large bite of ham and tomato, sandwiched between slices of crusty bread.

'Audacity, sheer audacity. They think we're bumpkins, and they'll walk off with millions.'

'Will they, d'you think?'

'Bound to, the scale of it all. And the planning department... well, they've got their eyes on the readies. They won't turn down the opportunity to say yes, put up more white-washed boxes and meet Government targets. You've only got to drive around any of the local villages and see the number of houses squeezed into back gardens and flanking the perimeter. So-called 'starter homes' but once up who buys them? What locals can afford them? I'll lay a pound for a penny they're incomers and weekenders. I wouldn't mind if the boxes matched their surroundings but most look like middle England landed here accidentally. They've no individuality! Now, if I had my way....' Pete, in full swing, seemed hardly to need breath. This was continuous oration but, reflected Marion, apart from being spirited it gave few leads for practical action. Except that it gave her opportunity to bite further into her sandwich and taste the coleslaw and potato crisp accompaniments. 'Hot-air man' was Luke's description of Pete, and this gas, Marion agreed, was good for stirring up local feeling, as long as you agreed with him of course.

'I've got a slightly different take on this,' she said.

'What, well, you surprise me,' Pete reacted vehemently, taking her comment as meaning she gave support for the plans which he so strongly opposed. 'Our culture. The bedrock of our civilisation for over a thousand years....' and Pete was off again, at a faster pace and higher volume.

Marion was starting to feel self-conscious. She had braced herself to meet him, put up with his verbosity and even the grovelling he exhibited at times, but she was being treated like a foolish child and others were starting to take notice. The barman was smiling as he replaced glassware into their slots above the counter from trays of the dishwasher, and people at the other end of the lounge were turning to look their way. Marion did not want to time-waste. She already had enough demands on her time and had to draw this peroration to a halt.

'Pete, I'm totally with you in principle, but I've been doing some arithmetic. Now, you take a sip of your ale and listen. We all need to do that sometimes.' She smiled sweetly and continued. 'I wanted to come prepared so our meeting could be really useful. I've looked through all the information you provided and done some analysis. If I can just take these out of my handbag...' But more fell out of her large leather bag than she intended. Across the table, in addition to the lunch plate, condiment set and drinking glasses, numerous items were scattered. A purse from which a few coins had tumbled found itself perched near the rim; combs, cosmetics, pens, a calculator, mobile 'phone, keys and driving glasses had fallen across the centre; and the debris of odd envelopes, assorted bills and receipts formed froth over it all. Marion rescued the plastic sleeves into which she had slipped the paperwork she had done on the development plans. She handed Pete a set and instructed him to read them through, while she reconstituted her handbag.

On reaching the last two of five closely written pages, he said, 'You can't mean that!'

'But I do!'

'It's incredible.'

'Surprised me, too, but that's what the figures show.'

'Well I'm blowed!'

'Yes, putting aside all the things both you and I care about, and just considering pounds and pence, even with estimated upper gains, Joe would be better off continuing to farm the land.'

'You've shown the profit would go to the builder, at least at the prices tendered.'

'That's right.'

'Then why is the farmer, I mean Joe Hartley, pursuing this?'

'I don't think he realises.'

'He's not naïve, Marion. He could have an interest in the building firm, of course.' Pete was showing himself to be shrewder than she had realised.

'Perhaps that information would be useful to us,' Marion countered.

'It could be, I suppose.'

'Let's not lose sight of our concerns, though. We're starting to question whether Joe has ventured into the building business. I'd like to ask what he thinks of the analysis I've done.'

A smile passed across Pete's face. 'I'll join you in that,' he said, 'and we can ask others too.' Before Marion could protest that the involvement of more people could blur issues, they were interrupted.

'So this is how you treat your hard working husband. Dining à deux with another!' Irritation showed in Marion's eyes, sufficient for Luke to realise that Pete was stretching her patience, so he relented and became jovial. 'Pete, meet my good friend Malcolm, and Polly you've probably seen around, she's been staying with us – and a veritable member of the family she is too.' Extra chairs were brought and the group enlarged. Luke purchased drinks and distributed menus. 'It's alright for some, but we've been denied our vittles. First, no food near the churchyard and then no aroma from the Aga. But we knew we could depend on *The Stag*.'

'Luke bothers too much. The last place – what was it called? *The Anglers Rest* I think. They sold good peanuts,' Polly said.

Pete displayed some knowledge of the inn they had visited, but none of the church.

'You should try looking for lichens, my man,' Luke said with cunning, 'gets you to the most remarkable places.' He went on to recount the villages he had particularly enjoyed, churches with novel features and he digressed to describe farms with chapels attached. Malcolm and Polly contributed with such vigour that Marion wondered whether Luke had forewarned them of Pete's propensity to be verbose and they were trying to out-do him. But their spate relaxed when the food arrived and, hungrily, they ate.

159

'My own local knowledge developed quite differently,' Pete interjected and told them of his accordion and the band he started in his student days. 'That's how I came to know the villages and Derscott too.'

It was refreshing to see Pete pensive, Marion thought. The anecdotes he recounted of circumstances a generation earlier, interested them all. 'The country's weathered change,' Marion said.

'And enough, I'd say, if we want to conserve the character of our countryside,' Luke commented.

'So your meeting is about rural England, I take it?' Malcolm had gathered from snippets of information, scattered through the discussion, that a meeting was planned.

'You could say that,' Marion replied, 'it's about a building development.'

'This is what we're chewing over,' and Pete spread out the diagram of the village, received from the local planning department and, as briefly as he knew how, explained about the location, kinds and numbers of the houses planned. Malcolm listened attentively, glancing occasionally at Luke and Marion for confirmation of Pete's account.

'So, the main point's the complete lack of infrastructure,' Malcolm observed, and then summarised, 'the density of houses; inadequate access because the junction with the main road would be hazardous; and the costing, which is not directly your concern but could undermine the venture. But wait a minute, d'you really think anyone can afford to build at the moment?'

'If it goes through in principle, they'll be building before you realise it,' Luke declared, and then lightened his tone, 'how about another round?' He took orders for refills and coffee, which he attempted to enjoy himself.

'What about environmental grants?' Malcolm asked, 'have you taken account of them as well?'

Marion explained the basis of her calculation; Malcolm was thoughtful. 'Can you send me some background information?' he asked, and went on to explain, 'I'm a surveyor by training and used to do a lot of work for local authorities.'

'That had slipped my mind,' Luke smiled. 'Marion would have involved you like a shot if she'd known.'

'I can't believe our luck!' Marion glowed.

'And what's happening next?' Malcolm asked.

'The council considers it. First, proposals are discussed in committees. And there'll be a consultation meeting – that'll be a face-saver,' Pete said cynically, 'little more than an opportunity for us to have a dig at the council. They'll have made up their mind already and it'll not make a blind bit of difference.'

'But when'll that be?'

Pete shrugged his shoulders. 'Depends what else they're up to. They only think of themselves when they plan their meetings. You can't trust the council, never could. Might be a fortnight, or even six months.'

Malcolm smiled. 'It would be useful to have a better idea of what it's all about, if that isn't too much of a bother.' Then he added, 'Can you send me the originals, from the council?' A glance through the window, damp with afternoon mist, and a glance at his watch reminded him of his own immediate plans. 'I must be going,' he said, 'if I'm to get home in daylight.'

'I'll walk back with you to your car,' Luke said, 'there's Janus to consider.'

Malcolm promised to stay in touch and left Marion, Polly and Pete to finish their glasses.

31   King's men on their way

The fire glowed and sparked casting shafts of brightness
over the settle and furniture as splinters of gnarled wood
burned and smoked alternately. The hall was quiet, save for
crackling in the hearth, until disturbed by the rapid footsteps
of a small child. 'Adam,' Jess, his mother, called. She had
been met by Toss, the oldest of the dogs at the farm and the
most tolerant and steadfast. The dog had recollected her as
part of the farm while it had been her home, as well as from
her frequent visits since that time, and he nuzzled his
welcome about her skirts. Adam in his eagerness had tripped
near the table legs, but plump and good-natured the infant
viewed the room from the floor. Jess chided him as she pulled
him to his feet. 'Now stay close,' she said to him as she laid
her baby, gently wrapped in a soft fleece and sleeping, into a
stout box her mother used for woollen threads, some still on
their spindles. She moved the box, with the baby well fed and
sound asleep, within reach of warmth from the hearth. Adam
was lifted by Jess onto a chair, his cap and jacket removed.
'Thy front's soaked...poor lamb.' He'd sat before her on the
pony and she'd sheltered the baby between them, in the fold
of her cloak. She went to his jacket, felt its wool fabric heavy
with moisture and spread it out to dry in a corner of the
hearth. 'Toss, where be they all?' she asked, surprised to find
no-one at home and wanting to see them. Toss, still
remembered as a lively young dog, was now tending to
decrepitude, his coat shaggy with matted fur. He was glad to
be in the warmth himself and tolerant of Adam's teasing. The
child, occupied by a piece of bread rounded by crust, played
with the dog's fur and fell asleep, lulled by the animal's
breathing and cosy atmosphere in the room.

'Jess!' Ellie, surprised by her sister's early return, busied
herself making some refreshment. 'Hush,' Jess put a finger to
her lips and pointed to the sleeping children. 'Why so soon?'
Ellie whispered and without waiting for a reply said,

'mother's following me just now wi' the cream, we've been working wi'....' But before she could explain more the door opened to show Tom and the elderly priest.

'We don't ought to have done it, that be one way o' thinking on breaking into thy prayers,' Seth's voice boomed from behind, 'but I bayn't have thee freezing alive in there!'

'My good man,' the priest protested but faintly so because he realised the sense the farmer spoke. The church had been chill, even for his cold bones.

'Why be thou 'ere?' Seth turned to Jess. 'We be glad to see 'ee, daughter, yet...'

'I know, Father,' she replied, 'but the King's men be on their way, more in line for us than Derscott, as also are Roundheads for the Parliament's side....so Matt, he bade me come.'

Her father understood. By coming here she'd brought useful news and also, at her family home, Matt believed she was safe. 'Ye're both damp through,' he said, noticing the vapour rising from her cloak and Adam's wet garment. 'This be no good for any of 'e.' He looked up at Catherine, 'More sup's needed,' and then faced his daughter, 'now, get thyselves warm!'

'They be not far away,' Jess said, shaking her head.

'Sustenance, that's what thou needs!' her father said with an eye on Adam who, wakened by voices, was demanding food.

'I, by being here bring problems,' the priest announced.

'Nay, don't speak like that,' Ellie replied.

The old man felt barely able to cope with all this turmoil, the country fraught between King and common men, and the farm busy with people and animals.

'Ye both be family while in this house, now think ye on!' Seth said, addressing Jess and the priest. But scarcely had he uttered this than hooves were heard, pelting towards the farm.

32 'Nothing happens here'

From a corner of *The Stag*, Polly learned more of Joe Hartley's reputation. She listened to her companions' comments about Malcolm; they were impressed by his knowledge of matters about development planning and wished he could be persuaded to lend advice.

'Valuable contact you have there,' said Pete, viewing the remainder of the coffee in his cup.

'We've had a useful discussion and thanks for suggesting it,' Marion replied.

'Aye, it has been good,' Pete said, as they prepared to take their leave.

But it was suddenly showering with rain and they thought better of it. Marion went to the bar to order refills of coffee, and this time with brandies.

'Cats and dogs outside.' Downie recognised Marion at the bar, and conversed with her. Downie's farm lay near the pub, with several fields put to grazing. 'This bayn't be what the farmers want.'

'The ground's getting too wet?'

'It's wicked! Work with nature! That's what we do, but nature makes it hard, at times.'

'How are the calves coming along? Have I seen them in the field by the copse?' Marion asked and Polly tried to recollect them, from the rambles she'd taken.

Downie looked at the group over the top of his spectacles. 'I be lookin' after 'em calves for the county show! Mind 'ee, competition's tough. There's no money in't, and we bayn't be in arable country, neither, can't compete. It ain't wot it used ter be. But it's rep'tation!' He paused to sip his ale. 'I bayn't believe some of the stories around,' he said darkly.

'Oh yes?'

'You knows what I mean.'

Marion looked blank and Polly stayed silent, as did Pete,

but his ears were working overtime. 'Nothing comes to mind,' Marion replied.

'Well, let me tell 'ee, then.' Downie paused for another sip and to remember proper English. 'My old acquaintance who visits nearby your 'ome... you knows who I mean?'

Marion and her friends kept their counsel, curious as to what Downie might impart.

'Well m'dear, let me tell you this. His own wife's the invalid, you'll know that I'll be bound and his best friend's been away too often, so he sees 'is wife, instead.'

Marion smiled. 'Downie, Mr Hartley has always seemed to me a friendly man.'

'Mr Hartley? He's been Joe Hartley for as long as I remember. But 'ees a bit too friendly, for some.' Downie's conversation was well punctuated by his need to quench his thirst. 'And I wouldn't trust 'im further than I could toss 'im.'

'Really?'

'You takes my word for it... Joe's a hard man and ee gets 'is way.'

'I don't know much about him. He's always been courteous, or considerate – considerate's a better word to describe his manner, perhaps.'

'You mind 'oo he be considerate of... that's wot I say. You know the farm across the valley?'

Marion thought for a moment. 'The one for sale last year?'

'That's the one. Guess who pocketed that for a tidy low price? And the old folks... what with the worries in farming, they didn't know how to do better for 'emselves, so 'ee got away wi' it!'

'That's sad,' replied Marion, her sentiments echoed by Peter, 'Hear, hear.'

'It's wrong. That's what it be, downright wrong.' Downie screwed up his nose, pushed his spectacles towards his forehead and emptied his glass. 'Must be getting back. There's more to do. And mind you mark my words!' Downie was off. He left without further ado and the bar seemed vacant once he was gone.

'Don't know what's come over Mr Downe,' the barman said. 'Never known him go on like that!'

Someone, overlooked so far, in a dimly lighted seat piped up. 'But 'ee's right, you know. Shouldn't be allowed.'

'Would you go as far as that?' Marion replied.

'There was a lot to say about it at the time, I mean. A lot most folks don't know.'

'Well… I've heard similar comments before, but nothing substantial,' Marion admitted.

'But be a lot of truth in that wot old Downie sez.' The voice emerged from a dim corner of the bar. 'I 'spect you live along the lane – round the corner from where the developments be planned?'

Marion nodded in agreement.

'Then you'll know 'is lady friend. It's a rum do, ter me. With iz wife, an'all.'

Embarrassed, Marion was silent. 'You can't believe everything you see in the papers,' Polly said as staunchly and pleasantly as she could.

'So d' ye 'ave much ter do wi' im?'

'No, not me, not at all.'

'Wise on you….And 'nother thing. With 'im lying cold. 'Ow's it happen? Bayn't be due to me or you, not the missus neither, to mi way o' thinking. But there be more to that story. Mark mi' words.' The dishevelled figure rose, plumped down his glass on the bar counter and addressed Marion squarely. 'We be off now,' he said, 'on mi' way 'ome wi' mi new mare. Came from 'Olsworthy, she do.' They watched him through the window. The engine of his large, overworked Rover spluttered to a start and then he glided forward, the horse box trailing behind.

Polly waited quietly for Marion to comment. Against the light, she had not been able to read the expression on the face of the man who had given his opinion so freely. They were silent for a few moments, sipping brandy. 'We're getting more than we'd bargained for,' Marion said.

'I wouldn't say that,' said Pete firmly, 'all useful propaganda, I believe.' With a wave, he was off, leaving Marion and Polly to finish their drinks.

166

'Whew,' said Marion, relieved their companion had left yet unsettled by comments exchanged.

Polly was thoughtful. 'How's money being raised for the development?' she asked.

'Well I suppose Joe's got capital tied up in land, he's bound to have, with his farms – and then there was Mike Townley.'

'So they were financing it together?'

'Knowing Joe Hartley's reputation I'm sure arrangements are watertight. He bought the land, we know that, and a company's been formed called *Vesta,* so rumour goes.'

Marion paused before adding, 'But of Mike's stake, I don't know any details.'

'D'you think Joe wanted out of the deal?' Polly persisted.

'What are you implying?' Marion lowered her voice and glimpsing a darker side to

Mike's death, she shivered. 'We'll ask Luke what he thinks,' she added and so they made their way home.

'I can't believe this is happening in Derscott, nothing ever happens here,' Marion said as she and Polly removed their outdoor clothing and joined Luke in the kitchen.

'Well something has happened, love,' Luke replied, 'and it's spicing up our village retreat.'

'That's what you say now, but you've been strongly opposed to the development. So have others. And now Mike's died.'

'You don't suspect me of lending a hand in sabotage, do you? I'm enfeebled with age.'

'Be serious for a moment. After you left we listened to rumours in *The Stag.* They're scurrilous!'

'Isn't that what bars are for?'

'You don't understand, Luke. Tell him what that man said, Polly.'

'Which chap?' asked Luke.

'We've seen him in there before. I don't know his name. About 70, I'd say, never shaves, always looks like he's straight out of a Ravilious' photograph and drives an old Rover that just about starts.'

'Sounds like old Bill from Merecot way. He's got a lot of

time for speculating, all by himself at the end of that lane. What did he say?'

Polly recounted briefly and as she finished Marion interjected, 'What he said was suggestive. It set both Polly and me thinking. And Pete was there; you know what he's like.'

'My love, we can't stop people thinking. It's human nature. And old Bill's entitled to think, along with the rest of us. We've got our village drama and we've got to expect speculation.'

'I don't like it.'

'But we have to put up with it. I don't see any alternative. People die, it happens to us all. You can say the opposite about building developments. They're mushrooming all over the place.' Luke's nose twitched. 'Do I smell brandy?'

'But did he die or was he murdered?' Marion said bluntly.

'You've had a tifter. It's set your mind racing, let alone your heart.'

'Let me humour you,' Marion said, reaching for a bottle of 103, and opening a box of mints to accompany it.

'I know what you're after, young lady,' Luke commented to Polly, 'the sweets. Well, you can have mine.'

'Luke, she's not a teenager,' Marion scolded.

'It's my glass he's after, not the mints,' Polly bantered.

'She's a breath of fresh air, that's what Polly is. Ask her what she's thinking now!'

'There's a series of circumstances, coincidences if you like, that are puzzling. Development could link them: that's what's intriguing. On the one hand there's Mike, working on large-scale projects abroad, and there's Joe, who may have embarked on something too big, at the wrong time. Perhaps they've both become involved in something that's gone wrong,' Polly explained.

'But Mike's dead,' said Marion.

'The police must think it's murder,' observed Polly.

'None of this is particularly unusual. Business deals go bottom up all of the time and people die,' Luke said cautiously. 'I think it's safest to stick to the facts.'

'Yes,' Polly agreed, 'but, for example, why should a busy

farmer like Joe spend a morning drinking coffee with Laura in Torrington? He's the first person Laura contacts when her husband dies: why? I know she might not have anyone else to turn to, but is there another reason, something she needed to talk to Joe about? Why did Mike 'phone Joe on arrival in Heathrow and then disappear? The report in the local paper about Mike's death: it was in print before he died.'

'No smoke without the proverbial fire,' Luke conceded. 'I can see where you're coming from. But let's be glad the police are here. It's their job to get to the bottom of this.'

'We've never had anything directly to do with them before. D'you think they will?' queried Marion.

'They've a better chance than us.'

'Than we.'

'You're starting to come round.'

Polly smiled. 'If we feel bad, Laura must be feeling a thousand times worse.'

'I agree with that,' Marion said.

'And perhaps Laura's the key.'

'Or knows more than she realises,' Luke added but, while the conversation closed, their thoughts ran on.

33 Cavaliers for the King

'In the King's name, let us in!'

The dogs barked and battering at the door halted Seth, his family and the elderly priest as they partook of their homely fare. Bowls of broth were nearly finished, and bread still lay upon the table with a ham, ready to be sliced.

'We've naught to fear!' Seth put down his spoon and moved to the door. He drew back the latch and faced six men.

'We be for Hopton and the King!' Weather dripped from the wide brims of the Cavaliers' hats and darkened the rich colours of their cloaks.

'What can we do for 'e?' Seth was stern and the dogs, their agitation quelled, slunk around his ankles.

In their tall leather boots, the intruders strode into the farmhouse and stared at all around. *'There be no more: we're all before 'e.'* Their eyes scanned the room and the table, also.

'Ye'll be wanting bread?' Seth asked.

'Aye, and vittles too.'

Seth recognised their weary looks. *'Ye're welcome here for sustainance. Tom, look to the horses.'* And the lad took with him the dogs, bar Toss, since he was old.

'Ye don't have long,' Jess said.

'But if a fight is comin', tis best we're fed!' The tension broke and a ripple of laughter spread among all present.

'It be urgent,' Jess insisted.

'Aye, mistress, we know.'

Jess went to help her mother. *'They be hungry and indeed look starved,'* she admitted.

'Ye'll come this way?' the farmer said, indicating places for them to be seated.

'We'll set these aside,' one volunteered regarding their arms: swords, pistols and carbines.

'Aye, in my house.' Then, in a quieter voice, Seth added, *'But there's no place for 'ee tonight, ye must move on.'* He

looked from Ellie to the priest. 'I have ye all to think of, this be our home,' her father said.

The King's men stood their ground. 'This be as good as any place,' they said. Their hats removed, their hair hung damp, shoulder-length.

The priest, in his corner, shook his head. Quietly, for the rest scarcely heard, he told them all it was not right. Only a stone's throw away, for a vigorous man, lay God's house and that should mean safety for him and others too. Though even he wondered 'bout its safety, in these times. He looked around the room. Jess's babe was sleeping unawares, protected yet not far from the fire, the scullery cats lay curled in hidden corners but Adam, the little boy, looked in wonderment at the intruders. 'Come here, my little man,' Father Patrick whispered. The child clambered onto his knee as he was used to doing with Seth. The priest rubbed Adam's arms and felt the warmth of the child's small hands on his face. 'Be still,' he said, adding, 'all is well,' as he prayed that this was true. The priest repeated simple words and the child stared, his wriggling calmed as the priest pointed at his eye, nose, the wood of the furniture and the dog. Both were distracted from the happenings around.

The six men towered before the fire, by the table and at the door.

'Ye'll be no good in here,' the farmer said again, 'pistol, or no.'

'We have the King on our side,' one staunchly affirmed.

'And what good be that, with twenty of the others on their way?' Jess chided as she sliced the ham and brought forth another loaf from the day's batch, still warm from the oven.

'Stay thyselves outside my house,' the farmer said.

'But how do 'ee know of t'other side?' Dick, the leader thought to ask.

'My Matt told me. 'Ee's got good eyes and ears too and knows what 'appens round these parts.'

'There be no sense in killing thyselves, if ye can wait an' win instead,' observed Seth.

'My men be hungry,' Dick stated, 'and fight or no we need nourishment.'

Catherine, wiping her hands on a cloth wrapped around her stout waist, cast a doughty figure in spite of being caught unawares. 'Be quick 'bout it and eat what's ready. If it be good enough for us, then it be likewise for thee. But listen: there's no safety 'ere. I say this not because of us, but because of Fairfax's men. Be on thy way.'

'Well spoken, wife,' Seth said. Then to the men, 'The choice is thine – stay here and die, or be away.'

'But barns thou has. Show me their space, to 'ccommodate my men,' Dick said. His few troops were tired. They had no fight in them, just words. And they knew the other side was likely just as spent. By assent they stayed their ground around the hall-room and one named Rob, who stood with his back to the fire, watched over them all. The farmer, resigned and unwilling to leave his family without protection, led Dick through the rear door, first to show him what resting place he could offer and then, in case of need, the passage that ran underground to the church.

The room fell quiet, except for the sounds Adam formed in response to the priest, who liked the child's simplicity and continued to provide amusement by repeating phrases. The gestures and eyes of the infant suggested some understanding, but the only word he uttered which bore resemblance to vocabulary was 'dog'. The soldiers, left alone, gradually relaxed their stance and finished any morsels of food which remained. They shook out their cloaks and tried to dry themselves, as best they could.

Jess, however, was nervous. 'They take no notice, yet the Parliament's be on their way!' she whispered to her mother.

'How many, daughter?'

Jess shook her head. 'Can't be certain, my Matt thought twenty – and yet, they could divide.'

'Or meet up wi more,' Catherine replied softly, pursing her lips. The room caught their whispers. The men fidgeted, the cats stirred and a hen flew down from its warm perch and strutted across the floor. Outside the rain continued and mixed with wind was noisy. Ellie, who had stayed quiet by a wooden screen, lifted logs still green, from a pile drying by

the hearth and made up the fire. It spluttered as flames shot around the mossy and lichen-covered wood.

'What do 'e 'ave for us?' Rob greeted Dick as he returned with the farmer.

'Be quick men,' Dick replied, accepting a rushlight from Ellie. 'Tis safe – but follow me,' and they were gone from the warmth of the room.

Ellie looked around and saw no trace that other visitors might note, save that chairs had been displaced and across the table platters had been spread and these she gathered up. 'Toss, come out,' she said to the dog, huddled under the table. 'And Nemo – where be thou?'

'Daughter, thou be talking at 'em as if they be us!' No sooner had her mother spoken than impatient knocking at the door signalled the arrival of Parliament's men.

In the yard at the back of the farmhouse the last of Dick's band hurried before Seth, who closed their way. The wind blotted out their sounds as they strode over wet cobbles, clutching their hats and weaponry. The pigs grunted as they passed, one large sow lying prominently on her side with sucklings lined around her and a second smaller one looking on with beady eyes. Dick went first and then in turn the men walked across the pen, over damp straw and through the stench to the solid fence at the back, apparently laid across a bare wall. Seth unpegged the section that closed the tunnel and held it open. The men, on Dick's urging, followed him and quickly entered. Those of neat and compact build had no trouble progressing its uneven length but the taller and the more rotund cursed as limbs and bodies brushed the rocky walls, lighted intermittently by the flickering of Dick's rushlights. From the farmyard end they soon looked safely stowed away. The farmer closed the gap behind the last and laid fresh straw across the floor. 'Ye'll be fine again,' he spoke to the piglets. 'Keep thy nose from me!' he added to the smaller of the sows, the more feisty of the pair, but she was satisfied as he pulled across a trough of food. Some sucklings squealed and others grunted. The farmer shook straw from his boots, secured the pen and returned, pausing for a moment before entering the farmhouse.

34   Parliament's men

'Where be they?' The Parliament's men swelled in numbers at the door and pushed their way past Ellie, filling the room. Crop-haired and weary, their manners were rough as they crowded into the hall, followed by the farm dogs that Tom had put outside, yelping in alarm.

'Why, sir,' Ellie started, but was unable to finish in the midst of such confusion, with the dogs barking and baby starting to wail.

'What be this?' asked Jess indignantly, picking up her child and striding o'er to stand by the priest. 'Be ye not good men? See ye not that we be looking after babes?' Adam whimpered at his mother's tone and clung to Father Patrick, by whom Toss the dog had also settled close, but Nemo was on his haunches and growled in warning.

'A posse for the King rode by – it is they we search. We have no quarrel with all o' ye.' So spake the one in charge, though among his men there was interest in the farm. The warmth of the scullery reached their faces and they felt some comfort, as the damp of outside rain was seeping through their clothes. Not armoured, their doublets were leather and coarse wool in dull colours.

Catherine added weight to her daughter's protests. 'Ellie, go find thy father and Tom. They be better placed to face our visitors than we, ourselves.' Sensing the feeling of the men, she added, 'Ye'll be wanting succour, I be certain...? We be poor but can find plain sustenance.' A murmur of assent spread around the room. The men took off their caps and cloaks and crowded around the table, on the bench, an old chest and the floor.

'My name is Hal,' the officer calmly said. ''Tis true, we mean no ill. But mind ye do not harbour any who call us enemies.'

The priest, whom the soldiers took to be an aged relative, cradled Adam on his knee. While weakened himself and little

174

active he believed that, through trust in God, right would prevail. The women, flustered at the number of their invaders and not sure whether they were ten or going on for twice as many, left the room.

'What mean thou, mother, 'bout the food? The best part's gone!'

'We'll give the rest.' Catherine eyed the remains of ham and a cold hen. The pot, as was the custom, was newly on the fire. 'Add all that,' she told Jess, 'and the turnip, too.' Jess checked another batch of bread which was already baking while Catherine filled pitchers with cider. 'We'll quaff their thirst,' asserted Catherine and she reminded Ellie to find her father.

Bewildered, Ellie went into the yard and, with great relief, came upon Tom though not her father Seth. 'They be here!'

'Aye – and all 'er horses too!' He had just returned from securing those of the King's men in a copse hidden from the house.

'Tom, mother's finding food for 'em.'

'But they've not touched 'ee?'

Blushing, Ellie shook her head.

'I be coming in,' he said.

'See mother first.'

'Aye, that I will.'

The priest, in part bewildered, hugged Adam to him. The soldiers recognised the scene from their own hearths, for some this farm being not dissimilar to their own homes. One spoke kindly to the child who stepped down and walked about. A cat stirred as Adam stroked its fur and this led to a little merriment, but the dogs stayed watchful. 'Here comes our apple brew!' Tom, bearing mugs of cider, strode in.

'And thou be the son?' Hal asked.

'Nay, sir, just the farmer's lad. Tending sheep 'til now – some lambs are come and others on their way.'

'Our horses,' Hal said, 'they need fodder.'

'We've grazing, sir, I'll see to 'em.'

'And oats?'

Tom knew the store held barely enough for their own

175

needs, but dare not resist their plea. 'All we have we'll share wi' ye,' he said.

'I'll come and see for us all.' One of the soldiers made ready to leave with Tom, while the rest opened their jerkins, stretched their legs and made free with the logs, heaping them onto the fire. Meanwhile, the pot bubbled, the loaves browned and the hall filled with the smells of homely cooking, damp clothing and sweat.

'Thy horses,' Tom asked the surly man who showed no consideration, save his own concerns.

'Five and twenty,' he said shortly. 'We ride with spares.' The rain dripped off the horses' manes as they stomped their feet, confined to the stoney lane in front of the farm. A ragged lot, they showed signs of hard riding with bruising and a few tears in their coats.

'Why, sir,' Tom said, 'in the field beyond there be plenty o' grazing with the sheep – yet they'll be easy to gather in.'

'Where be thy own?'

'We've not many, sir. They be mostly loose, along the stream.'

'Out of sight, I'll be bound.' The man made plain his thoughts about the grazing but assisted Tom who set about leading the horses down the track and freeing them.

'Wait here, I'll bring the oats,' Tom said.

'They'll wander not. I'll come with thee.'

Impossible as it was to lose the man who shadowed him, Tom led him around the farm towards the barn which was sheltered from the wind and weather. In the top storey were the remains of last year's oats, kept dry but raided on warmer days by over-wintering rats. Tom took down one sack, scarcely full. 'Call that three bushels?' his companion scorned, 'we need more'n that'.

'There'll be straw as well.'

'Enough for all? The horses, their bellies empty be.' The burly soldier continued, under his breath, 'Be thee satisfied with this? A boor is all ye'll 'mount to. My name, I'll have thee know, be Nathan.'

Tom stayed quiet through coarse mutterings and steadily persisted 'til satisfied that all to be spared was being fairly distributed. Nathan gave no hand in this, but watched. He was older than Tom, though not by many years, and troubled. Whilst giving allegiance to the cause to share government with the people, he had thought the task would soon be over and would be better finished by action than consideration. And while he had seen action enough, it had not always been to his liking.

Some years past he had fought and been beaten by Cornishmen supporting the King on Roundway Down. But, finding among the Cornish some of Parliament's persuasion, he had fled west with them to Bristol and further still, so now his roots were far behind. Sourly, he turned back with Tom, who led the way and opened latches for him while he stomped and clattered under his weight, combined of himself and of the arms he carried.

Inside the farmhouse pitchers were refilled, the soldiers relaxed and some dozed while others debated and connived about their next move. Hal had a mixed and troublesome bunch with most, like Nathan, joined from other regional armies and their loyaties were further afield than north Devon. They were due at Great Torrington but had gleaned knowledge of a group of King's men and were loathe to be outwitted. Catherine busied herself with kneading dough to replenish bread and cooking. She found herself wishing for a rabbit but again had to make do with scraps of ham torn into vegetables softened in the pot. Most of the soldiers, awkward or not, could be her sons and recognising this she wanted no nonsense, just common courtesy. 'The food be coming soon. Your turn next m'darlin',' she said to one who looked particularly ill-nourished.

The soldiers, humoured at the prospect of full bellies, helped her as she laid out the broth, thick and hot, into as many bowls as she could muster. 'Ye'll have to share!' she said. Those who waited their turn cut thick slices of warm bread, spreading it plentifully with fresh butter and pushing it through their hungry lips.

'Good day t' y'all.' Seth stood at the door. His hall-room had turned into a barracks mess, his food consumed by cavalry-men. Catherine refilled bowls, brought out more

177

loaves and passed Adam and the priest the juices, wiped upon fresh crusts.

'And thyself, my man.' Hal challenged him, 'Where's thou been?'

'Across mine acres, man. The farm takes walking and the rain blots out the senses, as ye must know.' Seth paused for a moment, 'Thy horses, where be they?'

'The lad is tending them. They're worn.'

Seth wondered how Tom had managed this, but knew the lad had a sound head and there was no shortage of pasture.

The horses, lightened of their loads, felt freedom. A few stayed close, at least at first. They munched on oats and straw, found the remains of hay left by a stile, then grazed as they spread between scattered trees. Tom and his ill-tempered companion arrived back at the farmhouse, satisfied there was enough nourishment to stem the horses' hunger and were hoping for some themselves.

'Ye do not so badly, hereabouts,' Nathan remarked. The low building, set against the hill, was protected from the worst of the weather along its back and they felt the benefit of shelter, as they reached the door.

'Enough for those living here,' Tom replied cautiously as he lifted the catch to enter the hall. The soldiers, having enjoyed their repast and warmed by the fire, slumped against the table, the screen and the walls.

Nathan's blood rose at the sight. 'Ye satisfy th'selves but be there aught for me?' he yelled.

'Hush, man, in my house,' Seth returned. 'Thou be as welcome as the rest. Use my place and be seated peacably,' and he sought Catherine to muster what nourishment she could. But Nathan's irritation grew, his stomach sounding discontent and he being angered at the comfort others had enjoyed while he had tended horses. Old grievances emerged. He kicked aside the leg of one of his companions to give himself more room. He was jibed in return, which led to further bickering and the dogs stirred. Tom, seeking to make him more comfortable, held out a mug of cider, fresh from the pitcher, cold and cloudy with last summer's apples.

178

'Is that the best thou can do for those that bring thee freedom?'

'Quiet, man,' Hal, slow to interpose, tried to soften him.

Nathan downed the cider in greedy gulps. 'Where's more?' he asked, 'and food? Or have those that call me friend consumed the lot?'

Tom, uncertain what to do, except give more, approached with the pitcher and Nathan lashed out with rage, sent the pitcher flying and Tom, as well. Soldiers, confused, landed on the lad, who found himself beneath others, larger and rougher than he himself.

'Quit this,' Hal said as Seth entered, disturbed at the noise and bearing a platter of food.

'Put order in thy men,' Seth said. 'Ye be visitors here.'

Nathan, dumbed at the sight of food, more than the rest had had, picked at it with his hands and licked the juices from the dish. 'Bring more,' he said.

Meanwhile, Tom disentangled himself from several men. With his shirtsleeve he wiped the blood running down his face and lifted himself up.

''Twas not I who did that, but the pitcher, man,' Nathan sniggered and was out of humour still. He picked up the handle of the broken pitcher and watched its cider running onto the floor. 'More of this be needed now,' he jeered.

The women, hiding their great anxiety, bustled about the scullery, peering in corners and opening the doors of half-empty stores, looking for more food to assuage the tempers of those who'd come.

'My men,' Seth said. 'Ye mean well, I know. Show thyselves fit to govern all.'

'Well said,' Hal affirmed and most around recognised the sense of this.

But Nathan was not easily appeased, 'What side be thou on?' he confronted the farmer.

'The side of honest men,' Seth replied.

'That no answer be,' Nathan, fuelled by cider, snarled. 'Ere 'ee be, at the foot of the church. We should ha' known.' Several men looked up at Nathan and wondered at his stance.

179

'We be farmers here,' said Seth. 'I want just rule for all –
and fear by no man of others.' Adam cried at the commotion
and was hugged by the priest, who quieted him with soft
words. But Jess could not rest without her child and snatched
the opportunity of a lull to take hold of Adam's hand and
lead him to join the safety of the scullery, where Catherine
barred the door.

Alert to simmering threats, Hal asserted himself. 'Tis time
to be off, my men. Gird thyselves to go.' Then he turned to
Tom. 'Young farmer, bring round the horses, tied in pairs.'

This being too hasty for those whose wick was up, they
wished to dally in the warmth and murmured among
themselves, 'The farm?' 'There's naught here.' 'Better wait
'til morn.' 'And what of the other side?' 'See for thyself –
we've eaten their all!' 'The church, it's scarce a stone's
throw away!'

'But be they here?'

At the thought of their enemies seeking refuge in the
church, the Parliamentarians' disquiet fermented. Hal
retrieved the horses and in dishevelled groups the men
remounted, leaving Seth, Tom and the women to wonder
about the Cavaliers, who stood for the King.

Meanwhile, Dick and his men had clung to their dark
underground. Dick had posted one at each end of the tunnel
and the rest straddled the distance between. They had the
barest sense of what was afoot. Seth's advice had been to
stay below as their isolation brought safety. The pigs at one
end and the church's altar at the other protected them from
both their enemies and the weather but apprehension trickled
through the soil and seams of rock. Inactivity bred their fear
of being trapped. 'Hush,' said Dick to their mutterings, 'we
need to listen and heed all sounds.'

'And how long do I stand the stench of pig?'

'What harm's a smell? Be glad none but that of a sow
offends thee!' came a rebuke and then a chuckle that carried
the length of the tunnel.

'What say 'ee?' Below ground, one man of less sharp
hearing puzzled at the mirth of his colleagues and asked, 'Do
ought sounds disturb 'ee?'

'It bayn't be sounds alone that share this resting place: so rich be the stench escaped from swine.'

'Be thankful it travelled without the snout.'

'Hush! Enough of all this jollity. Give our enemies time to satisfy their hunger and we'll be at the ready.'

During the course of these exchanges Hal's men had ridden from the farm along the lane, turning beyond the oaks into wind and cold, unrelenting rain. The churchyard lay along their left flank. 'There'll be naught around this place,' Hal said, and most agreed. The church looked a prominent, bleak monument and sanctuary to none.

'Ye can't tell,' Nathan brought his horse alongside Hal's. 'T'others might outwit us, still.' The men started to dismount and let their horses wander. The last few held the horses while some in the lead tried the church door which gave on the latch. Almost bare, save Ellie's early flowers and some wooden ornaments, it gave little scope for wrecking. Yet some wished to leave their mark and smashed a bench, then turned their eyes to a carving, which hung above the door. Another marched to the altar, to rip its cloth.

'Hold on,' said Hal, 'we've no quarrel with that, nor flowers, neither. Leave these quiet folk alone.'

Meanwhile, below the altar, the King's man crouched at his post in the passage and signalled to those behind. To them, each step above sounded louder by twenty-fold, as the heavy treads of Roundheads on the side of Parliament carried through the floor, their coarse boots echoing off flags and boards. 'If they come down, we top them, one by one,' the man whispered to Dick as the kicking of the smashed bench and broken carving into the middle of the church rumbled down.

'Make for off!' Hal commanded, 'How shall we convince these people we mean well if all we do is this?'

Nathan's anger was far from spent and with his sword he swiped Ellie's flowers from their place and looked around for more. Shards of pot with splashed water and petals fell before the altar. While he remained in troubled, stubborn mood, his comrades faced the rain again and rode south in fours to Great Torrington. Nathan, still fuming inwardly,

181

resolved to wait, so sure was he that those he had sworn against would show.

Meanwhile, at the farm they hastened about, putting everything to rights. 'And what of this?' Catherine remonstrated tartly, surveying the scattered bowls and crusts across the floor. Adam, who'd whined only quietly through most of the disruption now started to cry, and the baby too, at all the constant turmoil. Jess gathered up both and nursed them by the fire.

'Bread, we need more bread,' Seth said, realising that a focus could turn the women's minds from the dishevelled room.

'There'll be no more sustenance for 'ee today!' Catherine spoke despondently.

'Hush, woman, we've food a-plenty, though it be living,' Seth said, putting his arms round his comely wife to comfort her, adding, 'now see the hens, they'll provide more bowls of broth and pickings too.'

Nemo the dog wandered in, followed by Tom. 'Their ride be wet,' Tom commented, 'the sky's not let up.'

'Our other friends be still below,' said Seth, who shook his head. 'One lot be too fine and the other too coarse to rule o'er all of us.'

Ellie recovered the pots and with a broom cleared most of the rubbish off the floor. Catherine, meanwhile, put yeast to warm and measured handfuls of flour into a bowl. 'See there's enough,' Seth advised, 'we've more to feed than family alone, wi'em below and horses too.' He took Tom outside who slit two hens, to flavour stock for them all. 'Not cut thy best! Seth remarked, as he watched blood drip from Tom's fist as well as the headless birds. Ellie took them to be plucked for the pot. 'Want Tom to help thee, lass?' her father asked. Blushing, she turned away. 'On second thoughts, Tom come here and help me find the salve.' Seth searched for a pot kept close to the fire that held condiment mixed by Catherine from herbs known to heal wounds. 'Naught but a graze above thy brow and only a glance at thy thumb – thou'll live,' the farmer added. With that, his thoughts turned to other jobs.

By now, the farm was nearer its customary appearance. Logs heaped on the fire burned off the damp and carried the odours of bodies in sooty, grease-laden hot fumes up through the chimney and into the clouds. Adam slept and the priest, confused by all that had happened, stumbled from his corner. 'In Jesus's name,' he muttered, as he put weight on his legs and cats ran out from around his feet.

'Ungodly in my mind,' Catherine said, guiding Patrick to a sturdy chair. 'Here, Father, have sup o' this.' She had heated some cider, sweetened with honey. 'This be my trick, when I feel the need,' she added. Ellie watched, as with trembling fingers he clasped the mug and raised it to his lips. Slowly, he sipped the contents and felt its benefit seeping into his limbs and then his head.

Tom struck the panel at the back of the pig's sty. At first there was no reply.

'Say ought to them,' the farmer said.

'It be Tom,' the lad hissed into the panel.

'A stronger sign be needed,' said Seth. 'All clear! Come out wi'ee!' cried the farmer as he rapped the door.

Cautiously, the men unlatched the makeshift door. Then one, followed by others, gained their freedom, disturbing the pigs and making for the farmhouse door.

35   Ruminations

At first, Marion's thoughts were on village developments but later turned to Mike.

'How's the local council progressing with the development plan, I thought we'd know by now?' Marion asked at breakfast time. Luke coughed over his toast, but Marion persisted. 'Malcolm advised 'phoning the planning department. There can't be any harm in that.'

Links with the local council offices proved swift and straightforward. Marion's expectations of elaborate bureaucracy were unfounded and a single call, followed by an extension, enabled her to speak to the relevant officer who seemed well informed. After a short discussion, Marion relayed the main points to Luke and Polly. An application had been received, was under consideration and a senior planner had visited the site to assess the scale and context of the proposed development. The usual procedures were being followed. A public meeting was arranged to allow local residents to give their views; objections raised would be considered. Meanwhile, the planning committee was considering the application in relation to the overall area-plan to inform any future decision.

'It sounds systematic enough,' Polly said, 'but what does it mean?' Luke stayed silent.

'There's no time to be lost!' Marion said. 'I didn't realise the speed of the process; has this business gone further than I thought? Surely, it was an outline proposal at this stage. I wonder if Pete knows? I could ask him – or I suppose Laura may know.'

'I think Laura's past caring now,' Luke said.

'But we could ask.'

'Marion, I think she needs a bit of space,' Luke insisted.

'We'll give her that too.'

'Could Malcolm explain procedures?' Polly suggested.

'Luke, we might try him,' Marion commented, pointedly.

184

Marion did not relinquish the possibility of having a word with Laura. She spent a little time hunting through the freezer, found a home-made cake stored for unexpected guests, left it just long enough to thaw then re-wrapped it, as a comfort gift for her friend. After doing this, she wavered and mumbled under her breath, 'I wonder whether a bottle of wine might be more appropriate?'

'The cake will be handy; I reckon she's not eating much, but a tipple would comfort her. And she's bound to have visitors. Take both,' Luke said firmly.

Marion went alone, but in a few minutes had returned. 'I was resigned to a quiet afternoon by myself,' Luke looked up from his crossword. 'Polly's completing another sketch, or texting Haresh, Janus is dozing, but here you are scuttling back and forth. Where's Laura? Is she out?'

'Aren't you glad to see me?'

'I saw you only ten minutes ago.'

Marion looked disconcerted. 'It's the police,' she said. 'I saw them pull up in the driveway just as I walked up the lane.'

'Oh, I see. But it's come to a pretty pass if a law-abiding citizen is put off by the police.'

'Well you know what I mean; it's Laura I'm thinking about.'

'Not that she has anything to do with it. An innocent victim I'd say,' Luke added.

'Do you think so?'

'Don't you?'

'I don't know what to think,' Marion admitted, 'I'm getting confused.'

'C'mon, old thing,' Luke said, putting his arm around Marion.

'It's a long time since you called me that,' his wife smiled.

'I don't mean it, you know, about your being an old thing,' Luke spoke almost impishly, Polly thought, from her wicker seat under a window at the end of the kitchen. Just then the 'phone rang and Janus stretched his limbs out of the basket, shaking his head and wagging his tail, refreshed by a nap.

'Yes, Laura,' Marion spoke into the telephone, putting a finger to her lips and motioning to the others to be quiet, 'of course, just come round as soon as you're able.' She replaced the receiver with the eyes of Luke, Polly and Janus on her and she sank into a chair, a worn high-backed beech chair which Luke often occupied because its width was ample, but within which two of Marion could fit.

'I thought you said the police had arrived,' Luke commented.

'Yes, they have. They want to search and look at the computer.'

'Can't they take that away to look at it? And don't they want her there?'

'They've told her she's free to go and she's told them she'll be here.'

'So she's going to implicate us in all this,' grumbled Luke in a quiet voice, but deliberately loud enough to be heard.

'I think you're missing the point,' Marion snapped. 'Laura feels harassed and needs an escape.'

'Oh, we're a woman's refuge now, are we?'

Marion laughed, in spite of herself. 'You silly! And you're forgetting Polly's listening in on your rubbish.'

'Don't go, Polly. I don't mean you. Whatever mess Laura's got herself into I can't see why the police would want to worry you.'

Janus yelped his response to their lively interchange, giving Polly convenient escape. She put aside her water-colour and led Janus into the garden to play 'catch' with him, using a large rubber bone. But he became possessive and in a few moments clasped his paws around the toy, which he would not release.

The day was mild. Polly ambled from shrub to shrub, noting unfolding leaves, early blossoms and the perfect symmetry of a solitary pink *Camellia* flower. She kept an eye on Janus across the lawn and tried to recover the toy when his attention lapsed but to no avail. The dog was quicker than she and Polly did not wish to incite an angry reaction to her teasing. So she left him alone, and finding a small hand-fork half-buried in a flower bed she disturbed the top soil under climbing rose bushes which ran along a fence, and lifted intruding weeds. She moved on beyond the roses to a quiet corner where honesty plants were growing, their leaves vigorous and crisp with jagged points. And she remembered a corner of her grandmother's garden where they always self-seeded. She'd been happy there, in a world of carefree discovery and make-believe. She missed a garden. She kept a few potted plants at her flat and looked out over gardens that belonged to others, but she had no access to them. Her parents' 'yard' in a suburb near Chicago was typical American green space around their rented house, the grass cut impeccably and shrubs trimmed in spring and fall, part of a neighbourhood that was an easy drive to the university where her father was working on sabbatical. Lost in thought, she was oblivious to Janus until he pushed around her ankles, his jaws clamped across the dead stalks of early bulbs, their onion-shapes bouncing at the side of his mouth.

'And where did these come from, old chap?' Luke's deep voice came from behind her. He had slipped out of the house unnoticed, Marion still fussing about 'phone calls and arrangements. 'Don't worry, Polly, that's just what puppies do,' he said, noticing her embarrassment at Janus's attempt at gardening. 'I should have removed those weeks ago. C'mon, Janus, give!' And Luke explained for Polly's benefit that he was trying to train the puppy to obey. But they quickly recognised they were no match for Janus's playfulness, so they ignored him until his attention waned. 'My dear Marion,' expounded Luke, 'wants to put everything right. And she can't.' Polly smiled as Luke continued. 'I shouldn't moan. She's a good woman, in fact the best.' Luke screwed up his big face in concentration. 'It's not as if we don't have other things to do, Polly. She's running in circles now about those blasted inspections and the building development, let alone Laura. We should be getting out, enjoying ourselves and showing you a bit of the neighbourhood.'

'Then off you go! Don't mind me,' Marion interjected as she emerged quietly from behind. Restless and with conflicting thoughts on her mind, she had wandered into the garden. A determined glint in her eye and forced smile on her lips, Marion continued. 'Stop worrying about me – just go. Take Polly for the afternoon.'

'I can't do that, I can't leave you fretting about all these problems.' Luke looked remorseful.

'Fretting? I'm not fretting. I'm coping and everything's in hand. Polly, tell him to be off and enjoy a quiet afternoon in a churchyard.'

Polly looked from one to the other. The customary jocularity of her friends was dulled by the irritation each felt about the obligations of the other.

'It all comes down to the number of hours in the day,' Luke said.

'D'you know, I'm simply loving it here,' Polly said, 'and I'm happy with my sketch-pad.' The buds on an apple tree, showing the first signs of bursting, had caught her eye, yet after a moment's deliberation she sat on a wooden bench close to the house. Sheltered, she felt the full warmth of the sun and Janus, apparently tired of activity, flopped at her side, his chin resting on her feet. Luke and Marion meanwhile had wandered further down the garden which became bedraggled in its lower reaches, as if forgotten enthusiasm about growing vegetables had not been replaced by other gardening projects.

36   An arc of chairs

Relaxed, Polly might almost have slipped into a doze, but she heard the grating of the latch on the side gate and it slowly swung open. Manicured fingers held the catch at the top and then a pale-faced figure in light green trod carefully, finding her way along the shaded path into the garden. It was Laura. Her face, carefully composed, looked numb though her eyes betrayed the shock she felt. 'No-one answered, so I thought...' she started to explain.

'You're right; they've just walked towards the bottom of the garden.'

'So this is the puppy.' Laura held herself back from the attentions of Janus whose wriggling was curbed, only half-effectively, by Polly.

'He has little respect for clothes I'm afraid.'

Laura's expression softened momentarily. 'Perhaps I'll get a dog,' she said, stroking the silkiness of Janus's black and white fur until he settled. 'I'll join them,' she added quietly.

Polly watched as Laura walked stiffly down the garden, Janus following at her heels. Sniffing as he went, he retrieved a chewed yellow ball discarded some days past when it had ceased to bounce. Marion spotted her friend and moved forward to greet her, but Luke hung back, out of sight. He busied himself with a stack of garden chairs which had been relegated to the side of an old shed because long ago they had been displaced by furniture, itself now in varying degrees of shabbiness that graced the conservatory. He had been making use of the old seats occasionally, for a quiet break when gardening. He had been meaning to wipe away the cobwebs and rub down the wooden seats so they were fit for visitors and not just his gardening pants.

Polly felt she was intruding on confidences, excused herself and retreated to the conservatory. But the sun had moved round and it had become too warm. She decided to organise her own thoughts and few possessions, in readiness for her return to London the following day.

'It's only me,' Luke interrupted her thoughts. 'I'm sent back for cushions. We can't sit on gardeners' pews in our best frocks you know.' Polly watched him stuff the cushions under his arms and trundle back down to the bottom of the garden. She retreated to her room to check through her clothes and suitcase.

Meanwhile, Laura was explaining to Marion why she had come. 'The house is no longer my own. The police, oh they're very polite, but they're intent on hunting in every little corner. I'm in their way and feel displaced.'

'How many have come?'

'Three in the first car, but another car arrived just before I left.'

Luke interrupted. 'Are you comfortable enough?' but his mind was on the police numbers. As he gazed at the arc of chairs in the sheltered corner where it was sunny and warm, he puzzled why Mike's death warranted so much attention. He felt chilled, even on this late spring day that until a few minutes ago had seemed on the cusp of summer. Janus circumvented the group and then reclined with one paw on the ball he had recaptured, his dark beady eyes following the darting flight of an occasional early butterfly, before his head drooped and slumber overtook activity. Laura, silenced, felt recent events had confused all logic in her normally well-ordered life. She had become used to long stretches of time while Mike was away, when she could free herself and organise activities within an established routine. But the last time Mike had returned: she could hardly bear to think of that and clenched her hands around the arms of the chair. Luke watched, and hesitated about enquiring further.

'There's so much to say,' Laura tried to explain, 'all these people, and they keep coming.'

'You can stay here, Laura, 'til the police have gone,' Marion said, adding, 'I expect they know where to find you?'

'Oh yes. But they are only part of it. Manny arrived early today, unexpectedly, and it was only 5:30AM.'

Marion and Luke exchanged a glance. The name Manny

was new to both of them. After a moment Marion said in a kindly tone, 'What a surprise, at that time!'

'I almost didn't let him in. I couldn't believe the bell was ringing, a visitor, at that hour. I had 'phoned him, of course, but he didn't say he was coming.'

Reluctant to seem inquisitive, Marion and Luke were silent.

'I've only met him once before, he came to our wedding.'

'Manny?' Marion softly questioned the name.

'Yes, Mike's son Manuel. You know how young people are, well, he must be getting on for thirty now. But even after the flight and drive he's quite perky; though that's not quite the right word for Manny.' Laura did not smile. There was no warmth in her voice. She seemed ready to start a long explanation, but was having difficulty putting her thoughts into words.

'He went to bed, did he? I mean, you let him catch up on his sleep?' Luke asked.

'No, he didn't want to.'

'Then you should have brought him with you. Mike's son would be more than welcome here,' Luke said spontaneously.

Laura looked at him directly. 'I suggested he could follow me but the police,' she said, 'they're talking with him.'

'Well, I expect with his sudden arrival,' Marion started to reason aloud.

'Yes, that's probably it.' Laura found this explanation brought a morsel of comfort. 'Mike always felt an obligation towards him, you know.' She was quiet for a moment, before adding, 'But you never really know the children of others. They hold mysteries to themselves.'

'So do your own, often enough,' said Luke.

Laura almost smiled. 'Mike said it was an early love, a sudden impulse, a young couple's wedding...but it fell apart. Mike travelled even then and she was rooted in her village and part of its traditions. Though he always cared about the boy. And, of course, the man has come for his father.'

'It must have been a shock for him too?'

'Of course and it's right he's come, but I thought he might

wait until Mike was released, I mean, when I knew the date for…'

'The funeral?' Marion completed her sentence.

'Yes, that's right,' admitted Laura.

'It's so easy to keep in touch. I 'spect Mike and Manny used to 'phone?'

'And text and e-mail. Obviously, I spoke to Manny as soon as I could; I knew Mike would want him to know.' Laura's voice fell and, almost in a whisper, she added, 'Manny tells me he was also contacted by his local police. I expect they found him on Mike's mobile. And he's been called by Angie – that firm must have thought a lot of Mike.'

Luke pondered on what Laura was saying. Mike had a son, she called him Manny, and he heard through Laura herself, the police and Angie about his father's death. *We don't realise how closely linked everyone is*, he thought, but it was Marion who asked, 'How's Manny taking this?'

Laura phrased her response carefully. 'He's very charming and considerate of others. I think that masks his own feelings.'

Luke wondered what she meant. Hyperbole, that's what she was using. Taffeta phrases. But Luke's thoughts digressed. He had no idea that Mike had other family. There was no evidence around his house or from casual conversations with him – no photographs, mention of visits or reference to close relatives. Not that he had known Mike well, of course. It was just that the subject of family and children had never cropped up when he'd passed the time of day. He mulled over Laura's circumstances. She was clearly pained and shocked. And what sort of son could hide his feelings on the death of his father, he wondered, but perhaps the police had wanted him to come, suggested they might meet with him here? For a moment he listened while Marion exchanged some nondescript phrases with Laura, but he felt he needed an escape. 'How about some coffee, ladies?' he asked, 'or tea, if you'd rather; we have biscuits too.'

Marion knew from the expressions Luke used that he was perplexed and probably angry inside. A mundane task would occupy and distract him; it was a displacement activity. She could carry on conversing with Laura. The dog, Janus, had recognised the term *biscuits*. 'No, Janus mustn't have biscuits,' Marion insisted. 'Go with Luke, like a good boy, and he'll give you proper ones of your own.' She turned again to Laura. 'Do you need any supplies, Laura – you must take some salad and vegetables, and how about milk or bread?'

'That's very kind of you. I do have a freezer stuffed with food, but…'

'I know, fresh things. And perhaps Luke might bring us a glass of something, in a little time?'

They chatted on, Laura being fairly comfortable about everyday topics and house-keeping but guarded, almost mute, on circumstances surrounding Mike's death. She recalled humdrum snippets about house maintenance and reminisced about plans Mike had aired for further improvements. 'I think he has, I mean had, a vision about the house. You know what some people are like and he's never been one to run out of ideas. The proper computer, you know, that's in his study. So that's where the police have made their base.'

'The plodders are squatting, are they?' Luke had rejoined them.

'They're working hard on the computer but I don't know what they'll find. The one Mike mainly used, his laptop, he carried in his briefcase. But when they opened it up the laptop wasn't there. Can you imagine: there was a bottle of whisky in its place! I think that's why they're concentrating on the desktop, that's all they've got to go on.'

Luke was puzzled and imagined the desktop was accessed by Laura, as well as by Mike when he was home. He was used to Marion making extensive use of information technology wherever she happened to be and he had a good-enough idea of the stuff she used her laptop and desktop for: inspection evidence and reports. A shadow of a smile crossed Laura's face; it was as if she read his thoughts. 'I hardly touched the contraption, except to dust it. I realise, now, Mike was right, we should have had everything upstairs in his study. He wanted an office, properly organised. All those electronics and gadgets for his laptop look foreign in my little room off the hall. We were going to split one of the bedrooms into a bathroom and a shower room, and then....' Laura outlined possibilities and Marion, content that Laura was speaking more freely, listened attentively to the plans that now might never come to fruition. So there were six bedrooms but not as many bathrooms as they'd like. Laura's account confirmed there were six toilets, as the whole village believed. Why did they need more bathrooms? Admittedly, with some imagination plus a fair amount of money and a lot of dust, they could reduce the number of bedrooms and create more bathrooms. She thought she followed Laura's explanation of where Mike's enlarged office could have been. It would have allowed Laura to reinstate her pretty reception room by the front door. Luke was occupying himself with Janus: looking for lost balls, finding chewed toys and even a bone, and he reflected on the police's interest in the two computers Mike had owned.

'Could Mike's laptop be in his car, d'you think?' Luke interrupted, flopping into a chair next to Marion. This matter was serious and he felt better able to get the measure of it when seated.

'They've been through it once, but anything's possible. They're going through everything with a tooth-comb; they'll find it, if it's there.'

Marion saw quiet, desperate exasperation in Laura's face and tried to change the subject. 'So which room are you allocating for Manny?' she asked.

'Does the front room suit him?' Luke recollected this was spacious and had been Miss W's bedroom, in her day.

'Oh, no. I'm saving that for Juliet,' she replied. 'My daughter's coming.'

'I'm so glad she'll be with you,' Marion spoke impulsively.

Laura's face softened. 'She's coming a long way, from Australia, you know.'

'Yes, you've mentioned once or twice...'

'Oh, yes. Do you remember Mike and I going to Melbourne? It must be almost three years ago now, shortly after we'd moved in here. Juliet and her family had just moved into their present home on the edge of the city. The new baby's a bit older and things are more settled now; she feels she can leave them.' Laura was gratified to explain that she had family connections of her own. There were few of them, she would readily admit, and she had not been certain her daughter would be able to come with the extra tie of the second baby who was still so young. It was luck that Bob's mother was with them, visiting to see her new granddaughter. Yet it would have been humiliating to make excuses for her. She flushed slightly and continued, 'She says she understands how I must be feeling and she just had to come.' Laura covered her eyes for a moment and wiped tears away. 'It's not been easy, she's always been a rebel and I didn't care for her husband. I didn't think they matched. But he's got a good job and they're enjoying their little family. She's happy and I want her to stay that way, always.'

'If you carry on having visitors, there won't be room for the police!' Luke said.

'It's so sad,' Laura said, ignoring Luke's comment, 'I used to think it would be good to have both sides of our family together for a proper visit. And now it's happening Mike's not here and we can't relax.' Again, reminiscing as if explaining aloud to herself, she said, 'We always had other things to do. And with Mike's travelling, and that was sometimes unpredictable, we never got round to organising anything.'

'I know,' Marion commented, realising that in her own, much simpler circumstances, her children with their young families rarely converged. 'If we can help in any way, let us know.'

They had drained their coffee cups and sat, momentarily in silence as Laura tried to compose her thoughts. 'She'll be here tomorrow,' she continued, 'and will 'phone on landing.'

'Then she must be travelling now,' Luke observed.

'Yes, she's been in the air for several hours and is due to land at breakfast-time at Heathrow. She says she'll continue by train.'

'I could meet her in Taunton, Tiverton or even Exeter, if that would help,' Luke said.

'Thanks, I'll remember.'

'Have the police asked you about Joe at all, Laura?' Marion asked, but Laura shook her head. 'They've probably found out all they need by talking with him directly,' Marion conjectured.

'They talked with me about other things,' Laura said, wearily, 'practical things like Mike's blood-pressure pills and his travel plans. And some questions they just kept asking in different ways. What he said on arrival home that evening, for example. But he didn't: he didn't talk much at all. He just said he was tired.' A shy, reflective smile hovered around her lips. 'That's what was so odd. He hardly said anything. And we have our own funny little greeting. I said it. But he didn't reply, he just stared back at me,' Laura almost whispered, '*We be with thee…* and he looked so, so *haunted.*'

'They're being so very thorough, d'you think they have a hunch what happened? I mean about the lost few days, before he came home.' Marion immediately regretted airing her ideas.

Laura looked shocked. 'If so, they never breathed a word to me,' she said.

Luke put his arm around Marion. 'You're making too many assumptions, old girl. I think they're asking routine questions without having a clue what's happened, it's too soon yet,' he said.

'I expect you've talked with Joe about the police coming round?' Marion persisted in asking about Joe Hartley.

Laura shook her head. 'There's not been time,' she said. But her comment hid disquiet that someone she regarded as a friend might be avoiding her. 'I 'phoned his home yesterday. I couldn't speak with his wife, the nurse was with her. But I did speak with Heather, his daughter.'

'That's very good of you,' Marion commented.

'Well I hope it was taken in the way I intended. You can never tell. I was trying to find out if Joe was OK and to tell him not to worry about me, that I'm surviving, in a fashion. It did take an effort,' she admitted.

'Did Heather say how her father is?'

'She just said, *as well as could be expected. He is more*

concerned about her mother than himself.' In retrospect, Laura realised that Heather had not been clear about her father and, glancing at Luke and Marion, she was aware they too thought the family was being evasive.

'Have you ever met Joe's wife?' Luke asked.

Laura shook her head. 'She's in bed a good deal of the time, but sits downstairs on good days. Joe who told us once... I mean Mike and myself... that this started a very long time ago, when Heather was about two. And now of course, their baby is married herself. It's a slow, wasting disease and his wife can do very little, that's what he said.'

'Is Heather their only child?'

'No, well, they're all grown now of course. One son's in the Far East with a telecom company, and the other is married and farming with Joe. And then there's Heather. She's an animal nurse at the local vet's practice and has her own home, just a few miles away from her parents. But she won't have a family, that's what Joe said.'

'So the condition is inherited.'

'Seems so. It's sad, isn't it?'

'We shouldn't be talking like this,' Marion chided, 'it's Joe we're concerned about.'

'Perhaps it helps us understand,' said Luke airing his thoughts.

'Heather said – oh, you know, the usual things people say when you've lost someone. She was sympathetic.' Laura spoke quietly, 'And said that she or her father would give me a ring in a few days' time. I asked if there was anything I could do for her mother, but she said no. Heather had slept in the house herself for a night, to keep her mother company and to give her father a break, she said. I don't think she'd have been there if her father had not been worried by the police about what's happened to Mike.'

'Probably not,' said Luke, surmising that Joe could have been humiliated, confused or even angry by the plight he found himself in or by police questioning. He would want time to compose himself and to reassure himself that his wife had not suffered because of the episode. Putting a cheerful tone in his voice, he said, 'No wonder he's been interested in developments and building. With his wife an invalid I can understand his wanting positive, creative things and to make them happen.'

Marion held back from saying how much she wished he would find another outlet or activity and allow the village to remain as it was, but now wasn't the time. She left it to Luke to enquire about the progress of the development application.

'D'you know if anything is happening on that front, Laura?'

'Post has come from the local authority, but I couldn't face opening it. I'm forwarding everything to Mike's solicitor. I know I'll pay for it, but when I enquired the solicitor said he was used to dealing with such correspondence and would attend to everything systematically, no matter how small.'

'He sounds like a helpful chap.'

'He is. He handled our property purchase,' and here Laura paused, as if she was weighing her words carefully, 'when we moved in. So he knows about our circumstances.' Something about her intonation indicated there was more she might have said. After a moment, she continued. 'Funny you should ask about correspondence. So did Manny, almost as soon as he arrived. I expect he was just being attentive.'

As they were talking, the sun moved round. It was still warm but the light now fell on shrubs around them, previously unnoticed, and the conversation turned to gardening.

'It's the start of the season, Laura. D'you need any help?'

'It's all in hand, at least the heavy work; I've stopped him coming this week. Mike wasn't at home regularly enough to cope with it all so I found a local man. And I do like doing my own bits. Mike calls it titivating... but it's more than that.' Laura held back tears. 'It'll do me good to tend the plants. The effort always shows. I know I'm just taking my mind off all the rest,' she ended limply.

The conversation rambled on haphazardly. Laura had lost some of the tenseness she had brought with her and her friends skirted around issues they feared would upset her. But a central question nagged in Luke's mind and he quietly pondered how to approach this. Marion resolved the dilemma. She asked with innocent openness, 'D'you know the outcome yet of Mike's P.M.?'

They watched Laura withdraw into herself. Her hands, which had been fidgeting became still, her eyes hardly blinked and her breathing slowed. Considerately, Luke said, 'I expect you want to know for your own peace of mind. And then other arrangements can go ahead.'

'Mike's funeral and his affairs?' Laura spoke slowly.

'Well, yes, and to put an end to all the uncertainty you're having to cope with. It must be very difficult.'

'I do so hope it clears things up. I've asked my solicitor to let me know what we are able do. He tells me there may not be a medical report for some time, it's quite usual.' Laura calmed herself before continuing, 'And we should expect other investigations, as well. I wonder what he means.'

'You know what you've told us is confidential, Laura. We'll tell no one,' Luke said.

'I'm glad I have friends I can talk with.' Laura spoke without smiling, 'And you're right. I can't rest 'til I know the outcome. But what if something was the matter and I didn't know? Or did Mike have worries, dreadful worries, he was keeping to himself? The thought haunts me that I should have spotted something.'

'You were very close,' Marion said. 'I'm sure Mike would have told you if he'd been concerned about himself.'

'I do hope so.'

37   Manny

Polly put down her 'phone, happily anticipating from Haresh's message that he'd be home again soon. She returned to packing her case, now half-full. Funny, she thought, how she'd become used to the clothes she'd worn in Derscott: warm sweaters, jeans and waterproofs, folded in the bottom of her case. Soon she'd return to her working clothes and don the role that they'd impose, that of the busy science teacher. For a moment she thought of students' grades and assessments, yet to be confirmed, and wondered at the outcome of all her cajoling and goading and the targets she'd set. That part of her life seemed a world away. She reminded herself she was returning not only to work but also, thankfully, to Haresh, and she warmed to that, almost more than she dared to admit.

Enthusiasm for packing restored, she checked the remaining items, her sponge bag, nightwear and extra shoes, still to be fitted in. And she remembered her blouse and underwear included in Marion's washing load. The drying cycle should be complete by now, she realised, and the items retrieved. She went downstairs, through the kitchen and into the small extension that held household cleaning gadgets and machines: the washer, drier and freezer. It was then she noticed a figure in the conservatory. He must have heard her movements because his shoulders turned so that he could look at her directly. Smartly dressed, a dark brown jacket over cream trousers complemented his olive skin. His hair, brushed straight back, threw attention onto his dark eyes that were staring at her, openly curious. Who was this man, she wondered? For a moment they held each other's gaze and then, absently, she relaxed her hold and several items of laundry slipped to the floor. Embarrassed, Polly stooped to pick up a bra and some briefs and as she did so was aware that the intruder came forward to hold open the intervening door. She placed her laundry on top of the machine, leaving her hands free to assist; this door sometimes stuck. 'Hello, can I help?' she said.

'I'm Manny,' he said, extending his hand, 'and you are Marion?' He seemed bewildered, Polly thought. And there was something about his accent, a precision and the way he emphasised certain vowels that was foreign. He held onto her hand, which she clumsily freed.

'No, I'm Polly, a friend of Marion's and I'm visiting here.' Though her words distanced her from responsibility, she felt proprietorial and reluctant to let the stranger into the house. As she stepped forward into the conservatory, Manny, with obvious deference, made way for her. 'You came around the outside, did you?' She tried to sound as welcoming as she could, while wanting to find out how he had gained access.

'I understand Marion spends much time in the kitchen, where I might find Laura. I did not see a kitchen from the front, so I came around. And here I do not see a kitchen either.'

'It's not such an obvious kitchen, perhaps,' said Polly, 'but yes... I'm sorry, Marion hasn't mentioned you.'

'Let me explain.' He seemed in no hurry to find either Marion or Laura and preferred to talk. Polly felt increasingly aware of the warmth of the conservatory and how stuffy it had become. She was conscious also of the visitor's after-shave or toilet water, which had a lingering sweetness. Polly thought it was jasmine and found it oppressive. She opened the garden door and fastened it back to allow a draught. 'I am here because my father has died,' he said.

'I didn't realise, you must be Mike Townley's son. I'm very sorry about your father.' Polly sat on the edge of an armchair, which had seen better times in the house itself, but was comforting in its girth and sunken springs. From her position in a corner looking towards the house Manny, who had seated himself in a cane chair facing the garden, was illuminated by soft sunlight.

'He was a businessman.' He smiled at Polly, a sly, developing smile and she noticed how well-groomed he was, the clean lines of his jacket and the fine quality of his shoes.

She wondered at his reference to his father being 'a businessman' and why he should mention it, right now. 'He's been taking risks.' Noticing her puzzled expression, he explained, 'All those flights, hotel bedrooms and meeting strange people. It is stressful.'

'I'm so sorry I did not know your fathe... but I have heard so much about him. And I have met your mother, she will be glad you've come.'

'Ah, Laura. Of course, she is not my true mother. You will realise that.'

Since the visitor was swarthy and Laura was blonde Polly realised she might have suspected this to be so, though as she was uncertain of Mike's appearance she would not automatically have discounted Manny as their son. She should take him down the garden to where the others were gathered, but before she could lead the way he continued, 'I am, how do you say? A child of love.'

Polly spontaneously corrected his quaint language, '"Love-child", is that what you mean?' she asked and then paused, embarrassed about possible misunderstanding.

'Indeed that's what I am. I come with Czech, Italian and Russian blood in my veins and my father's too.' Uncertain how to reply, Polly smiled and waited for Manny to continue. 'I am romantic. Those are my origins.'

More silence followed. Polly knew Manny had not come to speak with her, but she was willing enough to give ear to him if that would help a grieving son. 'You kept in close contact with your father?'

'He was my best friend.' He spoke emphatically. 'Always he would 'phone me and he advised me on my business.'

'You've come far?'

'From the country of my birth: it is the Duke's land. We have suffered many wars but you call us Herzegovina?'

Polly hid her surprise and for a moment was unsure how to continue. Spontaneously she commented, 'In Bosnia, is that right?' To herself she speculated this could be one country to which Haresh had not travelled but, as Manny's face darkened, she commented on his journey. 'You've done very well to travel here, to this village. Look, I'll show you where Laura is…'

But Laura's stepson showed no sign of wishing to find her and his upper lip curled a little. 'She has brought in the police, did you know?'

'They're at Laura's house? Yes, my friends have mentioned that. I expect it's routine, in the circumstances.'

Manny's lips, molten in their smile, turned to an expression of distaste. 'Why bring in the police? People die every day, every hour, this is God's way.'

'The unexpected nature of his death, I expect that's the reason.'

Manny shrugged his shoulders but replaced his smile with an expression of resignation. 'I will be helpful. Is that not what you say?'

Conventional statements of sympathy did not seem apt. Still, Polly felt that she should lead him out of the house. 'Let's find Laura,' she insisted, 'I know where they'll be, in a wild bit of the garden.'

'Naturally.'

She stood and allowed him to precede her out of the windowed-doors and down the few steps that led to the garden. The heavy scent of jasmine floated with him and was at odds with the delicacy of spring flowers and cherry blossom on an old tree just by the conservatory. He lifted his shoes carefully as he walked along the path and avoided stepping on the grass, which was becoming muddy in places due to Janus scampering with his toys, and the weather. Manny showed no interest in his surroundings. The route was obvious enough and needed no explanation, thought Polly, as they walked in silence. But their progress had been detected and Janus came bounding towards them. With Manny ahead she could not see his face but he stopped in his tracks with no acknowledgement or friendly word for the dog, who barked. Janus was growing into a healthy adolescent sheep-dog, Polly realised, and he instinctively challenged intrusion. On his back haunches he gave a good impression of fierce defence, front legs outstretched and rapid barking so that his black and white fur quivered and enlarged his image. 'Silly

Janus,' Polly said, 'this is Manny, a friend.' But the man was scared and could not move and Janus, sensing he had the upper hand on his own territory, ran several times encircling them, until he stopped and barred the way.

'Please,' said Manny, and Polly went to Janus and stroked his back. Recognising her he was quiet for a moment, by which time Luke had appeared. In a crescendo, ending in a bellow, Luke shouted, 'That's a good pair of lungs – never heard so much. Now **go**!' The dog ceased barking but, head down, was not satisfied and whimpered. 'You must be Manny?' Luke was conciliatory. 'Laura is with Marion, come and join us.' They walked past old fruit bushes, Manny avoiding the outstretched twigs and ignoring Luke's comments about them needing to be covered with nets, while Janus ran around their legs. 'He means no harm,' said Luke, 'he's just a puppy. The garden's his own or at least that's what he thinks. But he'll get used to visitors now the weather's improving.'

The arc of chairs had been enlarged into a circle. While Marion talked with Laura, Luke was busying himself wiping down a suitable seat for Manny. They watched as Manny settled into the cushions protecting the faded, cracked plastic frame and then pinched the creases in his trousers and smoothed his jacket. Janus slunk under Luke's seat and gazed relentlessly at the new visitor. Marion offered Manny refreshment which he declined effusively, and for several minutes they exchanged social pleasantries, about the weather, the practicalities of air travel and of living in a small village.

'Have you been here before?' Marion asked.

But Manny didn't reply clearly. He shrugged his shoulders, dismissing the question with his hands as if it were superfluous.

'It must be very difficult for you, coming so far and in such sad circumstances?' Marion continued.

'Thank you, yes.'

'We're very sorry about your father,' Luke added.

Manny looked serious but said little.

'In my experience, you don't realise what you've lost, until they're gone,' Luke said.

An air of consensus was shared around the group except with Manny. Polly remembered his comments, about it being God's way, and hoped he found comfort in that notion. But she herself, she knew, would be devastated if similarly bereaved.

'How did you get on with the police?' Laura asked.

While Manny's posture remained tense – leaning slightly forward, his hands gripping his knees – his face assumed a mask of ease. Smiling, he said the police questions were routine. They had been considerate, they knew why he had come, that he was a loving son and it was his duty. He was welcome here.

'Did they ask when you last saw Mike?' Laura asked pointedly.

'Of course and I explained about the airport, there was delay, you know and it was my father's wish that we should meet.'

'Did you? I didn't realise,' Laura commented.

'Since I have come there has been no time to explain all. My father... he made a change in the flight because there'd been delay. It is natural he should wish to see me when he travels so close by. He was well. There was no sign of failure, of dying. He gave me this.' Manny displayed his left wrist for the group to see his watch, a gold Swiss-movement with a brown leather strap. 'It is Patek Philippe, my father says, and special. It belonged to his father too.'

Laura recognised the watch and was astonished. 'I knew nothing of this,' she said.

'It was spontaneous,' Manny said, 'one day before he let me know and I made the drive to see him when he arrived.' He extracted a small mobile 'phone from an inside pocket of his jacket.

'I expect you've told the police?' Laura asked, surprised.

'But of course,' replied Manny. Polly wondered at the officers' task, piecing together these diverse strands of information. Presumably there was a clear story here, if only she could see it; perhaps the gift of the expensive watch had required changes to Mike's travel plans; it must have been important to him. Marion sought to move the discussion on, to find a more comfortable topic, and asked Manny about his work and leaving it at short notice, to come to England.

'Ah, that is no problem. I am a businessman and arrange my own affairs.'

'What type of business are you in?'

Manny smiled with self-indulgent pride, 'Property, with my father.'

It was hard to interpret Laura's expression. She looked shocked but Polly wondered if this was due to grief and exasperation at the circumstances and developments following her husband's death, or resulted from Manny's conversation. His English was not reliable, that was obvious to all of them, Polly thought. But if the police were suspicious of an airport meeting, this would be checked, she assumed. Her conjecture was cut short. A sharp ring on her own 'phone summoned her attention.

'It will be your young man,' Luke said, 'go and find a quiet spot.'

Janus playfully ran with Polly until she reached the house where she returned to the conservatory, now shaded across one corner as the sun had moved around. The dog lay contentedly at her side as she greeted Haresh.

'My darling, is that you?' Haresh said. Immediately, she was transported into his world. 'There's still snow in this valley, and skiing too.'

'So that's what you're up to!' Polly teased.

'Now you know me better than that.' Haresh sounded remorseful, hurt even. 'Did you get my message? It's only another 36 hours and I'll be back. I've missed you – more than I can say. But the timing's so good for crafts, that's why I came, Polly, believe me. The people have started afresh after Christmas and they're very receptive to ideas.' He recounted the possibilities presented to him and choices he was making. 'And their use of electronics is very good. I've not seen better. A man, Ulrich's his name, devises neat and most clever effects. They'd look good in my catalogue but some pieces are big. I wonder if many would afford them at home.'

Polly giggled. 'So what are they like?'

'Well I've seen a picturesque house that's amazing. It has a working music system, a burglar alarm and an automatic garage door.'

'Wow! Some present for a kid. How much does that cost?'

'You haven't heard it all. On the outside it looks like a miniature schloss, just charming. Ulrich calls it *restorée*. Apparently he's taking orders from the French.' Polly asked about his hotel. 'I am invited to a schnaps party tonight,' he replied.

'I wish I were with you.'

'And I wish you were too, my darling. But it's only hours now and I can hold you!'

'Listen, I must tell you what's happening here.'

Haresh noticed the change in Polly's intonation. 'Your friends – are they well?'

'Oh yes, Marion and Luke are fine and they ask about you.'

'Please give them my regards.'

'It's their friends and happenings in their village.'

'In their village?' The signal faltered. 'It's snowing!' she heard Haresh say and then, through intermittent words, she thought he said, *I'll call you back,* before the line went dead.

She imagined a fairy-tale backdrop of middle Europe, trimmed with snow. The picture lingered of Haresh comfortable and warm in his alpine village with his business friends for company. It was time, she felt, to reconsider this way of life. How much longer would they maintain these separations, she wondered? She could join him. Instead of sitting here, missing him and dreaming of the next time they would have days or even a few hours to share, she could be with him. True, Haresh spoke several languages which was of course an asset, but Polly knew her French was passable and she would learn German, or even Polish or Russian if that would help them, the two of them. She craved his presence, sharing his bed and, deep-down, the prospect of children and having a family of her own. And then she recollected her own job. Both the enjoyment and pride in teaching science; she would have to give it up. The pattern of the school year meant she had barely a month in which to make up her mind if she wished to leave at the end of the summer term. She knew she should pluck up courage and give in her notice to the headteacher. She would miss her colleagues in the science department, and other Year 10 tutors of course. But it would be worth it, to be with Haresh. His business was developing well and he'd mentioned, more than once, that with her help it could grow faster. This would compensate for the loss of her salary she believed, although they hadn't worked through such details yet.

Her emotions were confused. She had become so used to the routines, the journey to work, unlocking laboratories and being the first to arrive. Making out orders, checking apparatus, marking books – they would all fade into oblivion. She recollected her Year 10 form. The young violinist, the boy who wanted to be a doctor, another who struggled with understanding English and with adapting to school because of a long time spent in a refugee camp. She wanted to help them on their way, to take each of them a step nearer their goal. Did she really have to give it all up?

'Don't let me disturb you. Oh, I see you've finished.' Luke stepped into the conservatory. 'Haresh didn't have so much to say today did he?'

'We had a snow shower – I mean he did and the line – it just went dead.'

'You sound weary, my girl. I could do with a hand, you know. They've sent me out for a round of drinks. I thought I'd open one of the bottles I've put by. I have some from a trip Marion and I took, oh, I don't know how many years ago...'

Polly followed him through the house and into the garage. There, at the back, in a cool, dark corner, beneath the stout container in which Marion's latest laptop computer had been delivered, was a store of bottles neatly stacked in rows, about five deep from the floor, in a simple wooden rack. Souvenirs from over the years, was all Luke said, as he lifted several dusty examples from the top row and proceeded to read their labels. He set these to one side and continued to unearth more. 'This must have been Sicily – or was it..?' He tilted his head in puzzlement. At his elbow he felt Janus's wet nose.

The dog sniffed around. 'Never sure what we're going to find back here, old boy, are we?' Then Luke recollected Polly's presence and the purpose of the search. 'They'll be wondering what's happened, I know,' Luke said. He rummaged elsewhere among his store, wiped off cobwebs and checked labels before, satisfied, he thrust a bottle of pale amber liquid into Polly's arms. 'Hold this while I reorganise a bit.' He found a second bottle from the same vineyard in his treasure trove. Carrying these two he returned with Polly to join the others at the bottom of the garden.

'At long last!' Marion said over-cheerfully, in an attempt to lighten the atmosphere.

'It's a serious business choosing tipple,' Luke replied. 'You've not to mind the date, but it was a good year when it happened.' Chairs again adjusted, they sat holding their glasses, the bowls of which were filled with a Loire-Valley white having a fruity, honeyed bouquet.

'Has this been chilled?' asked Marion.

'Just the right amount, as befits the *cave*,' was Luke's ready reply.

The sweetness of the wine lingered. Polly thought of peaches and then of aniseed. They sat in comfortable silence until Manny recounted a trivial anecdote from his journey. It was meant to amuse, thought Polly, though she did not get its point and wondered whether the smiles of others were anything more than polite gestures.

'You were saying you were able to change plans at short notice Manny, to make the journey here.' Manny's cheeks coloured in response to Luke's curiosity.

'I keep in touch, all the time. I speak, I text and I have my laptop, you know.'

'There's no end to communication now,' said Luke, a touch drily.

'Well, naturally. Always I am most attentive. I read messages on them all.'

'For your business?' Luke enquired.

'But of course.'

'So is business brisk?'

'He means busy,' Laura said.

Manny turned his head from right to left, in an arc. 'So so,' he said. 'I prepare chalets for the season. My father, he gives advice and investment too, and now I have cottages in our big forest, it is quite beautiful, by the sea.' Manny's explanation held everyone's attention. Luke and Polly, who were facing Laura, were aware of her stillness and her avoidance of catching others' gaze.

'Seems quite ambitious,' Luke said. 'I mean, you have a lot to manage.'

'My country, we are ready for this. We have land and mountains. All this brings visitors. I think it is a good time. And we have people to clean the houses and look after them, and to make sure people are happy with their holiday.'

'With all the travelling folks do nowadays, it seems like a very good time for a business like yours,' said Luke, encouragingly. 'And what's your role in this?'

'I am manager,' Manny said confidently, 'and receive payments. And I search out possibilities for new business.'

'Lucky lad!' Luke looked around the group as he said this. Marion had been quiet for most of the exchange and he wondered what Laura was thinking, if she was thinking anything at all; she seemed overwhelmed. The young man prattled on about the environs of the cottages and their facilities and Luke suspected this was news to his stepmother. For a moment his thoughts drifted to speculation, about Laura's feelings and Manny's circumstances, and he did not concentrate enough on Manny's diction, so he missed the gist of some parts of what was being said. When he looked up again he caught a chilliness in Manny's gaze that he had not been aware of earlier.

'You could do the same here,' Manny repeated forcibly, 'in fact, my father said...'

But before he could continue, Laura intervened, 'I'm sure Mike would have told me of the idea.'

'Perhaps I had not yet suggested it to my father,' Manny said smoothly.

'You're a charmer, we'll believe you for now,' Marion said a little sharply, but faint puzzlement and courteous laughter murmured around the group.

Seconds later, the telephone rang shrilly in the house. 'I'll go,' said Luke wearily.

'No, leave it,' chided Marion.

But Luke was already walking along the path, his steps plodding alongside Janus's eager bounds. The ringing had stopped by the time he reached the 'phone but he played back the message, returned the call and before rejoining the group he stood for a few moments in the conservatory. 'A good job I went,' he said, 'ought to appear conscientious in front of the law, and all that.'

'What do they want of us? It was the police, I take it,' Marion enquired.

'It'll be me,' intervened Laura.

Luke took another sip of his wine. 'It's alright, we have time for drinking up; they're an understanding lot.'

'Don't keep us in suspense,' Marion said.

'Well they sound fairly relaxed. I returned their message and spoke with that young woman officer. She was very patient about us all being in the garden. *Give them a few minutes*, I said.'

Laura flushed and glanced at Manny. 'So it's both of us they want?'

'The officer was courteous and said they'd be grateful if both of you would join them to discuss a few matters.'

'We'll walk round with you,' Marion said quickly.

'Not 'til we've finished our glasses,' Luke replied, and they sat quietly, before strolling together down the lane. Luke and Marion halted to watch Laura and her stepson walk into the driveway of their home. No sooner had they returned themselves than they were reminded of development plans. A note on pink paper from Pete had been pushed under the door. The date of the protest meeting was fixed.

38   Ellie is missing

The day slipped into night. The family fed, by outward appearance nothing had changed. The women busied themselves around the house. Seth and Tom looked to the animals. Jess stayed at the farm intending, under the cover of dark, to return. Tom, as had become his custom, offered to ride with her and then would make his way back fast.

Before night fell they picked good ponies, having more to choose from now with those of the Kings' Cavaliers as well as their own. Tom asked Adam if he'd like to ride with him as a second man, and the infant readily agreed, holding out his arms to be lifted up. Jess would not be parted from the younger babe who travelled close to her, secured within the long cloak that covered both herself and the horse's saddle. She cast a mysterious outline and with the cloth being dark she melted into the night. Tom, with Adam, took the lead and she followed close behind. As they turned out of the farm the moon's soft light was enough since they knew the way well. The rain had ceased but the ground was soaked and puddles lay upon the way. In stretches there was no dry footing. Each step the ponies took squelched in mud and Tom was careful that Jess safely followed him.

They had left the King's men ready to bed down. The family could spare neither tallow nor, in these days, the extra attention that rushlights might draw. Taking Dick with him, Seth had walked around the few suitable places for extra men and they had agreed on the cider house, with hay as bedding to supplement some straw already there. The cider house held stocks of apples on the upper floor, but they were more than half gone and would not be replenished until the next summer's crop, when ripe apples which were good and surplus to their needs for pressing would be stacked tidily and stored for winter use. The ground floor held barrels and pots of the cider already pressed and by the side of the press itself was the short ladder which led upwards, to the loft.

'This be not large,' Seth said, 'but ye'll be the warmer for't!'
He poked a fork through the straw which lay opposite the
fruit. 'To send rats fleeing away!' he said, and lay hay on
top. 'Make thyselves comfortable!'

Given the choice of here or the tunnel, the Royalists
were glad of the dry hay, with its lingering smell of summer.
Because of their small numbers, they deemed it best to wait
until the Parliament's men were well clear of this place,
before they went on their way. Seth pulled the door to and
returned slowly back to the farm. Nemo ambled alongside
and sniffed the ground. The farmer listened for sounds.
Unable to discern any, he prayed that Jess, with Tom's
help, was almost returned and that the lad would make
good time as he rode alone back to the farm. The moon
threw shadows from the trees with pools of light around the
church, which looked an eerie monument. There was little
wind, only the faintest movement in the trees whose
branches stood like arms against the sky, across which an
undulating white form swished followed by a screech,
reminding Seth of other beings out hunting food. He hoped
the owl had found sustenance, as he had managed for his
own dependants. All that should be were abed in the farm
by the time he heard sounds of the horse bringing Tom
home. The lad had cut a track wide of the farm to loose the
animal to rest with others along the stream. Then he'd used
the stairs to the loft where he lay at nights, as now did the
priest. Seth worried about the priest. He seemed more at
peace with the child, Adam, than with adults, who seemed to
bother him. This evening he'd let the food pass by and had
quietly left all those that supped. The times were troubled.
The farmer shook his head as he thought of the effect this
struggle for the land had on men – and women too.
Catherine was afraid to sleep some nights. He turned his
feet back towards the farm and his own rest.

'Where be Ellie?' The first glimmer of dawn shed a pearl
grey into the room, touching corners of the chest and
rushlight stands, reminders of how once they dared to light
the room. Seth stirred at Catherine's voice.

'Sleep on yet,' he said.

'Nay, our daughter, she's not abed.' Catherine had left Seth's side, pulling at the bed covers and causing draughts across him while he pondered on her words.

'Well, she were last night. Happen she's gone to see the hens.'

'Thy lad, more like!'

'Woman, thou hast no cause to think...'

'It's plain for all to see!' Catherine, alarmed by her anxiety, shed her gown and replaced it fast with other layers. Seth followed her example as he heard her steps down the stairs. 'Embers are low,' she called. Seth held his tongue. His wife's patience and accommodating manner had all been spent the previous day. Of course he knew of Ellie's attachment to Tom. But why would the girl leave her bed of a cold morning to go to him when she could nestle with him most days, easily enough, should she have the will? As he played with twigs and placed a log on top of them to coax life into the fire, he heard Catherine again.

'She's not there, nor Tom either!' Seth noted that the news, which could have been taken as good, did not seem to please her much, as she banged pans and put dishes in place for their simple breakfast. 'Strange though,' Catherine continued, 'the priest's gone too.'

Seth could understand Tom's absence; at least he knew of proper reasons why this should be. Because of the season he was out most mornings checking the sheep and lambs. Then there were the cows to be fed with their muck and straw pitched into a pile, as well as the horses to check. After his ride last night Tom had seen to his own horse quick enough though doubtless had been too weary to tend to the rest. With those of the troops, as well as their own, there were double the horses to be minded. Like as not, Tom was seeing to them now. Why had Catherine not recollected these tasks? Had the troops wanted for aught? Seth would expect them to come to him, but Ellie was a handy maid and perchance was aiding them. 'Wife, it's time to break our fast. I'll go and rouse our guests.'

'What – thou be worried 'bout them more'n Ellie – and she your daughter too?'

214

'It's not that, wife, but I'm as certain as can be there's a reason and an honest one at that.'

'If they've touched Ellie!'

'Nay, that's not what's on my mind.' Seth pulled on an extra garment to brave the cold and picked his way in the thin light across damp cobbles to the cider house. He pushed the door ajar and thought he heard a rustle within. No sooner had he entered than he felt a sword at his throat.

'For the King!' It was Dick's voice that apologetically added, 'Thou'll understand the need.'

'Not on my own farm I don't. Ye all know my 'ppearance. If ye wish to stay, be calm hereabouts.'

The troops had made a bench from odd wooden pieces stored in the cider house and their whispering ceased at Seth's intrusion. 'We be gone as soon as we can see our way,' Dick explained.

'Come by the house 'afore ye go. There be bread and porridge for all of ye.' As he left, Seth turned and said, 'Heard anything o'ernight?'

The men shook their heads. 'Naught, save the white owl,' one said.

39   Nathan

'Tom!' Seth exclaimed at the sight of the lad, returned and satisfying his hunger with food Catherine had spread on the hall table.

'I came across twin lambs needing some help,' he reported from his walk around the farm. 'The new ones in the upper field are doing well. An old ewe this morn....'

Seth interrupted him. 'Has Catherine asked – where's Ellie?'

'Ellie, what bothers thee?'

'Thou hast not noticed she be away?' Catherine said sharply.

'The priest – hast thou seen him about the farm?' Seth asked patiently.

Tom shook his head. 'This morning I did notice... but with my rounds....' His voice trailed off as the farmer comforted his wife so she stayed quiet. Seth doubted not Tom's commitment to the farm and its family and knew the lad would have flagged after his ride with Jess last night. With sudden insight Tom blurted out, 'There be only one place he would seek – and Ellie too, might go to find him there.' Her parents knew where he meant: the church.

Seth felt apprehension. Could Ellie not have led the priest back herself? Disconcerted, he had to search them out. Being wary, he thought it best to approach plainly, the open way, so he used the track from the farm to link with that leading from Great Torrington. By now it was light and as he rounded the hill on which the church stood he saw a horse, grazing within the hedge by the church. That should not be, he knew. Concern for his daughter hardened and his pace doubled, his steps barely touching the ground as he reached the porch. He leaned against the door to raise the latch and heard his daughter scream. Not thinking more he pushed and swung open the door to see the man who, of all the Parliament's men, had been a trouble: Nathan.

216

'Take care,' he heard the faint voice of the priest and saw him slumped to one side, clutching his arm.

'And the same for all of 'ee.' Nathan, inflamed in anger, smote the air with his sword. 'Though give thy daughter, if thou likes,' he said, coarsely.

Ellie was not to be seen and Seth froze in his place, considering no movement better by far than one too hasty. On his right, he saw Nathan with his back to the altar and face towards the tower. 'She meant well,' cried the priest with all the energy he could muster, though he still was faint, 'she fled, finding I was hurt.' Seth, looking around, noticed the door to the steps that led up the tower had swung open. The chime of a church-bell followed, it first to pierce the ears of those within the church, followed abruptly by the soldier's mammoth roar while the reverberations of the bell slowly died. Nathan, momentarily unnerved, kept his eye on the farmer and ear arched towards the tower awaiting a second peal. But this did not materialise.

'Collect thyself,' Seth quietly broke the silence. 'Why art thou here?'

'And why should I not be?' the soldier cried. 'The country's ours – or will be soon.'

Seth's eyes took in the broken woodwork, shattered pot, scattered flowers and disarray.

'And thou did this?' Seth's voice showed more surprise than admonishment.

'Such ornaments – the church has need of none.'

The priest started to remonstrate but Seth continued as calmly as he knew how. 'They be harmless enough – flowers be from the hedgebanks around and carving that's stood here for longer than any remember. They're the simple things of country folk.' The colour drained from his face. Before him, Nathan was scarcely rational, incensed with anger at finding the refuge he'd commandeered interrupted, first by an old man, then a maid and now her father. While Nathan had a sword, Seth had no means of defending himself and uppermost in his mind was his daughter who seemed to have taken flight to the tower, and also Father Patrick who was feeble with both age and injury. His daughter's place was senseless, since it offered no escape and he scolded her silently, as well as feeling pity for her panic. He could think of no immediate way of turning Ellie's bolt-hole to his own advantage. 'My aged man has wounds. Let them be tended to and leave us alone,' Seth said. 'What quarrel hast thou with us?'

'I have no quarrel, but ye two stay.'

'What want 'ee of us? What more?'

The question seemed only to anger Nathan, a vengeful tormentor. He cut a powerful figure, pale light through the window falling onto his shoulders, though Seth and the priest who was now leaning against the wall remained in the shade. Seth thought of his own absence from the farm and the single peal of the bell. Would this suffice to raise alarm? He hoped fervently that Catherine would not risk to come alone but the King's men, how would they respond? A hint of a wry smile crossed his lips, which Nathan caught, his voice rising as he challenged. 'What is there to laugh at, man?'

'I meant no harm.' Seth, seeking to prevent eruption, suggested, 'Thy horse, we can feed and water it so thou can leave?'

'I'm not done yet,' Nathan threatened.

Seth mused this perhaps was said more out of stubbornness than with reference to any plan. 'Then let us help thee, in any way we can.' After a moment's thought, he added, 'Thy comrades: they be on their way a'right?'

'A'right to them.'

Seth wondered how and why Nathan had become separated from his gang of comrades. But perhaps Nathan, a contrary man whose mind had become disturbed, wished to strike out on his own, or had quarrel with the rest.

'Ye for the Parliament still?' Seth enquired.

'Would thou suggest t'other? Where hast thou put them all?' Nathan added, brooding and suspicious.

'I know not what thou means,' Seth said. Before there was time to add more, the priest sprawled further and groaned. 'Consider him,' said Seth.

Nathan signalled with his sword for Seth to tend the priest, which he did. Much blood was soaking into the

218

garments of the elderly man from his arm that was badly cut. Aside from this, Seth could see no other injury save general frailty. Seth eased the old man's limbs into more comfortable positions and bade him rest. Silently, he supposed the priest had crept here to spend the day and that Ellie had guessed at this, from whatever clues she had perceived, such as the old man's faltering steps in the quiet of daybreak. Out loud, he told the soldier of the aid the priest was needful of.

'He'll get none such here,' was the curt retort. Seth held back his anger and said he'd tear off his own clothing, to keep the cut together. 'Get on wi'it, then,' was Nathan's reply.

Seth slipped off his woollen jerkin and rent a strip of cloth from the sleeve of his own undergarment. He worked quickly, conscious of Nathan's eyes on him. Gently he eased away the blood-soaked garments of the priest and tore further the rent the sword had made in the priest's linen, to see the gash in his arm. He brought the edges of the wound together and bound them, with a remnant of his own clothing.

'What be that?' Nathan, edgy, imagined he had heard a sound and that reinforcements were on their way. But he wanted none, not of his own side nor of any other.

'My mind's on this, I noticed naught.'

Nathan, however, was certain there were sounds around and switched his ear and eye 'twixt tower and porch for evidence. Seth, realising that while he was tending the priest he may have ignored signs that meant relief was near, sought to provide distraction. 'I query not why thou be here,' he said to Nathan, 'but the other two – my good man be weak through age and injury and my daughter came as fancy took her, as a young maid has mind to do. Both warrant care and warmth but there be neither comfort nor rest in this chill place.'

'Why be thou here thyself?'

'Looking for both of 'em!'

'Where ought thou be?'

'In the fields with the animals, tending their needs.' And then he heard the sound of a man's step, unmistakably a boot on the cobbles outside.

219

Nathan caught his eye. 'Thou think me dim. Come next to me.' Again, he signalled with his sword and made Seth stand between him and the door.

'This be not my doing,' said Seth calmly in the face of Nathan's blind rage.

'But thou may be the end of it!' Nathan retorted.

'Sounds up the tower?' Seth said, vainly.

'Nay, do not try to make a fool o' me.'

The priest lay by the south side of the church, apparently sleeping and, save for an occasional mewl, was quiet. The tower was silent. But the silence did not hold for long. With bangs, the church doors burst open and three men tore in. 'In the name of the King,' they cried.

'Hold off!' Nathan cried, 'or the farmer's dead.'

The troops edged closer.

'This is not all I have.' Nathan brandished his sword and stooped to recover with his free hand a flintlock he'd secreted, primed and ready, close by. 'There be no need for silence here.'

Sunlight gleamed off the Royalist breast plates and swords, but these rested in hands unwilling to risk the farmer's life. Seth, with intruders behind him, faced Nathan and saw fire in his eyes and smelt determination on his breath. Legs apart, Nathan held both weapons well and with these small numbers could inflict heavy damage, if he chose. Seth did not recognise the voices of those behind him and felt certain Dick was not among them. While he believed no reconciliation would come between the men of opposing sides, he speculated a further attempt to appease Nathan could bring no harm to others trapped within the church and so he spoke as calmly as he could. 'Thou's keeping us here, but what sense be in it? Allow us to go free – and be so thyself.'

'Nay, I tell thee again take me not to be a fool. About thee I care not and in them I see my enemy and my country's too.' At that, Seth felt a lurch at his back and a trooper ran forward with his sword set to deflect Nathan's arms but, faster than he, Nathan fired a shot which dented the attacker's plate and floored him. His companions stood back.

Nathan resolutely stood his ground. Though outnumbered, he had the more powerful weapon in the flintlock and had shown that he would use it.

Greg, the soldier fallen by the pistol, tried to right himself. The impact had bruised his ribs and winded him, but miraculously no worse than that. 'Stay down,' Rob on the Royalist side growled, sensing a good chance they'd get the better of this. The reloading time of the flintlock would bring them advantage though he realised that erratic movements of an injured man might incite Nathan to be impetuous. Greg stayed curled on the floor, his arm under him and bruises hurting but dared not move, not even to incline his head. He gazed across the cold stone floor with his eyes on Seth's boots, Nathan's form and the altar some way behind. Around him, feet were shuffled. He heard scraping and clashing of metal on metal and Nathan cursed.

'Stay,' Nathan spoke with rude brusqueness.

Greg sensed Rob and another comrade were close at hand. 'We want just rule, as dost thee.' Rob's tone was considerate and his words were measured. Then he heard Seth implore, 'We all be honest men – what good be served by this?'

'Thou spake thus, before,' said Nathan darkly, 'and I've patience for no more o'it.'

'Nay, good man, if just thou be why deny the right to speak?'

Greg wondered at the continued bantering and for how long Nathan could be distracted, when his mind was on the fight. He tried to turn to ease the pressure on his chest, slowly so as not to arouse interest. Then he suppressed a gasp as he noticed a tremble in the altar cloth. The plan, concocted by Dick, might yet save the day.

'Quiet,' decreed Nathan, he being mightily watchful sensed mischief in continued talking and was nearly ready to cock his pistol once again.

'What harm can words have? 'Tis steel does that.'

'Listen. Ye do well to listen now,' Nathan rumbled, quenching the murmurs of others.

The Royalists were deferential in their approach. Greg,

221

through half-closed eyes, watched as the cloth draped round the altar was held back, hands and then a head appeared. No longer could Nathan's attention be held. As he turned towards the rustling sounds, two fit troopers advanced with swords and Seth swiped a kick across Nathan's knees. With poor aim the flintlock fired again, this time the lead glancing off Rob, then Nathan was set upon with swords from front and back as troopers converged from both sides. Dick stood over him and the rest fell back.

'Father!' Ellie ran from the foot of the tower to Seth who hugged her close.

'Why be thou here?'

'The priest, I heard him leave and felt concerned since he had come to us for his safe-keeping ...' Ellie started to explain but Dick brushed her talk aside.

'Catherine, thy wife,' he said to Seth, 'be wanted here.' Blood was seeping from Rob's arm but Nathan was in a much worse way. The weakened tyrant was losing both blood and consciousness and they saw the need to act fast. Ellie was sent, with instructions to bring her mother, ointments, cloth and water to stem flesh wounds. The last Royalist stumbled out from the altar folds. All told, save scratches, the wounded comprised the only man they called their foe and three they counted as their own: the priest at a low ebb and recumbent on a bench; one trooper, Greg, who was winded; and Rob, with his arm gashed.

Catherine, panting from haste and wide-eyed in horror, stared at Nathan, grunting in pain. 'Husband,' Catherine spoke and shook her head, 'there's little I can do – a surgeon at the very least is needed here.'

Disgust showed on all their faces. Nathan had now collapsed with his wounded chest. As they watched, the scarlet patch across his front increased. He could not speak and lost interest in so doing. Life flickered out of him. He grew still and lay silent. He was dead.

Seth was the first to speak. 'And for all his show, this be how it ends.'

Catherine crossed herself. 'What now?'

'There's more to fear, we must act fast,' her husband

said. The troopers on the Royalist side eyed each other's injuries. The priest stayed quiet, apparently asleep among the signs of battle in the church.

'Quick, we must be gone,' Ellie panicked, 'what if the rest return?'

'I vouch they be as glad as we to lose him.' Dick looked momentarily at the body on the floor before turning his attention to the elderly man, silent save for an occasional groan. 'Our good man deserves a comfier place than this, as do we all.' He managed with the aid of his men to raise him to his feet, but the priest could not without aid support his own weight. 'I have a better plan,' Dick said, 'work together, men.'

Ellie held open the door and listened for sounds around the porch of the church, but there were none. She watched two men cradle the frail man, who weighed little more than a child, his slight frame cupped in a hammock improvised of a cloak. 'Once our good friend be settled, return as fast as ye know how. I here remain 'til ye be back again,' Dick said to his men. The troopers, with wounded comrades, set off to follow the easiest path to the farm guided by Ellie herself and followed by Nathan's horse, seeming both a curious and subdued animal. Remaining with the dead Roundhead, Dick removed the man's pistol, belt and sword. 'These be useful,' Dick thought aloud. Catherine, concerned at the damage in the church was overawed at the quantity of broken fabric around the altar and wondered at its repair. Dick insisted, 'Thou art needed at the farm, good woman, and there ye have a safer place than here.' And thence she and Seth returned.

The King's men, determined, kept alongside the hedge and made slow progress as they adjusted their load, conscious of the priest's fragility. Nathan's horse was constant in accompanying this small band back to the farm and there one man led him to graze, where he blended with Seth's own animals in a copse. The priest, who hardly had stirred through the gentle jostling of his return, was laid on a settle pulled into a corner of the hall and screened by a curtain to protect him from draughts. With Ellie's help the

King's men made him as comfortable as they might. The injury would not have been serious in a fit man, but his aged body bore it less well. His mind was troubled by the conflict that had disturbed him and he sought solace in prayer and escape in sleep.

Meanwhile, Seth's anxiety grew from witnessing conflict within the church itself and his fears renewed for his family and livelihood. Roughly, he locked an arm around Catherine's shoulders. 'We must ensure that all in our care be well.' In haste Seth stumbled as he half-walked, half-ran to check his fields and animals while Catherine surveyed the people who belonged at Derscott, Ellie in particular. They found a peaceful contrast to the church interior. The cats slept and hens were quiet in front of the warmth from the fire, in spite of the early hour. Ellie had gathered fresh water and torn clean linen and with her mother's aid she wound fresh bandage around the priest's injured arm. Catherine heated a herbal potion and with her daughter lifted Patrick's head and held the cup so he could drink. Slowly, the shock left his limbs and he became tranquil. 'Where am I?' he seemed to ask.

'Hush, save thy strength,' Catherine replied, making sure he was supported on cushions and swathed in covers to keep in his warmth. Finally, she realised he was sleeping naturally and signalled to Ellie to leave. In this corner he was no trouble and left peaceably, had the best chance of recovery.

Ellie looked about with thoughts of where Tom could be. Food had been given to the pigs so she expected to find him with the cows or feeding the youngest lambs in the new pen by the house, then seeing him neither place she considered the horses. Feeling she was bound to find him by their grazing she trod in that direction, though as she did she heard the rhythm of distant hooves. Coming from the Torrington direction, it sounded like a small posse and there was no telling of which side. Her parents would seem innocent enough in the farm, she knew – but she took fright remembering the church and Nathan still resting there. Panic giving her strength, she abandoned thoughts of the farm and made her way as fast as she was able to the church. Never having used the tunnel alone she returned by the lane, keeping close to the hedge. She ran so near to this that her skirts snagged on twigs and brambles. Often she had traversed this path, her mind full of flowers and birds or Tom, but now she thought of nothing save the progress of her feet across the tussocks. Panting as she rounded the low hill she paused to catch her breath. The sound of her own breathing filled her ears and, trying to calm herself, she listened for hooves. But all was quiet. Unnerved, she halted in her steps. She was sure of her own memory. She had heard a posse along the road, it should be at Derscott now and she had reached the church.

'Why be thou here?' Dick spoke kindly though he was greatly surprised that Ellie not his troops had returned.

'Did thou not hear?' she asked.

'What be thou telling me?'

'Hooves,' and between tears she recounted what she'd heard.

'Thou art shaken, Ellie, and 'tis my men I need. Return to the safety of thy hearth but urge my men forget their wounds and scratches and lose no time in finding me. The Roundhead's body still lies as it fell.' Ellie viewed the truth of what Dick said yet he had in mind hiding Nathan's corpse for a short time within the tunnel 'neath the altar and kept this to himself. Nathan remained a peril though he was slain, with his body a dangerous memento 'til night brought opportunity for burial.

40   Presumed innocence

Luke, recumbent from the effects of wine in the warmth of afternoon sun, stirred out of his dilapidated chair. He and Marion had returned to their places among the overgrown shrubs and bedding plants at the bottom of the garden where Laura with her stepson Manny had recently sat and talked in rambling fashion. The sound of the telephone broke through the myriad of notions he was trying to accommodate after their discussion; he picked up the receiver.

'Hello, this is Laura.' Her voice, could it really be the same Laura that less than an hour ago had been here, offloading anxieties and grief?

'Everything alright?' Luke was surprised at Laura's elated tone.

'I can hardly believe it.' Her tone was light, she sounded relieved. What had happened, he wondered? 'It's going to be alright, she says it is.'

'Tell me slowly, Laura.'

'Manny and I, the police....they've just left. It was the woman detective, Mrs Dewar's her name, she told us not to worry.'

The pause that followed was interrupted by Luke. 'That's really good news.'

'Yes, it was natural causes, that's what they've said and for us not to worry, we couldn't have known.'

'So was the other detective there – Inspector Marland?'

'Yes, but it was the woman who spoke to us while he was packing more of Mike's things.'

'You said 'they' so I thought it was both of them?'

'She told us what the pathologist said.'

'The wait for information hasn't been as long as you thought?'

'Oh no.' After an awkward pause Laura hesitantly acknowledged, 'Of course, it'll be confirmed in writing but that's just routine, Mrs Dewar said.'

'Does that mean Manny's free to go home?'

Dully, Laura wavered, 'No, apparently not yet.'

As cracks deepened in Laura's spontaneity, Luke tried to recover her good humour. 'You must both be very pleased and having Manny with you...you'll have a lot to talk about, it's a comfort.' He spoke hesitantly, sensing that with his every comment doubts were building in Laura's mind.

'Let me have a word with her,' Marion whispered, guessing the drift of the dialogue. 'I hear you have some good news, Laura,' she continued.

Luke listened as the conversation recovered its lightness: they would meet the next day and make plans for Juliet's arrival.

'She's much better,' Marion told her husband, 'would you believe it?'

Luke started to explain his worries, just small details that had been mentioned or left unsaid then thought better of it.

'We must build on positives,' Marion said, 'I think we need to move forward for Laura's sake.'

'I agree,' Luke acquiesced, but continued mulling over his thoughts in the peace of their garden.

Meanwhile, at the Townley's house Laura slipped her feet out of her sandals and wondered if this bewilderment could ever end. Manny, foreign to her life and a virtual stranger, still in his travelling clothes and polished shoes, stood over her as she sat in a kitchen chair. Oblivious to his sensitivities, Laura's thoughts were of maintaining her own existence, of managing her feelings of devastation as well as necessary routines, and satisfying demands made by the police.

Such humdrum imaginings were exploded by Manny's outburst, vehement at first in his own language and then in shocking, broken English. Laura stared in horrified amazement.

'All you nice people,' his pitch and volume rose, 'afternoons drinking wine, my father cold and my mother in Herzegovina living on scraps. We starve.' It seemed to Laura that he snarled and loomed, removing his jacket and prancing around the kitchen. His eyes travelled around the fitments and china and glassware on display. 'Look at these – the finest things. My mother keeps her mother's plates, her father's knives.'

With brutal suddenness Laura was scared. This confused man, swollen with anger and grief, filled her kitchen with torment. 'The police. Why do they see me? I travel and come all this way. You killed my father,' he shrieked. 'He was well when with me at the start of his journey but now he is gone. No soul you have, all these things around you and you kill him.'

Terrified, Laura watched him walk towards the knife rack and she became strengthened, stood from her chair and retaliated. 'How dare you! Go – leave. Mike I love, I loved him. I did not kill your father.' Shaken from her reverie, her rage matched Manny's. He reached for the edge of the worktop to steady himself, tired and hungry from his journey and wept, recognising truth in her words.

***

'Take that, will you please.' Marland's 'phone rang as he negotiated traffic along the Tavistock road on the return drive to Plymouth with Sophie Dewar and further evidence from the house, bagged and labelled. A laden tractor had turned in front of him by the Lydford turnoff, just where the road narrowed. It was as much as a sane body could do to drive this route at peak times and he was expecting a 'phone call from Courtenay, who was pursuing several enquiries connected with the case.

Reception as they drove was intermittent. 'It's a Dr Reid, sir.'

'That's the pathologist, the senior man. What's he have to say?'

Marland realised from the constable's brief interjections that matters were not as straightforward as their initial conclusions had indicated. Sophie reckoned honesty was the best policy and cleared her throat before explaining; an edge in her voice warned him of a problem. 'In Dr Reid's view, the preliminary report overlooks signs in his fingernails and possibly in body fluids. He's doubting natural causes and is sending material for more analysis. He apologises for any embarrassment caused.'

'And should there be – any embarrassment, I mean?'

'I have given Mrs Townley reason to believe…'

Marland drove in silence for several miles before pulling into a car park used by visitors to Dartmoor, his manner austere. 'Dr Reid's reliable and as thorough as they come. I want a report on what you've said and Mrs Townley's response on my desk tomorrow. One way or another, she's a crucial witness and I've a hunch will lead us to the truth.'

To find out what happens next in the CAVALIERS AND CORRUPTION Saga read FINAL WORDS – avalible in all good bookshops now!

Lightning Source UK Ltd.
Milton Keynes UK
UKOW03f1327020614

232708UK00002B/11/P